STONE AND SUNSET

RALEIGH HARMON PREQUEL MYSTERY #4

SIBELLA GIORELLO

For Frances and Belle.
My grandmothers and my best friends.

1

IF I DIED RIGHT NOW, it'd be okay.

I mean, yeah, I'd miss my family. Especially my dad. And I'd *really* miss my best friend—Drew Levinson—who at this very moment is riding on the handlebars of my bike. She is blindfolded.

"Raleigh." Her shaking voice rides the breeze back to me. "I can't see anything."

"That's the general idea of a blindfold."

"Can I take it off?"

"No."

"Please?"

"Drew, trust me."

I stand on the pedals and pump our way down Patterson Avenue, heading toward the high and majestic bronze statue of General Stonewall Jackson. I turn left and head up The Boulevard. The wind grabs the hem of my ugly school skirt, waving the hideous blue plaid uniform like it's some tribal flag for girls forced to attend private schools. I pedal harder.

"Why are you turning?" Drew sucks air in, blows it out. In-out-in-out. Like those heroic women who give birth without painkillers. "Raleigh, where are we—"

"Trust me."

Does this seem cruel—forcing my best friend to ride blindfolded on my handlebars? It's not cruel. Really. This is a perfectly nice Thursday afternoon in May and the spring sunshine has that powdery scent of blooming azaleas. But I can also smell the disinfected aroma of Lysol. The bitter scent of coffee. Both are floating from Drew's wild brown hair that's tickling my face. The last time my best friend left her house was January. By February, I got her to stick her head out the window. Early March, she stood with me on the front steps and looked like she might collapse from fear. But in late March, she walked down the steps—six steps, counted by twos—and by April, she let me lead her into the backyard. Three times—each for exactly six minutes. Drew has a thing for numbers, especially the number six.

Now, in this second week of May when the entire city of Richmond is lifting its arms to sing hymns to the coming of summer, Drew Levinson perches on my handlebars, knuckles white with fear, and trusts me to lead her to a surprise so big, so wonderful, so perfect that if I died right now, it'd be okay.

This surprise will change her life for the better. I know it.

As if hearing my thoughts, she turns her blindfolded face sideways. "If this surprise kills me, you're donating my brain to science."

"Drew, you're not going to die."

"You don't know that."

True. And science would definitely want Drew's brain. She is fifteen years old and getting straight As in her online math courses from MIT.

I lean forward, speaking through the long strands of her wavy hair. "You promised to trust me."

"I take it back."

"You can't."

"Why not?"

"Quantum mechanics."

She thinks about it. "This has nothing to do with quantum mechanics."

I tap the brakes, coasting down a gentle hill. "You told me energy can't be created or destroyed. Only transformed."

"So?"

"So are promises real?"

She faces forward, thinking about it. The wind blows her hair which tickles my face.

"Yes." Her blindfolded face turns sideways. "I suppose promises are real."

"And promises require energy."

"What?"

"It takes a lot of energy to keep a promise."

"Raleigh, you can't be seriou—"

"A promise is energy. And it requires energy. So if energy can't be destroyed, then you can't take back a promise."

That shuts her up.

But as I pedal us closer to the big surprise, her silence makes my heart ache. She's scared.

"We're almost there," I add.

I steer past the warehouses in the Scott's Addition neighborhood until the streets burst open with trees and wide sidewalks. I bike toward the iron gate that says, *Welcome to Sunset Gardens,* and lean back, letting the wind play with my ponytail.

"We're here."

"Where?" she asks.

I push the heel of my Converse high tops into my back pedal, slowing to a stop beside a wide white porch. Standing there is a cute and chubby woman with short blonde hair. She comes down the stairs, waving her plump hands like she's just joined some hallelujah chorus. But she doesn't say a word. Karlene Robertson. The woman who helped me plan this world's greatest surprise. She waits for my cue.

I brace the stopped bike and lean forward. "Drew, you can get off the bike."

"Where is *here?*"

"You have to get off my handlebars to find out."

Her fine-boned fingers keep a death-grip on the chrome. I glance at Karlene. Sympathy floods her round face. She wants to help, but we both know this situation is like dealing with a terrified animal— any "help" might just scare them more. Staying silent, Karlene waits while I peel Drew's clammy fingers from my handlebars and take her arm. It feels as rigid as the metal. "We're going to walk up six stairs."

"Six?" She turns her blindfolded face. "Not seven, or five?"

"No. Exactly six steps."

One of the benefits of having an obsessive-compulsive mathematical genius for a best friend is you learn about things like "six." It's considered a perfect number. "Okay, ready?"

"No."

On my left, Karlene hovers, there if needed. I lead Drew up the porch stairs listening as she counts each step with a quivering whisper. Karlene hurries ahead and opens the screen door. The hinges squeal.

Drew stops, cocks her head. "What was that?"

"You'll see."

I lead her inside the foyer of Sunset Gardens. The crowd has gathered—a sea of white hair, orthopedic shoes, aluminum walkers. And nobody says a word. I catch the eye of my grandmother, Frances Harmon. She gives me a wink and a smile.

"Okay, Drew," I tell her. "You can take off the blindfold."

Her face is pale. And perspiration dots her hairline. I glance at Karlene and see whole paragraphs of unspoken worry.

"Drew, you can take off the blindfold."

"No."

"You're here. There's nothing to worry about."

She swivels toward me. "Raleigh, I'm Jewish. I *always* worry."

Laughter ripples through the crowd. Drew tilts her head, listening as the sound evaporates as quickly as it came.

"Drew, please take off the blindfold."

She shakes her head, long hair billowing around her tiny frame.

Suddenly an elderly woman as tiny as Drew shuffles forward from the crowd. She is so old that her skin reminds me of stretched-out clouds, thin and transparent. But her eyes are clear and deep brown like the earth. Intelligent eyes, like Drew's. This is Myra Levinson. Drew's grandmother. She has not seen Drew since December, when agoraphobia kidnapped her only grandchild.

Myra looks me in the eye. For more than fifty years, the woman smoked like a foundry. Now an oxygen machine is her constant companion, with a plastic hose that clips to Myra's nose. The machine breathes, a mechanical wheezing sound that fills the silence.

I lean into Drew. "Hear that sound?"

She tilts her head again, listening. "Is that ..." She reaches up, ripping off the blindfold. When she sees her grandmother, she cries out.

"Bubbie!"

"Drewery!"

Drew and Myra rush for each other—which honestly is more like two snails hitting their highest speeds because Myra's lungs are black as coal and Drew's body is weak from hibernation. And yet when they embrace, the hold is so tight that Drew's long hair swings over her grandmother, making the tiny old woman disappear.

"Oh, Drewery." Myra's voice is shaking. "I've missed you so much."

"Bubbie! I can't believe it's you."

Drew calls her grandmother Bubbie. It's a Jewish thing. And I don't judge because I call my grandmother Gockey.

And now Gockey walks toward me, dabbing her eyes with a balled-up Kleenex. "I'm so proud of you, Raleigh," she says.

I don't reply because my throat's closed. Like somebody yanked a string and cut off my vocal cords. I glance over at Karlene. She's crying, too, but with a big white smile.

"You did good," Karlene tells me.

I still can't say anything, but the rest of the old people are seeping forward, encircling Drew and Myra, everyone buzzing with exclamations and happy tears and relief. They earned this moment, too. They've waited days—days being equivalent to dog years for old people—and only one resident here at Sunset Gardens was not in on this big surprise.

And here she comes, motoring down the hall toward the foyer.

Wilma Kingsford.

Former gossip columnist for the *Richmond Times-Dispatch*, Wilma can't keep a secret. Maybe it's some occupational hazard. Taking one look at this crowd, she pushes her way to its center. Drew and Myra are still in their sobbing embrace, but I can already see the upcoming headline in Wilma's *Sunset Gardens Gazette*.

Agoraphobic Teen Visits Ailing Grandmother!

"What's going on here?" Wilma demands. "Myra, is that you?"

There's no answer.

"Myra!"

Drew draws back, looking down at her elfin grandmother. "Bubbie?"

Myra's eyes are closed.

"Bubbie, are you alright?"

She's slipping from Drew's arms.

"Myra!" Karlene rushes forward. The plastic oxygen tube is sliding from Myra's nose. Karlene catches her falling body, pushing the tube back in place. "Myra, Myra—say something!"

"Bubbie?"

Myra says nothing.

Karlene spins toward me. "Call 9-1-1!"

2

"I WANT—*I can't*—I want—" Drew paces the front porch. "*I can't*—"

Six steps forward, touch the window, pivot. Six steps back.

Repeat.

I watch the medical guys at the bottom of the stairs, loading Myra into an ambulance on a stretcher. She seems groggy but alive. And she refuses to go to the hospital—hospitals, she murmurs, are full of germs. She's got some of the same obsessive-compulsive habits as Drew. The ambulance takes her across the courtyard grounds to the Sunset Gardens infirmary.

"Drew, you can do it," I tell her.

Tears glisten in her brown eyes. She shakes her head.

When the medical guys arrived, Myra was passed out on the floor. They checked her breathing, took her pulse, shined a penlight into her old brown eyes. Myra woke up. One of the medical guys started asking her all kinds of questions.

Who's the President?

"Who cares?" Myra replied.

What day is it?

"You don't know?"

How old are you?

"Sixty."

Karlene had tapped the guy's shoulder. "She's eighty-one. And she knows it."

I watch the ambulance motor across the lush property. Sunset Gardens looks like a park. Magnolia trees. Azaleas. Historic boxwoods. And the three-story plantation house that once belonged to a wealthy tobacco baron. He donated the house and land to a foundation that later went broke. Now this place is the retirement home for everyone who's anyone in Richmond.

Karlene comes out on the porch, having convinced all the old people—including my grandmother—to go back to their normal routines. They seemed more than happy to do that. The ambulance part isn't something they want to see.

"Drew, honey." Karlene's accent is a strong Georgia twang, but soft, like she knows how to talk to scared people. "Honey, I think it would help your grandma if you went to see her in the infirmary."

"*I want to.*" Drew picks up her pace. "*But I can't.*"

Karlene looks at me. My heart punches my chest. Back when I proposed this big surprise, Karlene told me to be very careful. Drew and Myra were both fragile right now. But did I listen?

"I'm sorry," I tell her. "I didn't mean to—"

Karlene reaches out, touching my arm. "You didn't mean any harm, Raleigh. We all know that."

I stare down at my shoes.

"Y'all have phones?" Karlene asks.

I look up. "I do."

Drew doesn't have a cell phone. For one thing, she never goes anywhere. And second, if she did go somewhere, she'd only call two people. Me or the MIT hotline for the geek knowledge.

"I've got an idea," Karlene says. "I'll go over to the infirmary with my phone. Y'all do that FaceTime thing, right?"

I nod.

"I'll get Myra on it and that way y'all can see each other."

Drew lets out the world's longest sigh. Answers mean a lot to her. Karlene gives me a kind of sad smile and goes back inside. Drew resumes her pacing. I continue to stare out at this perfect Thursday afternoon which has just turned into the Worst Day of the Year.

Worse than the February day when my boyfriend broke up with me.

Worse than the March day when I almost died in North Carolina.

Worse than all of that combined because Myra Levinson just *plotzed* on the floor of Sunset Gardens and could've died and now Drew is freaking out even more than when we left her house.

My whole grand plan completely backfired.

Way to go, Raleigh.

"Drew, I could take you home."

She shakes her head, pacing like a crazy wind-up doll. Counting her steps. *Three-four-five...*

"You might feel better in your own house."

"Raleigh, I can't leave."

"Not right this minute." I pull out the blindfold. "But after you talk to Myra."

She touches the window, pivots, walks six paces back to where she started. "You haven't even considered Moses."

My Old Testament knowledge is pretty good, but I'm not seeing any connection between this situation and the leader of the Jewish exodus—I mean, is Drew saying, *Let my people go?* I have no idea. Then again, confusion is pretty much standard hanging around Drew. Like spending time with a nine-year-old Einstein.

"Moses?" I ask. "What does Moses have to do with this?"

"Who'll take care of him?"

"I don't know—God?"

She crosses her skinny arms. "God's going to feed Bubbie's cat?"

Myra has a cat.

I forgot.

"Maybe Karlene can feed the cat."

Her brown eyes look at me so harshly I gasp. "What?"

"Leave," she says.

"Wha—?"

"Just go."

This day feels like somebody strapped me to a roller coaster. For weeks, I've been trying to coax Drew into this surprise. She kept saying she wasn't ready. Then today, as I sat alone in the lunch room at St. Catherine's School, my cell phone buzzed. Drew. Calling from the purple landline in her bedroom.

"Now," she said. "Right now."

I didn't hesitate.

Skipping my afternoon classes, I pedaled like somebody let Schwinns into the Tour de France. It took a full hour just to get her on the bike, but she did it. My big mistake was assuming the World's Greatest Surprise Ever wouldn't take long. I mean, all the agoraphobia advice books said, *Small steps, take it easy.* I figured we'd visit Myra, then I'd pedal Drew back home. I mean, how much time could a person spend in the real world after being cooped up in one house for five months?

"Leave." She points at my bike. "I know you have somewhere else to be."

"I have to—"

"So, go."

"You can come with me."

"Raleigh." She pivots. "I really don't want to be around you right now."

The knife sinks so deep that when I open my mouth, the words are gone.

3

I LEAVE my cell phone with Drew and ride away, my hands so numb I can't feel the handlebars. Stonewall Jackson's bronze statue passes by in a brown blur, and three miles later, when I reach the James River, it's like I can't remember anything about how I got there.

In the parking lot by the water, a red-haired madman waits inside a beat-up van. I coast down to the driver's side, catching the bitter stench of smoke wafting from the open window.

Teddy Chastain plucks a cigar from his bearded mouth. "Where the tarnation ya been?" he asks.

I left school so fast today I didn't have time to tell my geology teacher about picking up Drew. And, like Drew, Teddy shuns cell phones. Which wasn't going to be a problem because my Drew-and-Myra grand surprise was only supposed to last only an hour, tops.

I wave a hand in front of my face, moving the cigar smoke away. "I don't want to talk about it."

"I've been waitin' here forty minutes." He swings open the driver's side door. Rust rains from the hinges, leaving cinnamon dust on the gravel. "But I'm still not gonna go hood-rat-holler on ya."

"What?"

"Your lucky day," he says.

"There's no such thing as luck." I lean my bike against the van, where the paint is so scratched it looks like a can kicked down the road twelve times. Reaching behind his driver's seat, I yank out the wheelchair folded up back there. Yes, Teddy can definitely do this himself, but that takes longer.

"What buzzard climbed in your bonnet?" he asks, climbing into the opened chair.

I stomp across the gravel to the back of the van, pulling open the doors. More creaking hinges. More rust rain. And inside, science journals jumbled together with small plastic boxes. Wooden dowel rods scattered like busted Tiddlywinks. Seriously, this van really could be a can kicked down the road. I paw through the assorted rocks—most of which I've collected. Sedimentary, metamorphic, volcanic, petrified wood, dinosaur bones... you name it. Finally, I find a clean collection box and a rock hammer, hooked to a camping stove. I separate the tool, take the box, slam the doors.

"That's it," Teddy says, wheeling himself down the wooden ramp to the river. "Take it out on the universe. That'll change *everything*."

"Shut up."

His chair halts.

I keep walking.

Moments later, he starts whistling.

Teddy's been my science teacher for five years. In that time, I've learned he whistles for only two reasons. First, if he's super-duper happy. But I've only heard that whistle once. Last October. When Drew came back from the dead. More often, Teddy whistles because some student at St. Catherine's is proving she's the literal definition of an idiot. At which point Teddy will write the obvious answer to her question on the whiteboard and whistle—so low you can barely hear it— the tune "If I Only Had a Brain."

I turn around, glaring at him. "You think I'm an idiot?"

His red eyebrows rise up his wide forehead. "Eh?"

"You're whistling."

"That a crime?"

"It means you think I'm an idiot."

"Oh." A grin splits his red beard. "Not an idiot."

He rolls past me, moving to the dock over the river.

I stare at the back of his chair. "Then you're ... wait. You're *happy*?"

"Being happy's illegal?"

"No, but answering a question with a question is really rude."

"That so?"

"Oh, forget it." I pull off my Chuck Taylors, yank off my socks. "Tell me what I'm collecting so I can get out of here."

"Man a-*live*." Teddy's West Virginia accent lifts and falls on every other syllable. "You're actin' meaner than the cow chewin' barbed wire."

I leave my shoes and socks on the riverbank, pick up the sample box and hammer, and slosh into the river. The water's cold. I shiver and gaze at the current. The water's a turmoiled brown, a color like Drew's hair as it blew in the wind on the way to Sunset Gardens. I grit my teeth. "Just. Tell. Me."

"Quartz."

I look back over my shoulder. He's leaning forward on his elbows, expectantly.

"Quartz," I say. "That's it—just quartz?"

"Yerp." His green eyes look sharp as cut glass. "I need quartz from them beds in the boulders out there."

I look across the water. Fifteen feet from shore, dark granite boulders stick out of the water.

"And may the quartz be with you," he adds.

I groan. Happy Teddy. I don't like Happy Teddy. Especially on a day like today. Wading deeper into the river, I feel the fine-grained silt ooze between my toes. The current laps at my shins.

"Ain't you even curious?" Teddy asks.

"No."

"Teddy," he says, in a high-pitched tone that's supposed to be me. "Why're we collectin' this dag-gum quartz?"

"I don't care."

"Maybe you are an id-jit."

Hands down, Teddy Chastain is the best science teacher. Ever. But the man speaks in hillbilly lingo. He grew up dirt-poor in West Virginia and never lets anyone forget it. Personally, I think he enjoys how much the mangled English irks really uptight people. Same with the whistling.

Which, of course, he's doing again.

My jaw tightens. "Please. Stop. Whistling."

He stops.

I wade over to the jutting granite boulders. They are the geologic bedrock of Richmond. Eons ago, they entered the earth's crust. Today, the river flows over these rocks, churning in a powerful Class 3 rapids. I run a hand over the smooth eroded stone and find a deep cavity. Inside, white crystals sparkle like diamonds. I raise the rock hammer and clobber the quartz with a truly satisfying *whack*.

The quartz doesn't break.

I whack again, harder.

Teddy calls from the wooden landing, "I don't pay for bad attitudes."

For obvious reasons, he can't collect these specimens himself— Mother Nature never got the memo about handicap access routes. For the last couple years, Teddy's been paying me twice the minimum wage to gather rocks and mineral samples. He also acknowledges my contribution in some of his science journal articles.

I whack the quartz again. One hairline fracture spiders across the clear crystals.

"Whole lot easier if you quit havin' that tantrum."

I swing the hammer like a baseball bat. The quartz shatters. I pretend to find some worthy pieces but actually feel sort of nauseous looking at the smashed crystals. He's right. I'm having a tantrum. Like some kind of brat.

I turn my face to the side, not looking at him, but making sure he can hear my voice over the river. "Drew let me take her to Sunset Gardens. That's why I was late getting here."

"Wow-za!"

I glance all the way over my shoulder. Sometimes I can't tell when

Teddy's being sarcastic. But he's genuinely surprised. Maybe even glad because his bushy red eyebrows have shot all the way up.

"Ain't right to quit the story there—what happened?"

"It was a wonderful surprise for her and her grandmother."

"Giddy-up."

"So wonderful that her grandmother almost died."

He says nothing.

"The ambulance showed up. Now her grandmother's in the infirmary and Drew refuses to leave Sunset Gardens." I face the river, the swift current nudging my legs, like some invitation to ride it all the way to Virginia Beach. I could disappear, one more piece of life's flotsam. "She told me to leave."

"Ain't yer fault," he says.

My whacks have destroyed these crystals. I wade to the next boulder. Around the back, I find an outcropping of perfectly formed prisms with 60-degree angles. Like icicles growing up instead of down. I tap the bases, carefully, *tap-tap-tapping* until clean lines crack across the crystals. I place the prisms in the rock box and wade back to Teddy, not daring to lift my face. I only lift the specimens. "That enough?"

He doesn't reply. I look up. The afternoon sun is dipping behind the gum trees so all I can see is the fuzzy outline of his misbehaving red hair and beard. Below that, the square of his wheelchair.

After a moment, he says, "You did good."

He takes the box and the hammer while I climb up the soft-soil riverbank and wipe my muddy toes on the velvety spring grass. Teddy is rolling down the wooden planks, pushing the wheels even harder as the chair comes to the parking lot gravel. I feel so alone, tugging on my shoes, following him to the van.

He opens the rear doors. "How'd you get Drew outta her house?"

"Teleportation."

"Come again?"

"You know, when a person's in one place then suddenly appears in another. Einstein's experimented with it."

"You built some kinda time machine?"

"Very funny." I take the collection box, clamping the plastic top shut and set it in a somewhat safe corner of the mess. "I told Drew that wearing a blindfold was as close as she could get to experiencing teleportation. You're in one place, then you take off the blindfold and you're in a completely different place."

"Used your noggin," Teddy says. "Good job."

I slam the back doors, grab my bike. "Except for the fact that I almost killed her grandmother."

"Stay stubborn."

"What?"

He flings open the driver's door and lifts himself into the seat, folding the wheelchair and storing it behind him. He closes his door but glances back at me through the open window. There's no humor in his eyes. Only a fierce green light that kind of scares me.

"Stay stubborn, Raleigh."

"I don't get it."

He starts whistling, and drives away.

"Thanks for nothing," I tell the empty air.

4

TEDDY'S JUNK-VAN drives away from the river, belching black soot from its rusting tailpipe. Watching him leave, I feel a powerful urge to bike back to Sunset Gardens. Drew's probably losing what's left of her mind.

But I check my watch.

Because crazy lives at my house, too.

It's almost dinner time and I can't call home to tell my parents I'll be late because Drew has my phone.

"Great."

I bike up Huguenot Road, winding through the West End of town until I reach The Street Where Time Stands Still— Monument Avenue.

I steer my way onto the sidewalk, avoiding the bumpy cobblestones that pave the four-lane road. Matthew Maury's statue goes by, then Stonewall Jackson. Then the Greek columns around Jefferson Davis, and finally I reach Robert E. Lee, the Confederate general riding his regal horse Traveller into eternity. I coast into the alley behind our three-story brick mansion and unlock the carriage house. Inside, the exposed brick walls still hold leather horse bridles and buggy whips. My dad added a hook for my bike. And a mirror. I can check my appearance.

My ponytail is its usual mess. I take out the hair band, finger-combing my long brown hair, and wipe the river soil off my chin. I ignore the dark circles under my eyes which are not going away now that Myra's in the infirmary. Aside from Drew, my closest companion is insomnia.

I stare at myself.

Myself scowls back.

"You messed up," I tell myself. "Again."

As I cross the alley to the back gate, my mind goes over all the excuses that might explain why I'm home so late. But my desperate thoughts are interrupted by the scene on our back patio.

My parents—both of them.

They are sitting at the wrought iron table.

Holding hands.

Smiling.

My *mom* is even smiling.

At me.

Several geologic eras pass while I try to make sense of this development. But I can't. My dad, the judge, isn't giving me any hints. Usually his smile comes with a silent warning attached— *Act like nothing's wrong.*

But now?

"Hey there, kiddo," he says, smiling in a way that's totally disturbing because it's like nothing's wrong.

I take one step forward. Slowly. Like walking down a long diving board that hangs way too high over the deep end of the pool.

He's still smiling. "How was your day?"

"Fine." I glance at my mom. Also still smiling. I glance back at Dad. "How're you guys?"

"We are terrific," he says, with so much enthusiasm it almost scares me.

"It's a gorgeous spring day and I get to be here with my gorgeous bride."

I nod.

My mom tilts her head. "Is everything alright, Raleigh?"

I freeze.

All across America, parents can ask this exact question of their kids and it's no big deal. But in this house, that question is like a lit fuse leading to an explosion. The best way to answer, I've learned, is to act like it's an essay question for my English teacher. He always makes us restate the question in the answer's first sentence.

"Everything is alright." My voice sounds like a robot.

"Did anything special happen today?" she asks.

I glance at Dad. Is she testing me? I can't tell. My mom is paranoid. Like, *clinically* paranoid. She believes weird ideas and gets suspicious about things that aren't really happening. Like the CIA is bugging our faucets and listening to our conversations. Like I'm not her "real" daughter. Sometimes she asks me things that Raleigh *should* know, but if I suddenly don't remember some tiny detail from eight years ago, then I'm an impostor, sent to spy on her. Which is why there is no way I'm telling her I skipped classes today and biked my agoraphobic best friend to see her ailing grandmother at Sunset Gardens. I just keep looking at my dad, pleading with my eyes.

Help?

He just keeps smiling.

So I respond the way my horrible English teacher makes us answer message questions—by restating the question in the answer. "Nothing special happened today."

"That's about to change," my dad says. "We're ordering pizza for dinner."

Pizza.

Pizza is made somewhere else by *complete strangers* who then come to the house—*right to the front door.* They could *poison* us. We haven't ordered pizza in four years.

"From Pagliacci's," he adds.

My mother accused the delivery guy from Pagliacci's of putting gasoline in the cheese because Exxon or Chevron or whoever was trying to kill people who didn't drive cars—my mother doesn't drive

—and her rant scared the delivery guy so bad he dropped the box right there and ran.

"Great," I say, feeling so scared and so happy all at once.

"Let us know when you're ready," he says. "I'll call for a large with everything on it. Just the way you like it."

I force my feet to move. But it feels like I'm still on that diving board only now clunky rubber flippers are strapped to my feet. To get to the kitchen door, it feels like I have to lift my knees really high to not trip over my own numb feet. Pawing open the kitchen door, I cross the room and glance over my shoulder, making sure the weird creatures are not coming after me.

I pick up the wall phone and dial my own cell number.

It rings.

And rings.

And rings.

Then my voice comes on, telling myself to leave myself a message. I hang up on myself and call the main number for Sunset Gardens. The call goes directly to Karlene's office.

"Sunset Gardens," she says, in her sweet Georgia accent. "How can I help you?"

"It's Raleigh."

"Oh. Where did you go?"

"I, uh, had a school thing to take care of." I hesitate, praying for good news. "How's Myra?"

"Much better. Turns out she only fainted. Maybe a little too much excitement."

"Right."

"*Very* good news. She'll be fine. When are you coming back?"

"You mean, for Drew?"

She doesn't even need to answer. I glance at the patio where Mr. and Mrs. Perfectly-Happily-Married are still holding hands, chatting away. "I'll be there as soon as possible."

"Raleigh, she can't stay overni—"

"I know, I'm sorry. This is all my fault."

"That's *not* what I meant. You tried to do something nice for both of them. And don't forget, Myra begged you."

That's true. After Drew's agoraphobia took hold in December, she stopped coming to Sunset Gardens to visit Myra. Every time I visited Gockey, Myra looked more and more depressed. Drew's her only real family, what with Drew's parents being so useless and selfish. When I told Myra about my idea to bring Drew to Sunset Gardens, her wrinkled face lit up like a Hanukkah candle.

"I'll make sure she goes home tonight," I tell Karlene.

"Thank you," she says. "And please, don't beat yourself up. Everything's going to be okay."

As I'm hanging up the phone, my sister Helen wanders into the kitchen. She's in her first year at Yale University and somehow is already home for the summer break. Maybe she skipped her finals—that would be just like her. In Helen's world, rules are for other people. Nodding at me sleepily, she goes straight for the coffee maker —because who doesn't need a blast of caffeine at five p.m.

"What's going on?" she asks, yawning.

I point to the patio. "We're ordering pizza. From Pagliacci's."

Helen nods, stretches like a cat. "Dad found some new meds for her."

"Really?"

"Started kicking in yesterday. Didn't you hear her humming around the house?"

I shake my head.

"You might want to stop paying so much attention to rocks," she says.

I glance at the patio. My handsome dad. My beautiful mom. They look so...normal. Which seems totally abnormal. "That's good, about the meds."

"Yeah." Helen slaps the coffee maker, impatient for the machine to start gurgling out the bitter brew. "But don't get your hopes up. Who knows what she'll be like tomorrow."

5

HELEN LEAVES before the pizza arrives, claiming she's got to be at some art gallery shindig. And even that required sleeping all day, getting amped up on caffeine at night, and ditching me here with a lit fuse on a ticking bomb.

I set the dining room table for three. My dad answers the doorbell and brings back the everything-on-it pizza from the restaurant which was previously accused of poisoning us. My parents sit across from me, full of more lovey-dovey. But I barely notice as I savor three slices and shove away Helen's comment that this peace won't last.

After the meal, I clear the table. My parents wash our dishes at the sink, my dad drying, both of them singing Frank Sinatra tunes. They even ask if I want to play an after-dinner board game. Because now we are normal.

"Thanks," I tell them. "But I've got homework."

I climb the servants' stairs to my third-floor bedroom and run my index finger under the door's bottom edge. My Scotch Tape trap is still intact, which mean no sign of entry. Maybe that sounds paranoid but my mom tends to "inspect" my room, looking for evidence of her "real" daughter. I suppose it could be worse. When Gockey lived here with us, my mom kept accusing her of putting bugs in our laundry soap. Not insect-bugs. Surveillance bugs, FBI bugs. I yank off the tape, open the door, and listen. Downstairs the new normals are singing about the summer wind.

I change into my pajamas, leave my door open a crack, and sit on my bed, muscling through Latin conjugations (ugh), World History (meh), Geometry (ugh *and* meh), and as I'm starting my poetry assignment for English, Dad appears at my door.

"Good night, Kiddo." He walks over, kisses the top of my head. "Sleep well."

My mom stands at my door, too, but doesn't come in. It's been years since she said good night to me.

"Say your prayers?" she asks.

I nod, staring at her. Even when depression hovers over her like a black cape, my mom's stunningly beautiful. But when she's happy? Holy quartz crystals, I'm finding it hard to believe how good she looks. And I want to memorize how she's looking back at me. Because it might be a long time before I see that look again.

"Sweet dreams," she says.

I want to say something back, let her know how much I like her this way. But the only thing that comes out of my mouth is one almost useless word.

"Okay."

They walk down the stairs. I hang my head. This day. This horrible, weird, frustrating day.

I can't even get the good stuff right.

But I say my prayers—because, frankly, today all I've got is prayers —and then lay on my bed, watching out my window overlooking the back patio until their bedroom light goes out. I check the clock. Just past nine. At 9:20, I tiptoe over to my bureau and change into shorts, T-shirt, and sweatshirt. More tiptoeing down the servant stairs, then carrying my shoes into the kitchen. It smells of dish soap. And my dad's fresh happiness.

Within three minutes, I've got the bike out of carriage house and am cruising through the quiet dark, past the empty warehouses in the neighborhood known as Scott's Addition. Past the empty city baseball diamond where Drew and I used to spend so many Saturdays watching the Richmond Braves. I slow down at the best burger place in town—Big Man Burgers—searching the black windows for any sign of light. Drew and I used to spend every Friday night in there, eating and challenging each other with fresh science news.

Seven blocks later, I coast down the long driveway toward the large plantation house full of old people—and Drew. I heel down my kickstand, climb the six front steps, and find that the front door is locked. But a light shines at the end of the porch. I walk down, look in the window.

Drew Levinson is playing chess in the recreation room. Her opponent is Bill Goddeau. He's a retired mathematician who likes to quiz Drew about theories I can't understand. I lift my hand and rap on the window. Neither of them looks over. They are fixated on the chess board. I bang my fist on the glass. Drew glances up, stares at me for a long moment. After another long, long moment, she stands up and walks out of the room. I move back to the front door. When it opens, Drew stands there, holding it open only wide enough for me to see her purple shirt. It's covered with gray cat hair. Moses, I presume.

"Need something?" she asks.

"Yeah, I need to come in."

She gives me a hard look then walks away, leaving the door open. I step inside and follow her down the hall. The strange hush that always hangs over this place feels heavier than ever. Usually it's just the quiet of old people not talking. But right now it's like old people are dreaming, remembering. And you can feel their regrets. I talk to the back of Drew's hairy shirt. "Karlene says Myra's going to be okay."

She keeps walking.

"Drew?"

"I'm about to win this game, do you mind?"

In the recreation room, Bill Goddeau glances up and smiles. His white hair looks like it was probably last combed in 1982.

"Check," he tells Drew.

She sits down at the chessboard, then picks up a real silver knight —some medieval soldier riding a chain-mailed horse. Drew leaps the knight over two silver pawns that resemble medieval peasants and lands on a white square. I think the square is white marble. The black squares look like onyx. Or obsidian. But with those real silver pieces, it's a stunning chess set.

Drew positions her knight next to a bishop holding a Bible. "Checkmate," she says.

"I was hoping you'd forget that move." Bill gazes at the board, shaking his head. "Well played, Levinson. One more match?"

Drew raises her wrist to consult her purple wristwatch. Purple is her favorite color. "I'll play, provided we finish within twenty-two minutes."

"Why twenty-two?"

"We've played two games in forty-four minutes, minus the interruption from Raleigh."

My head swivels. *Interruption?*

"If we finish the next game within twenty-two minutes, we can achieve a perfect sixty-six minutes of play."

The suddenly excited math people begin rearranging their fine silver figures on the polished stone board.

"Uh, Drew?"

She places her peasant pawns on the squares. Each one has a painted white hat. Bill's pieces have black hats.

"Can I talk to you?" I ask.

"I'm busy," she says.

"Hey." Bill leans forward. "Ask her about my king."

She turns her narrow face toward me, dark eyebrows cinched down into a frown. "Someone stole Bill's king."

"Sorry?"

Bill picks up a stump of foil, positioned next to the queen who is wearing a bejeweled crown. "My king was spirited away. Absconded. Purloined."

I wait, making sure he's done being a thesaurus. "I'm sorry to hear that."

"Me, too." He shakes his white head. "Theft violates all the moral laws of the universe."

"That is true," Drew says. "And don't forget about Stan's cuff links."

I look at Drew. "Stan?"

"Stan Pillink." She says the name like he's some old friend.

I look at Bill, since he's the talkative one.

"Stan lives in 3H," Bill says. "Always wears cuff links with his dress shirts. Monogrammed with the initials S and P. One for each link. But now that somebody stole all the S links, Stan only has the Ps. And believe me, nobody around here wants to be known as PP."

Drew guffaws. "Bill, that's a good one."

I clench my jaw—mostly to keep my mouth from falling open. My obsessive-compulsive best friend, the girl who Lysols even her own germs, is laughing at potty jokes?

She sends a silver peasant across two squares. "I told Bill you'd look into the theft."

"Really."

"More accurately," says Bill, the mathematician, "Drew said, 'Raleigh can find all these missing objects.' She said you'd find them before I could say, 'Forsyth-Edwards Notation.'"

I pry open my jaw. "*What?*"

"Forsyth-Edwards Notation—FEN." Drew keeps her gaze on the silver pieces. "That's the notation system for recording positions on the chess board. See, the squares run from A8 to H8, and the ranks are—"

"No. The other part."

She waits. Bill moves a peasant-pawn forward one square. "You mean, finding the cuff links?"

"Bingo."

"Chess, to be accurate," Bill says.

Drew laughs again and an out-of-body sensation sweeps over me. It feels like I rode my bike through the fourth dimension. Drew Levinson, sunshine and light, laughing at jokes that would normally make her swab her fingers with rubbing alcohol. And the strange feeling only grows stronger as she turns toward me, wrapping one wild strand of brown hair behind her ear. She gives me a look.

Oh, dear God.

I know this look. It's the same look she gave me when our class-mate Sloane Stillman died. The look I got when I refused to enter a science competition in North Carolina. The look that kept ruining my relationship with the most gorgeous guy in town. My stomach knots. "Drew, my bike's outside. I can ride you home."

She slides a castled-rook across the squares. "I'm not leaving."

"But Myra's better—"

"No thanks to you."

I stand there, waiting for...what? I don't know. Maybe I'm waiting for normal to come back. For everything to snap back into reality.

Drew looks up.

"You can leave," she says. "But I'm staying."

6

I WALK AWAY from Drew and Bill and their twenty-two-minute chess game, feeling like my heart's hiccupping. I even hold one hand over my chest, like that might make the pain go away. But it doesn't.

I take the stairs to the second floor and lean my ear against the wooden door of apartment 2B. I hear English voices bickering.

I knock.

"Enter if you dare!" cries Frances Harmon.

My grandmother sits in a yellow armchair that's way too big for this small apartment. She's watching TV but as soon as she sees me, she mutes the Brits and stands up, opening her arms.

"Raleigh, the perfect gift!"

My dad's mom isn't related to me by blood. David Harmon, her son, married my mom and adopted me and Helen. We were little kids and moved into the big house on Monument Avenue, the house where Frances Harmon had lived for more than forty years. And yet she always acted like we were her natural-born grandchildren, even when Helen took one look at the tall old woman who was all elbows and angles and said, "You're gawky." Helen was eight. She'd just learned that word and probably didn't realize it wasn't a compliment. Probably.

Instead of being offended, Frances Harmon took it like a badge.

"You're right," she said. "You can call me gawky."

We only changed the spelling.

Tonight, Gockey's face looks shiny from cold cream, framed by a soft cloud of white hair.

She looks at me, carefully. "Everything all right at home?"

I nod.

"And yet you ran over here in the middle of the night?"

"I biked." Like that makes a difference. "I just wanted to check on Drew."

Gockey waves her long hand, swatting away my gnat-thought. "A little dehydration, that's all. Myra's going to be fine. Wilma confirmed it. Her 'sources' told her." Gockey makes air quotes around the word *sources*. "But everyone knows the source, Dr. Boatman."

"Who's he?"

"The doctor in the infirmary. Wilma hounds the poor man. She knows all the health scares make us read her silly *Gazette*. You should've seen her at dinner tonight, clinking her glass until everyone paid attention. She said the *Gazette* is doing an upcoming story on dehydration. Very important, she said. Dehydration is apparently bad for our electronics."

"Your electronics?"

"Drew said Wilma meant *electrolytes*. Whatever those are."

I sit down at her tiny kitchen table. There are only two chairs, because this apartment is so small.

Gockey sits down across from me. "What's wrong?"

"Drew was at dinner?"

"Oh, yes. And life of the party, once we learned Myra was going to be alright."

I stare at the television. British men in tweed suits drive a miniature car on the wrong side of a narrow road. I can feel Gockey's gaze on me.

"Raleigh—"

"It's nothing."

"You need cake," she says.

"Gockey, I have school tomorrow. And it's almost eleven o'clock."

"Just in time!" In two steps, she's in the kitchen. "Chocolate with cherry-vanilla frosting. According to *my* sources, it tastes like Cherry Coke." Gockey bakes cakes for the kids on the cancer ward at the Medical College of Virginia.

She places the glass-domed plate on the small round table and my salivary glands spring a leak. When she turns around, rummaging in a drawer, she says, "Frances, where did you put that knife?"

She opens another drawer.

"Where do you think it could be?" she asks herself.

Gockey talks to herself. After we'd been living in the big house about three years, my mom's paranoia got really bad. She decided Gockey wasn't talking to herself, but to those surveillance bugs in the laundry soap.

"Don't you worry," Gockey tells herself. "It'll turn up."

"Can't find your cake knife?" I know this knife. It was an anniversary gift from Grandpa Harry. It has an ivory handle and their wedding date is engraved on the sterling silver blade. "When did you last see it?"

"I can't remember and it doesn't matter." She reaches into the drawer. "We have forks. We can eat the whole cake with forks."

We dig in and I'm humming after the first bite. It tastes like Hershey's started making bread. And the cherry vanilla icing makes my tongue feels carbonated. Between creamy bites, Gockey tells me another Wilma story, her long arms gesturing to make it even funnier. I take another bite and decide there is comfort food—and then there is food made by people who want to comfort us, even this late on a Thursday night of the worst day of the year.

"Thank you," I tell her when I'm too full to continue.

She reaches over, giving my hand a squeeze. She doesn't say anything. But then, she doesn't need to.

That cake said it all.

7

THE NEXT MORNING, exhausted from late-night biking and sugar-crashing in my sleep, I shuffle through my classes like I'm one of the old people at Sunset Gardens.

And because I skipped English yesterday to spring Drew from her self-made prison, I know that Sandbag—a.k.a. Mr. Sandberg—is going to punish me as soon as I sit down in English.

Standing at the front of the classroom, Sandbag lifts the poetry book in one hand like a burning torch and reads aloud. He reads the way a bad stage actor spirals into a major death scene.

"TELL ME NOT, in mournful numbers,
　　Life is but an empty dream!
　　For the soul is dead that slumbers,
　　And things are not what they seem."

TINSLEY TEAGER SITS to my left. The moment Sandbag sucks in a deep breath for the next bellow, Tinsley leans toward me, whispering. "Things were *never* what they seemed."

Behind her, Norwood Godwin, her lackey, giggles.

At a low moment like this, I used to be able to glance over at Drew for some good eye-rolling. But Drew now takes all her classes online with MIT. Everything except English. Sandbag refused to let her go. Every week, I bring her the homework and then Sandbag quizzes her over the phone.

"Miss Harmon."

I knew it.

"Yes, sir?"

He peels his shoes off the floor, coming toward me like I'm magnetized. "What literary device is employed in this first stanza?"

I look down. The book is open on my desk but the poem swims across the page. I look up again. Sandbag's cold heavy eyes hold me in a death grip. He's going to stand there until I answer.

I take a blind guess. "Declarative?"

"*Declarative?*" Sandbag makes it sound like something stuck to the bottom of the garbage can. "For one moment, we will bypass the dubious irony that you uttered the word *declarative* as a question."

He smiles, full of pity.

"Instead, we shall ponder whether Longfellow, genius of the Western cannon, would employ a prosaic *declarative* opening at the beginning one of the world's most classic poems."

Sandbag.

The guy can take any piece of literature and turn it into a special broadcast for his own supposed intelligence.

Tinsley raises her delicate hand, making sure to shake her wrist so we all notice the new white-diamond tennis bracelet. I know it's totally wrong to hate people—*I know it*—but it's also wrong to lie. But the truth is I hate Tinsley. Same way I hate rats, snakes, and people who stab you in the back while saying to your face, "Bless your heart."

Sandbag's sagging face shifts toward Her Snakiness. "Miss Teager, you would like to offer an insight?"

"Yes." Tinsley's smile spreads icily, like frost spidering over winter glass. "Longfellow's saying you only live once and it's only the losers who go around moping. Those people end up all alone." Tinsley turns to me. "*Alone.* Totally *alone.*"

Sandbag looks confused—naturally, since Tinsley isn't talking about the poem.

"I see," he lies. "But that insight is rather tangential to these particular lines, especially when stated in such colloquial terms."

I would like to smack my head on my desk. Ten times.

The only good news is that since Sandbag's already humiliated me, I'm off the hook. For now. The next forty-three minutes are spent watching the time. When the bell finally rings, everyone bolts. I slowly make my way to Sandbag's desk. Drew's homework is waiting.

"Please remind Miss Levinson that I will be testing her memorization on Monday evening."

"Yes, sir."

I turn to leave.

"Miss Harmon?"

I glance back.

"I trust Miss Levinson is improving?"

I head for the door. "Never better."

MY BIKE IS the only one in the rack outside school, now that Drew's purple Schwinn stays in her garage. I wrap the coil-lock into my backpack, and wonder if my mom's meds will work long enough for my dad to finally teach me how to drive. But that hopeful thought gets burst to bits by the sight of a familiar truck turning into the St. Catherine's parking lot.

Quickly, I turn away. But my heart still manages to mule-kick my chest. I yank my bike from the rack.

The school's side door whips open. Tinsley totters out, her blue plaid school uniform replaced by a white skirt, black tank top, and four-inch sandals that make her walk like a starving panther on the prowl.

I hop on my bike.

From the corner of my eye, I can see DeMott Fielding getting out of the truck. He's wearing his white St. Christopher's School baseball uniform, and his cleats make clickery sounds on the pavement as he opens the passenger door for Tinsley.

I start pedaling like my hair's on fire.

The truck door closes.

I pedal faster, quads in flames. Up ahead, the stoplight is green. I spin my feet—*faster, faster*—my dork-skirt fluttering in the wind.

The truck is coming up behind me.

Do not look up.

But somehow, I refuse to listen to myself.

I look up.

Tinsley smiles at me from the passenger seat. I look down, watching my front wheel as it spins.

Keep your head down.

And yet... as the truck passes, I glance up again. Through the cab window, I can see the back of DeMott's head. Brown wavy hair, shoulders of his baseball uniform. I'm just about to look away when his blue eyes appear in the rearview mirror. One single glance. One split-second of time.

He looks at me.

And then, he looks away.

8

It's just before three o'clock when I arrive at Sunset Gardens.

Mrs. Donner is waiting in her pink bathrobe.

"Where's the milkman?" she demands, as I come through the front door.

I shrug off my backpack. "The milkman is on his way."

"I can't send the children to school without breakfast." Her gray hair smushes against her face, like she just woke up. "Where is that milkman?"

"He'll be here any minute."

Mrs. Donner wanders back to her chair beside the front door, already forgetting about me.

People say time is like a river. And I agree—time never stops. But here in Sunset Gardens, time is also sort of circular. Moments come, moments go—and then the exact same moment comes around again, like it never happened before. Every afternoon, Mrs. Donner repeats this milkman routine. Every night, dinner is served at 5:00 p.m. Time rolls forward but on the same schedule every day, each day just like the day before, and the day after. Which is why everyone in here was so excited about Drew's surprise visit—something different was going to happen.

And boy, did it.

I check the recreation room. The TV is playing to a crowd of white-haired people, all napping in their chairs. I don't see Drew. Or Bill Goddeau. I walk back down the front hall, assuring Mrs. Donner that the milkman is coming, then I cut down the shorter hallway to Karlene's office. Her door is open. She's at her desk, typing with a landline phone propped between her shoulder and ear.

"Of course," she says into the phone. "Thank you."

When she sees me, she waves me in. "We couldn't do it without your help," she tells the person on the phone.

Waiting for her to finish, I stand at the front window. A brown UPS truck is coming down the long driveway.

"We are deeply grateful," Karlene says.

The brown truck stops at the front steps. But for several long moments, nobody gets out. Finally, the driver appears in his brown shorts and shirt. He stands in the truck's opening, staring at the front door, holding a cardboard box like it might contain a pipe bomb.

"I'll make sure all the paperwork's taken care of," Karlene says.

She hangs up. I can't take my eyes off the UPS guy. Karlene comes over, standing beside me at the window.

"That poor guy," she says.

"No kidding. They should pay him extra for dealing with Mrs. Donner."

"By the way," Karlene sighs, "would you like a cat?"

Some kind of dread creeps over me. I'm not a cat fan. I hold my gaze on the UPS guy who is bravely stepping out of the truck, getting ready for Mrs. Donner. "Did something happen to Moses?"

"Moses—Myra's cat?"

I nod.

"Moses is fine. But Mrs. Donner says somebody keeps putting a cat in her apartment."

"And, let me guess, it's her cat?"

Karlene nods, sadly. "Her mind's getting worse."

The UPS guy slowly makes his way up the stairs. "But Myra's better, right?"

"Yes, thank God. But, Raleigh…"

I look over. Another wave of dread.

Karlene touches my arm, preparing me. "Drew came in today and asked to move in. Permanently."

"*What?*"

"She's taking Myra's spare bedroom."

"She can't be serious."

"Oh, Drew is quite serious. And I'm hesitant to say no because everyone loves her, including me. I called our insurance agent, begging. But he said our policy doesn't cover teenagers."

"What's that mean?"

"He said Drew's a liability risk."

I shake my head, still not getting it.

"If anybody gets hurt while Drew's living here, even if it's not her fault, we could get sued."

My dad's a judge. And I spend a lot of time sitting in his court-room. I know that "getting sued" is pretty much the legal equivalent of being told *you've got cancer*. "I'm so sorry, Karlene, I never thought—"

"Raleigh, don't. You had the best intentions. That's what counts."

I look out the window. But guilt wraps its chains around my heart. "What about another insurance agent?"

"I thought of that, too. I called around. Nobody wants to insure a group of elderly people plus one teenager. We're already what's known as a bad risk. Old people tend to have accidents. They fall, break hips, get sick—"

"And pass out from too much excitement."

She looks at me with sympathy. "You've got to stop beating your-self up."

I turn to the window. My eyes sting. And it's not the sunlight.

"I did manage one compromise," she says. "Our insurance agent agreed to write up a temporary policy. We can have three days' guest coverage for Drew. By then, Myra should be back in her apartment and I'm sure you can get Drew home—"

The UPS guy leaps off the porch, sprinting for the brown van.

Right behind him, Mrs. Donner stands on the porch, giving him an earful for not bringing milk for her children. She stays there until the brown van is speeding down the driveway, squealing back onto the main road.

"If Drew doesn't leave after three days, what happens?"

Karlene sighs. "Let's think positive," she says.

9

MYRA LEVINSON'S apartment is on the third floor—number 3G—but when I knock, there's no answer. Opening the door, I poke my head inside. And cough.

"Drew?"

I can hear her voice, somewhere deep in the apartment. I step inside. Cough again.

"Drew, it's me."

"What do you want?"

"Fresh air."

Myra's apartment is three times the size of Gockey's—the Levinsons have a lot of money—but it feels smaller because of Myra's smoking habits. The whole place smells like an ashtray.

I find Drew in the living room, kneeling on the carpet. Apparently talking to the dust ruffle on the floral couch.

"Polycyclic aromatic hydrocarbons," she says.

"What?"

"Hydrogen cyanide. Nitrogen oxide. Benzene—"

"What are you talking about?"

She glances over her shoulder, dark brows pulled into an angry frown. "I'm giving you the chemical components in tobacco smoke.

That's what you're smelling. But never mind." She turns back to the couch. "Moses, I want you to come out. Now."

A thick gray cat tail twitches from under the dust ruffle. Probably also full of aromatic hydrocarbons.

I look around and find my cell phone on the coffee table next to an empty ashtray. Picking it up, I check the battery. Still almost full charge. Drew has nobody to call—she probably didn't even call her parents, who probably didn't even notice she was gone. I drop the phone into my pocket.

"I have your English homework."

"On a scale of one to ten, how bad is it?"

"We need to memorize a poem by Longfellow."

"That's an eight," she says. "Do I have to figure out what it means, too?"

Drew doesn't mind working on literary architecture—poetic meters, for instance, are almost like math. But getting her to see what the poet's trying to say, that's always a struggle.

"Don't worry," I tell her. "Tinsley already figured out the meaning. She says Longfellow meant I'm some kind of loser."

Drew stands up. Dust clings to her jeans. "Tinsley's so dumb she can't even comprehend her own ignorance."

She holds out her hand.

"What?" I ask.

"The homework?"

Amazed, I reach into my pack. Normally she acts like the homework is coming from a leper colony—she makes me spray the papers with Lysol before she'll even touch them. But now she takes the pages, reading the poem, and pulling her wild hair behind her ears.

"This is long," she says, already defeated.

"But look at the structure." I stand beside her, reading aloud over her narrow shoulder.

"TELL ME NOT, in mournful numbers,
    Life is but an empty dream!

For the soul is dead that slumbers,
And things are not what they seem."

"ONE AND THREE," she says. "Two and four."

"Good." Drew Levinson can count rhymes like nobody else. "But remember, Sandbag wants you to say A-B-A-B."

"I'm using numbers."

Yeah, preparing Drew for these Monday night phone calls with Sandbag has drained entire weekends from my life. Which didn't exactly help my relationship with DeMott. "The whole poem needs to be memorized by Monday night. So if we ride back to your house right now, we could start—"

"No."

"Drew—"

"Raleigh, I'm not leaving."

"You can't stay here."

"Why not? Bubbie has an extra bedroom."

"Drew, this is an old folks' home. You are fifteen."

"So?"

"*Fifteen.*"

"Age is a state of mind."

"You're a math person. Age is a number."

"Bill Goddeau and I decided that conscious reality exists in a state of perpetual motion. That makes numbers subordinate to reality."

My head is swimming. "Okay, you want reality? If you stay here, Sunset Gardens loses its insurance and then wha—"

The cat squawls.

We both look down.

From under the dust ruffle, the long gray tail emerges. Followed by a cat with really long gray fur. And a white beard. Like his human namesake. He meows at Drew.

She scoops him up—and buries her face in his fur, even though he's covered with dust from under the couch.

"Oh, Moses," she coos. "Let's get you something to eat."

I stand totally amazed. Drew has lectured me for years about the biohazards of dust—dust being primarily composed of dead skin cells, which even I think is gross. And yet, here she is, toting a hazmat-level cat into the kitchen as if nothing's wrong.

Moses, perched on her thin shoulder, gazes at me with sharp yellow eyes.

Drew snuggles him closer. "I love you, Moses."

I follow them into the kitchen, which is as big as Gockey's whole apartment, and sets the cat on the floor.

"Liver and chicken feast?" She opens one of the cabinets.

The smoke stink is bad enough. But canned cat food? At the back of my throat, my uvula starts hopping up and down.

Drew dumps the marinated meat goo into a food dish that has *Moses* painted on its side.

"You really need to open a window," I say.

"More importantly," she says, "did you consider the missing objects?"

"No." I yank down the sleeve of my white blouse, pulling it over my hand so I can cover my nose. "I'm not interested."

"I checked Bubbie's jewelry. She's missing one earring from several sets."

I start to tell her that doesn't mean theft but—oh, man—*that look* is back on her face. "Drew," I say through my blouse, "you can't be serious."

She watches the bearded gray cat scarfing up the goo. "I've performed some calculations."

No.

Please.

No.

"Bill's sterling silver king chess piece, plus Stan's cuff links which are monogrammed and made of gold, plus Bubbie's missing earrings equals $11,252. And seventeen cents." She turns to the sink, rinsing the empty can. "Does that amount meet the threshold for grand larceny?"

"And Mrs. Donner believes the UPS guy is the milkman."

She looks over her shoulder, dark eyebrows cinched together. "Your point?"

"Old people forget things."

"That is not what is happening here."

"Really? Gockey can't remember where she put her favorite cake knife."

"I'll add that to my list."

"Don't."

"Oh, she found it?"

When I don't reply, Drew nods.

"That's what I thought. The cake knife goes on the list."

"Drew, at least admit it's possible all these people just forgot where they put things."

"For the sake of science, I will admit it's *possible*. But Bubbie has two PhDs in chemistry and reads an entire book every week. She's not going to forget where she put one earring in each pair."

"Your grandmother is on oxygen."

Drew glares at me, brown eyes like amber knives.

"I'm sorry, Drew, but we both know memory is part of the brain. And the brain needs oxygen. *That's* science."

"I see." She places the sparkling clean can in an immaculate recycling container that makes me wonder if the Levinson DNA is programmed for OCD. "So you think Stan forgot where he put all the S cuff links? And Bill Goddeau forgot where he put that *one* chess piece. You want to tell me that's possible?"

I pause before answering. I don't know Stan. Or Bill Goddeau, who doesn't seem senile. But I know Drew, and I know how she gets these ideas. These theories. Hypotheses. Formulations. Like her massive brain didn't come equipped with an off switch. The busy brain that was the last straw for DeMott.

"Why would anyone steal those things?" I ask. "One chess piece—what good is that? One earring, one cuff link? What's the point?"

She turns her back to me.

"Drew, this is logic."

Moses looks up from his bowl with bits of meaty brown disgust-ingness clinging to his white beard. I gag and back away.

Drew smiles down at him. "Do you want another can?"

I could throw up. Or scream at her.

I back all the way out of the kitchen.

"I'm going to get some fresh air."

10

THESE THIRD-FLOOR APARTMENTS are the penthouse suites of Sunset Gardens, and Myra has a balcony. I slide open the glass door and step outside, breathing in spring air that never smelled so good.

Down the long driveway that leads to the street, I can see the city baseball stadium. It's surrounded by steaming smoke stacks, including the Sauer's spice factory. I take another sniff. Nutmeg. Or cloves. I glance back to check on Drew, but the only thing there is my reflection in the glass. A wind-blown girl, still in her school uniform. Looking frustrated. And lonely.

I turn back around.

When Drew and I were nerdy middle schoolers—instead of nerdy high schoolers—we met every Friday night for "Burgers and Brains." Weird name, I know. But we tested each other with new discoveries and ate cheeseburgers and fries—mine dipped in Duke's mayonnaise. At first, we just microwaved frozen burgers at Drew's house because her mom didn't care what we did. But later we moved to Big Man Burgers, which is right behind that baseball stadium. The owner, Titus Williams, was a major league baseball player. Baseball was Drew's obsession, back when she used to leave the house.

I pull out my phone and tap the memorized number. Titus answers.

"She still locked up in that house?" he asks.

Hello to you, too.

"No, I got her out."

He waits. "But."

Titus has this way of talking—actually, of not talking. For instance, if a meteor was hurtling toward earth at 500,000 miles an hour and aimed right at your head, Titus *might* say, "Duck."

"Now she's stuck somewhere else," I say.

"So you walked her to first."

"I don't speak baseball."

Titus makes his weird grumbling sound. Like muttering without words.

"I was calling," I tell him, "because I thought if you could make another delivery, it might help." Back in April, Titus delivered burgers to Drew's house. "And we're not that far from your place."

More grumble-mutter. I only half-listen because down below, a familiar truck is coming down to the driveway.

No.

Please.

Not—

"Where?" Titus asks.

"Uh, her grandmother's."

"This ain't Little Red Riding Hood. Gimme an address."

The truck parks near the stairs and DeMott Fielding gets out. My heart slams into my throat.

"Sunset Gardens. It's..."

DeMott's baseball uniform is clean. And Tinsley doesn't seem to be with him. I listen as his cleats click up the front stairs, then turn my back—only to get a really good look at my own lonely reflection in the glass door. Me gives me a nasty look. "Sunset Gardens, it's a retirement home. About six blocks from your place."

"Sunset Gardens."

I want to reply: *That's what I just said.* But with Titus, you act like a smart-ass at your own risk. "Yes, Sunset Gardens."

"Sunset Gardens."

"Do you want me to say it again?"

"Get to the kitchen," he says.

"What?"

"The kitchen."

I squint at my reflection. My hair's scrunched into an almost useless ponytail. "What kitchen?"

"Tell Toots I sent you."

"Who's Too—?"

He hangs up.

11

WHEN I STEP inside Myra's apartment, coughing again, Drew says, "I hope that you were calling the police. *Somebody* needs to start investigating these stolen objects."

It seems entirely possible to me that when people adore their pets, something happens to the brains. Because here is Drew Levinson, Miss OCD America, cradling hairy Moses in her arms, not even flinching at his meaty beard, not to mention the still-attached dust bunnies.

"We need to go downstairs," I say.

"Is this another surprise?"

"But it's a really good one. I promise."

She sets Moses down and walks into the kitchen, washing out the second can of cat food. Then dries it with a paper towel and sets it inside the sparkling clean recycling bin. But then she turns the water back on and washes her hands. Over and over again, like she wants to scrub off the skin. *Bad sign.* Finally she turns off the water but goes through the ritual with the paper towels—each finger gets a fresh towel. She's stressed.

"Just downstairs," I say, trying to assure her. "Not outside. And you'll be glad."

She folds the paper towels into perfect squares, lays them in the recycling bin. "Show me your trick with the Scotch Tape."

Fine.

In Myra's "junk" drawer—which is so organized I'm certain about OCD in the Levinson DNA—I find a roll of Scotch Tape and stick a strip of it to the bottom edge of Myra's front door. Drew steps out, I close the door behind us, and attach the tape to the hallway floor.

"That's all?" she asks.

"Sorry."

"No. I'm glad. Einstein said things should be as simple as possible, but not any simpler."

We walk down the hall to the stairs, Drew counting our steps in multiples of six and whispering the numbers because she's still stressed. I really want to apologize for what happened—*I didn't think Myra would pass out.* But I can tell she's not ready to hear that from me. Maybe an apology would even make things worse. We take the stairs—more counting—but Drew halts at the bottom.

"Do you hear that?" she asks.

It's some kind of music playing, those old-fashioned tunes my parents like to listen to. "What about it?"

"Dance lessons," she tells me. "Mondays, Wednesdays, Fridays at 3:20. I can learn the rhumba."

I smile, but inside I'm thinking, *I've got to get her out of here before she turns into an old lady.*

The dining room is located on the first floor, way in back. A big open space, it has a dozen round tables all set far enough apart that wheelchairs and walkers can maneuver around them. As I start crossing the room, guessing where this kitchen might be, Drew grabs my arm.

"This is all wrong."

"What?"

"Dinner is served at five." She lifts her arm, pointing at her purple wristwatch. "It's three fifty-five. We need to stay on the schedule."

"It's okay, really."

Her thin fingers tighten around my arm. So tight it hurts. But you know what hurts more? Knowing that I almost killed her grand-mother. And that Drew's now full of new fear and Sunset Gardens might have some serious financial problems if she refuses to leave. *What if they have to call the cops, forcibly remove her?* I place my hand on hers and guide her toward the swinging doors on the far wall. When I've eaten dinner here with Gockey, I've seen a waiter come out of those doors.

"Raleigh—"

"Drew, don't worry."

"I'm Jewish."

"Pretend you're not." I push open the swinging door. "This is a really good surprise."

But it's not.

On the other side of the large kitchen, a short black woman stands holding a pen and a clipboard. Bright red eyeglasses perch on the end of her wide nose. Beside her short frame, pallets of shrink-wrapped food look like towers. To her right, pots of water steam on an industrial stove. The same kind of steam that seems to rise from her dark eyes.

"Hi," I say.

The woman lowers her chin. She glares at me, eyes above the red frames. "Help you?"

Drew shakes her head. She is standing so close to me, her hair tickles my face. Shakes and shakes.

I try to smile. "Somebody told me we should come here."

"Somebody?" The woman moves slowly, like a python slithering close, ready to squeeze you to death. She sets the clipboard on the stainless steel island. "*Who* said come into *my* kitchen?"

"T-T-T." I try again. "Titus, Titus Williams."

Drew gasps. "Titus?"

I nod.

Her fingers squeeze my arm even tighter. "Titus, is he the surprise?"

I nod.

Without moving her head, the woman shifts her heated gaze to Drew. "Y'all know Titus?"

It's as if she said a magic word. The kitchen's back door swings opens and in walks a giant black man with skin so dark it could be forged iron. He wears a white-and-black referee's uniform. And in his huge hands, he carries three white bags.

My mouth waters.

Titus stares at Drew. "Best on-base percentage?"

She whispers, "Ted Williams."

"What else?"

"Ted Williams had the best on-base percentage for a single season."

"How long?"

"Sixty-one years."

The black woman still hasn't moved one centimeter but her eyes —round and large and the color of night—follow every volleying word as they keep talking baseball.

Finally, Titus sets the white bags on the stainless steel island near the clipboard. I lick my lips.

"Gehrig in '34," he says.

"Forty-nine home runs," Drew replies, "while playing for the New York Yankees."

"RBIs."

"One hundred and sixty-five."

"Drew." He smiles. "You alright."

She smiles back and lets go of my arm. Titus reaches into the white bags and pulls out the treasure. Cheeseburgers. Fries.

I close my eyes, humming my grace. *Thank you.*

"What's up with you?" Titus asks.

I open my eyes, expecting to see him asking me that question, but he's talking to the woman.

"Inventory," she tells him. "And I just lost count."

She harrumphs.

That sound. I know that sound. It's that grumble-mutter-with-no-words. I pick up one of the warm, paper-wrapped cheeseburgers and steal a glance at Drew, hoping she's catching on. But she's only staring down at the burger like the stainless steel island is for dissecting frogs.

"What's wrong?" I ask.

"I'm going to need a fork. And a knife."

Silence.

Silence, but I can hear the question popping into our minds. *Who eats a cheeseburger with a knife and fork?*

"Can I have one?" she asks.

The woman walks over to a large closet. On the shelves, small appliances sit near pots and pans, cups and glasses. And some plastic bins. The woman reaches into the bins. I hear metal clattering. She carries a knife and fork back to Drew. "You gonna wash 'em yourself, hear me?"

Drew nods. She's holding the knife and fork but still staring down at the steamed bun, glistening burger, and melted cheddar cheese. Carefully, she cuts the food into tiny pieces.

"Somethin' wrong with my son's burgers?" the woman asks.

Drew shakes her head.

Son.

But—hold on—Titus has a *mom*?

If I wasn't eating the greatest cheeseburger in town, my mouth would be hanging open.

Titus looks at me, maybe realizing my shock. "This is Toots," he says. "Y'all can introduce yourselves."

"I'm Raleigh." I nod toward my fearful best friend. "And this is Drew."

Titus picks up the pen and clipboard. "Mama, you gonna thank me."

"How's that?"

He offers Drew the clipboard and points to the pallets of food. "Count it."

"Count?" Drew's eyebrows slant up, excited. "All of it?"

"Every ounce."

Drew takes the clipboard and walks toward the pallets like they're holy. Like she can't believe this honor.

Titus leans down—way-way-way down—and kisses Toots' cheek. "Gotta ref a game. Thank me later."

She swats his muscular arm. He walks over to the back door. But at the last moment, he turns around and looks at me. His brown gaze seems as intense as his mother's.

"You done good," he says.

And then, he is gone.

12

WHILE DREW STUDIES the clipboard and the shrink-wrapped food towers, I finish my cheeseburger.

Toots moves around the kitchen, throwing handfuls of salt in the steaming pots of water on the stove, pulling huge foil-wrapped pans from the super-big refrigerator.

"Titus told me 'bout you girls," she says.

Oh, boy. Last October, we were the reason Titus got thrown in jail. "I'm sorry. We were wrong."

She makes that no-word-mutter sound. Which, if I had to translate, would be, *You better be sorry*. She fills a tall pot at the sink that runs across the left wall, then plunks it down on the iron stovetop. She flicks on the gas, opens a huge bag of rice, measures out cups and cups. But she keeps glancing at Drew. She harrumphs only once more as a small square packet plops from the rice bag into her measuring cup. Toots plucks the thing from the grains, holding it up. The cover reads, DO NOT EAT.

"Don't gotta tell me Do Not Eat." She tosses it into a jar beside the stove. It's half-full of more DO NOT EAT packets.

"I need to point something out." Drew waves the clipboard. "Your inventory system isn't efficient."

Toots stirs the rice pot with a wooden spoon. "I *like* my system."

"You won't after I demonstrate how it could be better."

Toots glances at me.

I shrug, eat a fry. I would really like some mayonnaise for dipping but I'm too scared to ask Toots. She's already at a slow-boil with us being in here.

"For instance," Drew continues, tapping her pen on the clipboard. "You just used six cups of rice for tonight's dinner."

Toots hesitates. "So?"

"So do you use that same amount each day?"

"What if I do?"

"Minus Sunday, because dinner isn't served here on Sunday, you are using thirty-six cups of rice per week." Drew points the pen at the stacks of food. "Each rice bag contains forty-eight cups. That means each week you have nine cups of rice remaining. So if you ordered five bags of rice, it would work out better."

Toots waits. "Say what?"

"Five times forty-eight is 240. Divided by 36, which is the number of cups you use weekly, you would have 6.66666667 cups of rice. That's a truly great number. Nearly perfect."

Toots holds the wooden spoon like a monument of somebody cooking. The only thing that moves are her big round eyes—and they move toward me. But I don't know what to say. This is Drew. Math machine extraordinaire.

Finally, Toots says, "Tell it again."

"I can also perform the same calculations for green beans, mashed potatoes, rolls. You name it. Just tell me what you want."

"What I want?" Toots shakes the wooden spoon at her. "I wanna know why you don't eat nothin'."

"I'm just..." Drew stares down at the clipboard. "I'm just not that hungry anymore."

Toots harrumphs. "Know what your problem is?"

"Not really."

"You're lettin' your imagination hold you hostage."

Drew's mouth opens into a silent *Oh*. The face she makes whenever a new truth bursts into her overworked brain.

Toots, however, is already heading back to the stove, and suddenly the back door opens again. It's a young white guy wearing a bike helmet over dark hair. And he's reading a book.

"Niko!" Toots yells.

The guy keeps reading.

"NIKO!"

He glances up, slowly, one hand absently unclipping his bike helmet. He looks around the room, like he's just noticing us. "Did you say something?" he asks.

"Lawd!" Toots snaps the green beans, throwing them in the steaming pot. "You gotta live on another planet!"

Niko continues to read, hanging his helmet on a nail by the door.

"I want those tables set," Toots tells him, decapitating more beans. "And that book stays in here!"

Niko takes a large round tray from the wall and carries it to the closet, loading it up with forks, knives, spoons. The book lays open on the tray. He's still reading when he goes through the swinging doors.

"Always with his nose in a book," Toots grumbles.

I finish my food—and Drew's cut-up burger—then clean up the wrappers and bags. I also take Drew's fork and knife to the sink, washing and drying them. And, since we're already skating on thin ice, I take them back to the supply closet. I see bins of salad forks, serving forks, even tiny forks for shrimp and oysters. Very Southern. Finally, I find a regular fork bin and drop Drew's fork in there. Then I go through the knives. Southerners are all about entertaining. There are little butter knives, and salad knives, steak knives and...

Wait.

I reach into the bin.

The ivory handle feels cool and smooth in my palm. I lift the blade. On the sterling silver, the engraved words read, *To Frances. The sweetest of sweethearts. Love, Harry.* And below that, my grandparents' anniversary date.

I glance over at Toots. She's leaning down into the oven's open door, checking the foil-wrapped pans. I try to get Drew's attention but she's penciling something on the clipboard like it's a nuclear code. When Niko comes through the swinging doors, book open on the tray, Toots hollers at him about paying attention.

Carefully, I push the cake knife up my sleeve. And for several moments I stand there, paralyzed by the thoughts zinging through my head. I'm so lost by the thoughts that when my phone buzzes in my pocket, I jump.

With my non-cake-knife hand, I take it out and read the text.

It's from Karlene. **Where is Drew?**

I type, **With me. In the kitchen. Why?**

The cursor on the screen pulses, mimicking my pounding heartbeat. Something's wrong. I can feel it.

Myra isn't doing well. Asking for Drew. Can you get her over to the infirmary?

13

I OPEN the kitchen's back door and tell Drew what is very possibly a big fat stinking lie.

"You can do this."

Her purple Converse are stapled to the floor like she's a kitchen appliance. Behind her, Toots is hollering at Niko the waiter who still doesn't look up from his book.

"Drew." I gently take her skinny arm, trying to coax her down the back stairs, to the lawn that leads right to the infirmary. "Myra's asking to see you."

The green lawn. The leafy trees. The warm late-May afternoon of Virginia. But the way Drew's looking at it, this is the Bermuda Triangle. And yet I know deep inside this frightened girl is my best friend who called me yesterday and said, *Now.*

"Drew, remember how—"

"Hey!" Toots calls out. "Close that door!"

"Drew, c'mon, you need to move."

Toots stomps over, pointing that wooden spoon at her own face. "You see me? I'm sweatin' over boiling water. Don't let my air conditioning out!"

"Just one minute—"

"I don't got no one minute." Toots grabs Drew's arm and lifts her off the floor like she's nothing but another wooden spoon. She sets her down on the brick landing outside. "Don't you two be holdin' up my meals. Hear me?"

She slams the door.

I stare at Drew, wondering if she'll break down, freeze, go catatonic? A bird twitters from the leafy trees.

"Drew?"

In my dad's courtroom, I've seen some really weird human behavior. Sometimes eyewitnesses will take the stand but get so nervous they can't speak. That's how Drew looks right now, sort of shock-frozen-what-is-happening. But I've also seen how attorneys can snap people out of it.

"Drew, do you remember what Toots said?"

"Get out?"

"Okay, she did say that. But *before* that. When she asked why you weren't eating."

She blinks. "My imagination is holding me hostage."

"Right."

She shifts her gaze until she's looking me at directly, a look that sinks so deep it feels like a fishing hook just snagged my heart. She is in so much pain. But the Old Drew, she's in there, too.

"Myra wouldn't ask to see you unless she believed you could come. You can do this."

Her nod is so small I would've missed it except for the hair moving back and forth. I push Gockey's cake knife deeper up my sleeve, and take Drew's hand.

"Come on, I'll go with you."

FOR A MEDICAL PLACE, the infirmary doesn't smell all that bad. Definitely better than cigarette smoke and canned cat food.

"We're here to see Myra Levinson," I tell the nurse who is standing behind the front counter. She wears bright pink scrubs.

"Are you family?" she asks.

I point to Drew. "She is."

Pink Scrubs pushes the sign-in sheet toward Drew. I pick up the pen, placing it in Drew's shaking hand.

"Room 137," says Pink Nurse. "Down the hall to your right. But family only."

"Okay," I tell her. "Thanks."

I lead Drew down the hall by the hand. White halls, gleaming bright lights.

"One-thirty-seven." Drew whispers. "Raleigh, did you hear that? Room 137."

"Let me guess. Prime number?"

"Not just prime—*Pythagorean* prime!"

"Well, there you go." I have absolutely no idea what Pythagorean prime means but, hey, Drew sees it as a good sign. *Thank you, God.*

We pass several rooms. Beside the closed doors, plastic wall boxes hold medical files. And small windows run vertically down the sides of the doors. As we pass each room, I glance through the windows. Old people are sleeping through television shows.

Room 137's door is closed, too. I look through the side window. All I see is white—white floor, white bed, white blanket. And under the white blanket, some feet poking up. But it's got to be Myra. This is room 137.

"Okay." I start to turn the doorknob. "Pythagorean prime, custom-made for you."

Drew's breathing fast, her thick eyebrows yanked tight over her dark eyes. I'm pretty sure she's now imagining all the germs that are cruising through our cardiovascular systems looking for a good home. And I'll be honest, when Pink Nurse said I couldn't go into Myra's room, I wasn't exactly upset.

"I—I—I—" Drew stutters, goes silent.

I feel a temptation to pull the cake knife from my sleeve, maybe even use it as a weapon to force her into the room because I know she'll be fine—as Toots said, it's just her imagination holding her hostage. But the fear on her face makes me feel like the cake knife is nicking my heart. I glance through the window again. Myra's in there, waiting for Drew.

And it's my fault.

I look back at Drew. "You want me to go in for you?"

"Yes." Her thin shoulders slump with relief.

WALKING INTO MYRA'S ROOM, I get a bad-bad-*bad* case of both looking back and seeing forward. Like *deja vu* meets *preview of coming attractions*. Drew's own hospital visits suddenly merge with the sight of this elf-sized woman who looks just like Drew with sixty-six more years. And both of them have olive-colored skin that turns a puce-green when they don't feel good.

I tighten my clammy grip on the cake knife. "Myra?"

Her heavy eyelids flutter but don't open. The oxygen tube snakes under her nose but now there's also a clip on her index finger, connected by a cord to a heartbeat monitor. Her heart is beating very, very slow. That doesn't seem right.

"Hello, Myra?" I stare at the eerily familiar face, willing her wrinkled eyelids to open. "Myra, can you hear me?"

She lifts her left arm, the one with the monitor clip. Skin drapes off her arm bone like Spanish moss. I take hold of her hand, feeling the cold arthritic fingers curl around mine. She opens her eyes, looks directly at me, and says, "I love you, Drewery."

Her eyes close.

The monitor *beep, beep, beeps.*

I swallow that tightness in my throat. "I love you, too."

I stay there until her fingers uncurl from mine.

14

I STEP into the infirmary's hallway, glance down the hallway, and close the door to room 137.

"How is she?" Drew whispers, her voice urgent.

I glance down the hall again. No sign of Pink Nurse. "She seems really tired."

"But okay, right? She's okay?"

"Well, yeah. I'm sure it's nothing to worry about."

"Raleigh, I'm Jewish—worry is like a hobby."

I nod, my palm cupping the cake knife. I want to pull it out, show it to her, prove my point about no thefts here. But not now. Definitely not now. I need to get her into that room. "Why don't you come in there with me?"

She glances at the window, then back at me.

"Drew, it's ten more steps. If you lunge, we can make it six steps."

I open the door.

She stares across the space to Myra. "Bubbie?"

The eyelids flutter again.

"She can hear you," I say. "Go."

"Bubbie." Drew takes one careful step. Then another. She walks to the bed, not even counting her steps. "Bubbie, I'm here. It's me."

"Drewery, I know."

The oxygen machine wheezes air into that nose tube. The monitor beeps the heartbeats. And Drew Levinson stands there as rigid as a No. 2 Ticonderoga pencil.

"I'll go get you a chair," I tell her. "Hold her hand."

She nods and nods and the brown hair flows and flows, moving like that river of time that will never come around again.

THERE ARE no chairs in the hallway so I head back to the nurse's station, praying Pink Nurse will let me have one. But Pink Nurse is busy talking to an old man. And a young guy. And—

No.

Please. No.

"I just called Dr. Boatman," DeMott is telling her. "He's on his way over."

DeMott's great uncle, Cabell Fielding, is the black sheep of their family. Tall and thin as an iron rail, Uncle Cab is known for saying whatever pops into his head.

"I need a drink!" he tells Pink Nurse. "Not a doctor."

"He was clutching his chest when I got to his apartment," DeMott says, sounding stern. "He called my girlfriend's cell phone because he thought he was having a heart attack."

I tell myself to turn around *right now. This minute.* But do my feet obey? No. My feet are too busy listening to my heart which is climbing into my throat.

"I'm just thirsty!" Uncle Cab bellows. "Get me a drink."

Pink Nurse shifts the sign-in sheet toward DeMott.

I take one step back. Two. Three...

"Raleigh?"

"Oh, hi." I stand there, still wearing my dorky school uniform—with a cake knife shoved up the sleeve of my blouse. "What's going on?"

Pink Nurse says, "Mr. Fielding, please be patient. I'll have a room ready shortly."

"I don't need—"

DeMott cuts him off. "Thank you," he tells her.

Pink Nurse suddenly shifts her gaze to me. "Something wrong?"

Lady, I want to say. *You have no idea.*

Using my non-cake-knife arm, I point down the hall toward Myra's room. "We need a chair for room 137."

"Myra Levinson?"

I nod.

"Myra!" Uncle Cab pipes up. "She's one smart cookie. Hey, you got any cookies in here?"

DeMott stares at me. "Is Myra alright?"

"She's a little ... dehydrated."

"That's what I'm talking about!" Uncle Cab says. "We need whiskey around here. You got any?"

"Fresh out," I say.

"Dagnabbit." He tugs on his blue cotton shirt. The front is splotched with drops of grease like fake buttons. "Hey, aren't you Frannie Harmon's granddaughter?"

"Yes, sir."

"Woman broke my heart," he tells Pink Nurse, who is doing some kind of paperwork and looking frustrated about it. Uncle Cab goes on and on about my grandmother—which is exactly what he did the last two times I met him, which he doesn't seem to remember. How they went to school together, how she was "prettier than Donna Reed," how that "ol' scoundrel Harry Harmon" asked her out first. "Luckiest man in Richmond, may he rest in peace."

Pink Nurse keeps moving the papers around, scowling.

Uncle Cab winks at me. Just like before. "Put in a good word for me with Frannie, will ya?"

"Sure."

Pink Nurse tells them to wait there. She walks down the opposite hall, signaling my chair request isn't a priority. But I'm not staying here. I move toward the entrance and lift one of the molded plastic chairs that surround a short table with magazines telling old people how to enjoy retirement.

I pick up the chair and head toward the hallway.

"Need some help?" DeMott asks.

"No, I'm fine. Thanks." I carry the chair down the white hallway, awkwardly because of the knife splinting my forearm. But before I reach Myra's room, Uncle Cab's booming voice rolls down the hallway, rumbling past me, bouncing off the walls like a wild bowling ball.

"DeMott," he says. "You're making the same mistake with her that I made with her grandmother."

I don't hear any reply from DeMott.

15

AFTER DELIVERING DREW'S CHAIR, I decide to leave the two of them and take Gockey her cake knife. But as I'm coming across the courtyard, Karlene is standing under one of the big elm trees, hands on her plump hips, gazing up into the umbrella of green leaves.

Standing beside her, I look up and see something white stuck to the tree bark, about fifteen feet off the ground.

It's a cat.

A white cat with its claws gripping the bark.

"How do you feel about cats?" Karlene asks.

"Same way I feel about humans."

"Which is?"

"Depends on the human."

She looks over. The cat meows.

"Whitney," Karlene tells it. "Come down here. Now."

Whitney only glances down with eyes as blue as the clear sky above.

"How'd she get up there?" I ask, assuming Whitney means a female.

"Mrs. Donner."

"She opened the front door?"

Karlene sighs. "It's her cat. She told it to go home."

The front door opens, and I look over. Old people are streaming onto the front porch. The men wear paper napkins like bibs, tucked into their shirt collars. Dinnertime.

"It's gotta be Whitney," says one of the old men.

"Whitney got out again?"

"That cat needs help."

Karlene, sighing again, looks at me with a flat expression. For some reason it reminds me a lid placed over a boiling pot. "Did Drew go see Myra?"

"Yes."

Karlene lets out a long breath, not a sigh. Just relief. "Thank you. And when do you think she will be leav—"

"Karlene!" Someone is yelling from the porch. "What's wrong with Whitney?"

Karlene looks up at the cat—still in vertical cling—then calls back to the porch, telling them the cat will be fine, go back inside, finish their dinner. But nobody moves and I'm not really paying attention anymore because a car's coming down the long driveway. An old black car. Trouble.

"Whitney—*no!*"

Like a cotton ball shot from a rifle, the white cat bolts up the rough bark. Karlene gives an exasperated cry, just as the black car rattles to a stop near the porch. A woman gets out. She has bright red hair and wears a tie-dyed dress large enough to double as a circus tent.

My Aunt Charlotte.

"Frannie," someone calls out from the porch, "your daughter's here."

Gockey appears as several residents lift their wooden canes, pointing first at Aunt Charlotte then at the tree, then giving Gockey a play-by-play of the cat's movements like it's a football game between Virginia Tech and University of Virginia. One thing's for sure—Wilma Kingsford is definitely going to write about all this in the *Gazette*.

My aunt traipses past the porch, her clothing billowing in the humid afternoon. She walks right up to Karlene and demands, "Is that the same cat as last time?"

But before Karlene can answer, my aunt says, "I'm calling the fire department."

Karlene starts to protest, but my aunt only traipses back to her old black car and starts rummaging around inside. Aunt Charlotte believes cell phones "contaminate" our auras or something weird like that, but my dad made her get one to keep in her car. I was in that car in March when it broke down and we had to hitchhike to our hotel in North Carolina. What's even weirder than the whole contaminate-the-auras idea that is my dad's sister can afford anything she wants—new cars, cell phones, real clothing. She's married to one of the richest men in Virginia. His family owns a famous pork company and they have houses stretched across Virginia, from the mountains to the beach. All of them smell like bacon.

"Hello," Aunt Charlotte almost yells into the phone. "This is Charlotte Gwemes."

Whoever's on the other end probably recognizes the last name. Gwemes are really famous around here. They give a ton of money to charity.

"I want a fire engine to come to Sunset Gardens. Right now. Immediately. There's a cat stuck in a tree. And don't even try to tell me how much this trip will cost, I've donated to the firemen's fund before you were bor—"

Karlene, walking over to my aunt, politely tries to get her attention. "Charlotte, please tell them it's not an emergency. Please?"

"There's no fire or anything like that," my aunt says into the phone—when she suddenly notices me. "Oh, hi, Raleigh."

My aunt.

My aunt is a lot of ... *everything*. Impulses. Energy. And many many odd ideas. But she means well. My dad even says Aunt Charlotte's good intentions could single-handedly pave the road to Hell.

"Do you understand me?" she says into the phone. "Right now.

This cat's suffered enough trauma. And it would be dead already if it wasn't all for love."

Aunt Charlotte disconnects the call.

"Raleigh," she says. "Pray for that cat. Right now!"

See what I mean?

But I do pray. I pray for this dim-wit feline Whitney who can't figure out how to get down from the same tree she just climbed up. I pray for Karlene who looks just as stressed as when Myra collapsed. I pray for DeMott's uncle and Myra and Drew. And I pray for my aunt who is taking charge of this situation which only means something is about to go even more wrong.

Cautiously, I move over to the porch and find Gockey. I pull out the cake knife and she exclaims.

"Oh my heavens! Wherever did you find it?"

"In the kitchen. You must've left the knife in the dining room. Did you make a birthday cake for someone here?"

"Well..." She thinks about it, but the white-haired crowd encircles us. Everyone wants to know the story. Because this is all they have— stories. And this will probably wind up in the *Gazette*, too. So I tell them. And the way they're listening, you'd think finding a knife in a knife bin in a kitchen means we can land men on Mars.

"Hey, Stan, what about your cuff links?" asks a man wearing a blue bowtie.

Stan is wearing a green suit. He kind of looks like an elderly leprechaun.

"Stan's sick of being PP," the blue bowtie points out.

"And how about Halvorsen's ring?" someone else asks.

"And Bill's chess king."

The comments are coming so fast that they barely notice the fire engine barreling down the long driveway. No sirens are blaring, but the red and white lights are flashing, probably just for my aunt and her donations. When the truck stops by the porch, everyone suddenly forgets about the cake knife, cuff links, ring, king, and once again, remembers the cat and the tree. And now, the fire engine.

Sometimes I think old people behave like little kids.

But not one of them notices the handsome guy in the baseball uniform crossing the courtyard. His head is down and a comma of brown hair hangs over his forehead. My heart plummets.

I look back at Gockey, but Aunt Charlotte is already heading toward her, pointing at the cake knife in Gockey's hands.

"Mother," she says, coming up the stairs. "What are you doing with that?"

"Charlotte, I can explain."

"When was I born?"

"Oh, for heaven's sake."

"*When?*"

"April first. I thought it was a joke."

"What year?"

My aunt's on this hyper-alert thing for Alzheimer's. For the last couple months, this question-and-answer routine is happening with every visit. "What year was I born?"

"Same year Kennedy was assassinated."

"Oh, Kennedy," the man in the blue bowtie says. "Now *he* was a president."

"Camelot."

"Remember Jackie's pink suit and a pillbox hat?"

Once again, the entire porch has changed the topic, talking about John F. Kennedy and how much they miss him and how America isn't the same. Aunt Charlotte is waiting—barely—for them to stop so she can ask her next rude question.

A fireman walks over to the porch. Despite the heat and humidity, he wears a helmet and heavy yellow jacket.

"Mrs. Gwemes," he says. "Could you please move your vehicle?"

"Yes. Yes, I can." Aunt Charlotte turns and floats off the stairs. "And don't forget, this is all for love."

"Yes, ma'am. I know."

Whitney seems to sense something other than love because she lets out a tortured yowl—then scrambles even further up the tree.

Gockey makes a *tsk-tsk* sound. "That poor animal."

"You mean, living with Mrs. Donner?"

"Well, that doesn't seem to help. But even before that, someone left that beautiful cat on the side of the road. Abandoned it. I would've taken her in myself but I'm allergic."

A fireman standing inside a metal bucket signals the truck's driver and the bucket rises. An expectant silence hangs over the porch—like little kids waiting for Santa—until the fireman reaches the same level as Whitney. He starts speaking to her but her white fur puffs out until she looks like an albino porcupine. The fireman slowly leans toward the cat, his gloved hands open, and Whitney jumps—up.

The fireman snatches her mid-air.

The crowd cheers.

It's the biggest thing that's happened since Drew came to see Myra.

The bucket descends and the cat puts up a fight, squirming, digging its claws the man's thick gloves. But the fireman never lets go. And the crowd applauds and applauds.

What a small thing. What a big thing.

And all for love.

16

I'm heading back to the infirmary when Drew comes out. Her hair looks wilder than ever, like she picked up static cling from Myra's medical devices.

"What happened?" She points at the fire truck, driving away.

"Cat drama." I'm telling her about Whitney and the tree and my aunt when I hear my name called.

Karlene is walking toward us. In her arms, she carries the white-furred troublemaker like it's a baby.

"Speak of the devil," I mutter.

"Oh, that poor cat," Drew says, not hearing me. "It looks so sad."

"Girls," Karlene says. "I've got a job for you."

"Raleigh can't take it," Drew says. "She already has a job."

I turn. "I do?"

"Yes." Drew reaches into the back pocket of her purple jeans and pulls out a small notepad, the kind doctors give away. There's an ad on the top page for constipation medicine. Below that, Drew's precise block handwriting.

Oh. No.

She's made a list.

"Bill's king, Stan's cuff links, Frannie's cake knife, Bubbie's earrings." She looks up. "And Larry Siegel's service revolver from the Korean War. Somebody stole that, too. But Raleigh's taking the job. She'll find all of it."

Karlene looks at me. "You think these things are stolen?"

"No, not stolen." I give Drew a warning look. She's already in enough trouble around here. "They're just things that are missing. And I'm sure they'll turn up. I just found my grandmother's cake knife in the downstairs kitchen."

"Cake knife, check." Drew takes out her pen and crosses that item off the list. "But the monetary amount still remains an issue."

Karlene adjusts the cat digging its claws into her shirt. "What 'monetary amount' are you referring to?"

"Grand larceny."

Karlene looks at me. Like she wants to burst out laughing, except she's too annoyed. "Grand larceny?"

Drew holds up the list, tapping it with her pen. "The total replacement value of these stolen objects makes it a felony. Raleigh confirmed it."

Karlene looks at me.

My face feels really hot. "We were just talking. You know, hypothetically."

"Because the hypothesis is the only way to begin," Drew says, totally missing what's actually happening here. "Richard P. Feynman once said, It's better not to have answers than to have wrong answers."

"Well." Karlene smiles politely. "Isn't that nice."

I know this smile. It's the smile people give my mom when they hear her talking about how carpet fibers can be turned into high-tech listening devices that allow the government to spy on everything that's going on in your house. I glance at Drew. The girl can do all the advanced math at MIT, but simple social cues? Right over her head. She doesn't see that Karlene is humoring her.

"You said something about a job?" I prompt, hoping we can stop talking about the missing stuff.

"Yes." Karlene strokes the cat's lush fur. "I need someone to look after Whitney until I can find her a new home. I was wondering—"

"I'll do it!"

Drew snatches the cat from Karlene's arms. And miraculously, Whitney goes with no protest, probably because cats can always sense who loves them. Karlene looks like she's about to change her mind—Drew being off her rocker and all—but Drew's already carrying the cat toward the main building, cooing into the pointed pink ears. "You are so beautiful," she says. "You come live with me."

I give Karlene an apologetic smile. "Drew has a cat at home."

Karlene raises an eyebrow. "Her real home?"

"Yes. And she'll go back there."

"Soon?"

"Yes," I say, hoping that's a promise I can keep. "Soon."

And on that note, I take out my phone and text my dad, telling him I won't be home for dinner.

17

WITH THE BUNDLE of white fur purring in Drew's arms, we head upstairs.

"I'll make you a deal," Drew tells me. "Since your grandmother is allergic to cats—"

I stop. "Wait, how did you know? *I* didn't even know that until today. "

"Simple deduction." Drew keeps walking up the stairs.

"How simple?"

"Everyone at Sunset Gardens keeps a cat, unless they're allergic. Frances doesn't have a cat. Therefore, she must be allergic."

I follow her up the stairs. "*Everyone* has a cat—are they all crazy?"

"Don't try to change the subject." She walks down the third-floor hallway to Myra's apartment. "I'll be taking care of this beautiful cat. That means you'll be talking to them."

"Talking—to who?"

"The innocent victims of these horrible thefts."

"What?"

"Stan, Mr. Halvorsen, Wilma Kingsford—"

"Wilma?"

"Somebody stole her priceless brooch."

"But why do I have to talk to them?"

"Because you'll see things and I won't."

I start to protest again, but two things strike me. One, Drew isn't counting our steps by sixes. This is a very good sign. And two, maybe just as importantly, she's recognized one of her biggest flaws. Drew doesn't pick up on social cues. So this is a start. Maybe by going along with her plan, I'll be able to show her why staying here is a problem.

"Okay, I'll talk to them."

"Thank you."

Another shocker.

Thank you? Drew doesn't even say *hello* or *goodbye*. I know she needs to get out of here, but if the insurance doesn't run out for two more days, why not help her, calm her down, then ease her out the front door. "You're welcome."

She opens Myra's door. "And I want you to grill these people."

"*What?*"

"Like they're witnesses in your dad's courtroom."

I wave a hand in front of my face, coughing through the tobacco's chemical compounds. "I can't grill them, they're old."

"But we need to narrow down the hypothesis. I can tell Karlene doesn't believe my theory."

Wow.

I stand there, stunned, while Drew carries Whitney into the living room. Moses is laying on the floral couch and takes one look at the white cat and lets out a horrifying sound, as if he just caught us worshiping a golden calf.

"Are all these cats crazy?" I ask.

Drew doesn't answer. She's talking to Moses while he leaps onto his carpeted cat tower by the sliding glass door. Climbing and climbing, he opens his bearded mouth and lets out more tortured noises. Drew places Whitney on a chair. The white cat is suddenly so mellow, she spreads across the seat like a puddle of milk.

"Moses," Drew says, shaking a finger at him. "I expect you to behave. Raleigh and I have important work to do."

~

FIRST UP—MR. Halvorsen and his missing ring.

"Ruby," he tells me.

Mr. Halvorsen lives on the third floor, but his living room has the view the opposite of Myra, over the infirmary. Drew stands at the sliding glass door, staring at the low building down below while I take a seat across from our host.

Mr. Halvorsen—naturally—has a cat. It is striped and orange and fat. As soon as we enter the living room, it waddles away. Like we're not good enough.

"I'm sorry," I tell Mr. Halvorsen. "What did you say?"

"Ruby," he says, tapping his knuckle. "My college ring has a big ruby, right in the middle."

For a guy who's so old he has more skin tags than actual skin, Mr. Halvorsen seems pretty spry. Popping out of his reading chair, he grabs the pencil I'm holding in my right hand. Drew's pencil. One of the black pencils she special orders. The pencil nobody can touch except me. I glance over. Her dark eyes watch him. Her left eye twitches.

"I'll draw you a picture," he says, taking the notebook, too. Drew's notebook. The special notebook—

"And when you find the ring, you'll say, 'Hey, that's Halvorsen's college ring.'"

He starts to draw a picture of a thick men's ring, ruby in its center, engraved lines around that. I cut my eyes toward Drew again and see she's coming toward us. I'm expecting an OCD freak-out over the pencil and notebook, but she only leans over Mr. Halvorsen's stooped shoulders, looking at his sketch.

"That's the ruby." Mr. Halvorsen taps an arthritic finger at his drawing. "More than three carats, that ruby."

"And thus," Drew says, "the ruby adding to the ring's value."

I open my hand, hoping he'll give back the pencil. "When did you last see this ring?"

He thinks about it—*by sticking the pencil in his mouth*!

Drew gasps.

I hold my breath.

Mr. Halvorsen bites down. "Let's see," he says, removing the pencil. "I got my Master's degree in Business in fifty-nine. Which means I got the ring the year before, fifty-eight..."

Drew sucks in a breath. Blows it out. In-out-in. Just like when we rode my bike here.

"Yeah, okay, great," I tell him, my gaze flicking between the two of them. "But the last time you *saw* the ring, when?"

He sticks the pencil *back in his mouth.*

Drew is now making some kind of gurgling noise. Then sucking down another breath. I'm nauseated, but I can't tell if it's from the impending doom or the thick saliva he's leaving on the pencil.

He yanks it out. "March 7. Last time I saw the ring was on March 7."

I can barely breathe. "You're sure?"

"I took it off that morning 'cause my fingers swelled up." He holds up his other hand, displaying the fingers. He's not a heavy guy, but his fingers look like plumped-up sausages. He shoves his hand closer to Drew's face, so she can appreciate the disgusting deformity. She lets out another gurgling sound.

He glances at me. "She alright?"

"No..."

"Put it on a milk carton."

"Pardon?"

"My ring. You should put it on a milk carton. Like they do with missing kids."

"Right."

"It's not like I got a lot of time," he tells me. "Eighty-four years old. My will says I'm to be buried with that ring."

It's odd to me how some people get more attached to their stuff as they get older. And other people do the exact opposite. Gockey lived in our house on Monument Avenue for more almost half a century but when she decided to move in here, she didn't take much of anything with her. "Raleigh," she told me, "Where I'm going, I won't need any of it." For a long time, I thought she meant Sunset Gardens. She didn't.

"Mr. Halvorsen, when you lost this ring—"

"You mean," Drew dabs perspiration off her forehead, "when it was stolen."

"When you last saw it," I clarify, "was anything else going on?"

"Like what?" he asks.

Here comes the delicate part, the other reason Drew's not asking the questions. "Anything that might cause you to forget where you put it?"

"I don't forget anything."

"Like Bubbie," Drew says, pointedly.

"There's nothing you forget?" I ask him.

"Nope. That's why I was a successful accountant. People paid me top dollar, partly because of my excellent memory."

"Okay." I smile, thinking, *You forgot to give me back the pencil.* "Maybe someone came to visit you around this time?"

He stares down at the pencil. The black paint displays a perfect dental impression of his mouth. "I don't get visitors."

"Oh, I'm sorry."

"Ask me something else."

"Was anything else missing from your apartment?"

"My wife."

"Pardon?"

"My wife, she died two years ago. So she was missing on March 7. But the cat's here, and all for love. Ask me something else."

I ask him more questions, and still more, and pretty soon none of the questions have anything to do with this ring. But he keeps saying, *Ask me something else.* He tells us about his wife, his work for big corporations, but I'm only half-listening because there is something so very sad about sitting with someone who has so much time on their hands, yet doesn't have much time left.

Finally, the fat orange cat waddles back into the room. It heads right to Drew. She is standing by the glass door again, staring down as if willing her grandmother to get well. The fat cat winds itself through her ankles, turning left and right, making the sign of infinity. Drew looks down, and smiles.

I close the notebook. "That should do it."

Mr. Halvorsen nods, sadly. He offers me the pencil.

"Why don't you keep it," I tell him.

18

WE WALK DOWN to Larry Siegel's apartment.

He's the one missing that revolver.

But Larry doesn't answer Drew's knock.

"Larry likes a good nap after dinner," she tells me as we continue down the hall. "Let's try Wilma. She stays up late."

I don't even want to know how she knows these things, but it would be nice if she realized seven o'clock isn't "late." Except in an old folks' home.

"Does everyone on your list live on the third floor?" I ask.

"Ninety-nine percent."

"So one person doesn't?"

"Scratch that," she says. "I need to recalculate. You found the cake knife."

"Because the cake knife wasn't stolen. And neither are these—"

Pretending not to hear me, she lifts her thin hand and knocks on Wilma Kingsford's door. Wilma is next door neighbors to Myra.

The door swings open immediately.

"Please step inside," Wilma says.

Half past six on a Friday evening, Wilma Kingsford is fully dressed for work. Red blouse with a big bow collar. Linen skirt the color of July peaches. And cream-colored one-inch heels that are one shade darker than nurse's shoes. I'll bet when Wilma Kingsford was our age, she was the Tinsley Teager of Richmond. No wonder she became the city's gossip columnist.

"Please have a seat."

Her apartment looks like a memorial to her days at the *Richmond Times-Dispatch*. Perfectly lined-up photos cover the walls. Wilma is in every one, always with some famous figure from Richmond, including tennis great Arthur Ashe who looks like he might jump three nets to get away from her.

"Let's begin."

Her living room is decorated with shiny satin chairs that look like nobody ever sits on them—except for an elegant Siamese cat curled on a black velvet cushion. The animal stays so still that I wonder if it came from a taxidermist.

Drew sits near the cat. I take the chair farthest away from it and open the notebook. "Would you happen to have a pencil?" I ask.

"Pencil!" Wilma throws me an eyeful. "Never!"

"What?"

"Young lady, did your parents teach you no manners whatsoever?"

"Oh, right. Pardon?"

"Now I forgive you." She pats her hair. It's brown and teased into still waves, sort of like burnt meringue. "You must never use a pencil. Do you hear me? Only pens. Interviews such as this should be etched in ink, not the fading silliness of a pencil."

"Yes, ma'am." I force my eyes not to roll. "But I need something to write with."

Wilma gives me another eyeful, then strides across her large living room. At an immaculate inlaid-wood desk, she picks up a clutch purse that has that creepy texture of lizards. The cat's cool blue eyes in its tiny triangular head track her motions. But otherwise, there's no other sign of life from the thing. From the purse, Wilma removes a rectangular box, bringing it over to me. She lifts the top like we're about to enter Tutankhamen's tomb.

"Please, do be careful," she says.

The pen is gold and heavy. Maybe it's real gold and I should be impressed. But my fingers hate it. "I understand your ivory brooch is missing."

Wilma pats the meringue hair again. "I'll have you know that my family is among the First Families of Virginia."

Uh-oh.

First Families of Virginia. The FFVs. Families who landed in Virginia back in the colonial days. The Harmons belong to the FFVs but my dad and Gockey hardly ever mention it. DeMott's family never lets you forget it. Wilma appears to be waiting for me to exclaim, or at least write down this extremely important crucial never-to-be-forgotten historical fact.

Moving things along, I write on the page *FFV.*

"This particular brooch," she then continues, "first appeared in the year 1687."

I knew it. I attempt to signal Drew. *Buckle up, my friend. This will be a lonnnng interview.*

But Drew's focused on the cat, so over the next seven million years, I pretend to listen to the many branches of the Kingsford family tree, the people who first arrived in the "Old Dominion" in 1600. Wilma tells me who lived where, who married whom, who was related to any of Virginia's eight presidents. To say my mind wanders is an understatement. My mind actually turns into a full fugitive and runs wild, reminding me about upcoming homework assignments, that I am hungry, that I need to get Drew out of here in two days ... and when I check back in on Wilma, she's only 150 years from getting to the point.

"During the War of Northern Aggression," she is saying, "my great-great-grandmother wore this same brooch every single day. But when the damn-Yankees broke through our line at Richmond, she cleverly placed the brooch in her brassiere—"

Drew asks, "Brassiere?"

"Bra," I explain. Something Drew won't wear for several years because her chest is as flat as a geometric plane.

I look back at Wilma. She's giving me that eyeful again.

Rewinding the mental tape, I decide she got offended by my vulgar use of slang. *Bra.*

I smile. And cut to the chase by skipping right over the Civil War. "When was the last time you saw this brooch?"

"I can give you the exact date."

Wilma and her proper heels walk to the desk where a wall calendar shows the month of May, displaying a photo of the Jefferson Hotel in downtown Richmond. Each square of days shows a red check mark. Wilma lifts that page—April is matched to a photo of Agecroft Hall—and more red check marks show on those squares. Then March—President Tyler's plantation house—but now Wilma sticks a manicured fingernail onto the first box without a red check mark. "March 12th."

"You're sure?"

Eyeful. Times one hundred.

"I'm just asking."

"Young lady, I reported this crime to the Richmond police. On the evening before it was stolen, I wore the brooch to the Richmond Garden Club's spring dance. The ivory and onyx match my houndstooth dress, which, you should note, belonged to my late mother. She purchased it at Montaldo's on River Road."

I sternly order my eyes *Do. Not. Roll* as Wilma launches into stories about her mother, the history of Montaldo's, how this houndstooth dress attended two luncheons with First Ladies of The United States. "And I always accessorize the dress with that brooch and the pearl-drop earrings given to me by my husband, Marchant. His mother belonged to the Benjamin Harrison family line."

God, I pray. *Please, make it stop. No more historical name-dropping.*

And right there, God answers my prayer.

Wilma says nothing more.

"So you lost the brooch at that dance?" I ask.

"Incorrect."

She walks back to her chair, sits, hands clasped in her lap.

"Then when did you lose it?" I ask.

Drew says, "It wasn't lost."

"Correct," Wilma says. "I was still wearing the brooch when my gentleman caller walked me to my apartment at ten o'clock."

"Who was that?"

She squints. "You're rather forward."

I lift the notebook. "Just trying to get the facts."

"Carleton Willis, if you must know."

"And he's...?"

Drew pipes up again. "He teaches the dance lessons."

I shake my head.

"Blue bow tie?" Drew prompts.

Ah, yes. I turn back to Wilma. "Did Mr. Willis come into your apartment that night?"

"Dear Lord!" Wilma clutches the string of pearls around her neck. "Who taught you to be so forward?"

Then Carleton came into the apartment.

"I'm just trying to narrow down the time when the brooch went missing."

She lifts her face, so high it starts to look like something on an ancient Greek coin. However, she refuses to speak. So I try another topic. "I understand all these apartments are unlocked, is that right?"

"No. My door is locked."

"Just your door?"

"Young lady, when I moved in here, I informed the management that should anything happen to even one of my treasured family mementos—which are of historical importance, I would be devastated. Karlene has allowed me to put a lock on my door."

"But," Drew adds, "the other apartments are unlocked. In case someone needs emergency medical help."

Wilma's head rises even higher. "Should I perchance require such immediate medical assistance, Karlene placed several buzzers around my apartment. They go directly to the infirmary."

I could ask more questions. Like, *how many cans of hairspray does it take to turn hair into a helmet?* But I really want to stop this charade of pretending I'm looking for stolen stuff.

"Thank you." I stand up, offering Wilma her gold pen. "I appreciate your time."

"Young lady, find this brooch," she orders. "The Museum of the Confederacy is anxiously awaiting its arrival, since they already have my great-great grandmother's brassiere."

Oh, lucky them.

19

As we're leaving Wilma's apartment, Drew says she wants to check on Moses and Whitney next door. Which is fine because I could use a pillow for muffling the primal scream that's hanging in the back of my throat after listening to Wilma go on and on. And now I realize her brooch is even less likely to be stolen, since she has a lock on her door.

"Moses?" Drew steps into Myra's apartment.

The place still smells like a damp ashtray, but there's a new odor, too. Bitter, almost oil. I'm thinking it's the scent of feline anxiety because Moses is perched on his cat tower, staring down at Whitney like he's going to pounce.

"Can we take a cat break?" I ask. "I'm hungry. Let's eat."

"Check the fridge." Drew walks over to the cat tower, reaching up to pet his long gray fur.

I open Myra's fridge. One package of smoked salmon. One stick of butter. A jar of kosher pickles. A half-empty bottle of Manischewitz wine that's the color of grape juice.

"Any food here for Gentiles in here?" I ask.

"Try the cupboard."

One loaf of rye bread. One box of Matzo crackers. I lift the orange box of crackers. Maybe I could smear that whole stick of butter on these things and—

THUNK!

My head swivels toward the living room, thinking Moses finally dive-bombed Whitney. But the bearded cat remains on kitty Mt. Sinai. "What was that sound?" I ask.

Drew is already sprinting for the front door. She flings it open and yells.

"Wilma!"

～

ONE WHITE SHOE ASKEW, Wilma Kingsford's body splays across her living room floor. Her eyes are closed. Drew drops beside her, patting the old woman's hand. "Wilma?"

There's no response.

"Raleigh, call—"

I'm already tapping 9-1-1 into my phone screen. But the ringing sounds so faint that I rush into the next room, trying to get a stronger signal. The dispatcher picks up. I explain what happened, give our location. "She's on the floor, I think she fainted. Or something." The dispatcher asks me to stay on the line.

While I wait, I glance around the room. It's a bedroom, full of antiques. There's also a red cord dangling on the wall, with a large button. I reach over, pressing the button. This must be the alarm Wilma was talking about. I press it again. Then a third time. Seeing Myra Levinson collapse was one thing—Myra's on oxygen. But Wilma Kingsford? We were just talking to her. She was fine.

The dispatcher comes back on the line, tells me help is on the way. I hurry back into the living room and see Wilma's legs are still bent at a weird angle. She hasn't moved. A sudden numbness creeps over me.

"Wilma." Drew's mouth is inches from Wilma's ear. "If you can hear me, squeeze my hand."

Wilma's manicured nails twitch.

"Good!" Drew says. "Please hang on."

Wilma's purse is also on the floor, the contents spilling across the carpet. I reach down, replacing everything—the box with its gold pen, some prescription bottles, a small reporter's notebook, one tiny antique photograph of Robert E. Lee. When I look up, the Siamese cat is staring at me.

"Wilma!" Karlene rushes through the open door, dropping to the floor next to Drew. "Wilma, honey?"

The burnt-meringue hair shifts. "Kar-Karlene?"

"Yes, I'm here," Karlene takes her other hand, the one Drew's not holding. "The medical folks are on the way. Don't you worry. We're all here for you."

I close the purse, replace it on the desk. And glance at Drew. She is watching Wilma the same way she gazed out of Mr. Halvorsen's glass door to the infirmary. Like one of those people who can bend spoons just by thinking about it. Only now her dark eyes glisten with tears.

In all the years I've known Drew, I can count on two fingers the times I've seen her cry. She didn't even shed a tear when her parents divorced. And yet here's Drew, sorrow brimming in her eyes, kneeling beside this old woman, holding her hand, when all I did was secretly mock this same person during an entire interview.

It makes me wonder. Who's got the real personality problem here —Drew, or me?

The answer comes.

And stings my eyes.

20

THE EMERGENCY medical guys appear and hook one of those plastic IV bags of clear fluid to Wilma's arm. When her eyes open halfway, the men start asking her questions—the same questions they asked Myra. Although Wilma's answers are all correct, her voice sounds really weak. And her lips are as white as her face.

Lifting Wilma onto a padded cart, the medical guys wheel her to the elevators. Karlene stays right beside her the whole time, holding Wilma's hand and encouraging her. But as the cart moves down the hallway, all the apartment doors start opening. The old people stand in the doorways, silently watching. The familiar hush is back in the air, like the only sound we can hear is time passing.

The elevator door opens, Karlene steps in with Wilma's cart and turns to look back at all of us. Her plump face seems ten years older than yesterday. The elevator doors close and the old people fade back into their apartments, softly closing the doors. My eyes burn.

Inside Wilma's apartment, Drew walks over to the elegant Siamese still on its velvet cushion. "I know you're scared." She reaches down carefully, lifting the cat into her arms. "But you're not alone. You can come with me."

Drew carries the cat and its velvet cushion next door into Myra's ashtray-apartment. Whitney is still zonked out, laying on her back, white paws in the air. And while Moses continues to perch on the cat tower, his gray fur seems to vibrate with animosity.

Drew sets the velvet cushion on the other end of the couch.

"Moses," she says, "this apartment is six hundred square feet. Taking into consideration your relative size, that's roughly equivalent to a half-acre per person. Now behave."

Moses flicks his long tail.

"I'll take that as a yes." She turns to me. "Do you believe I can do it?"

"Get a cat to behave?"

"No. Go to the infirmary."

"Yes, and I'll go with you."

"No." She walks to the door. "I want to go by myself."

She closes the door.

I stare at the cats.

This day feels like I've been trapped in the world's worst race. First, a bad day at school. Then DeMott and Tinsley. Then watching my best friend make even better friends with people who are more than three times our age. I suddenly feel a powerful temptation to run to Gockey's apartment and eat an entire chocolate cake by myself.

But Aunt Charlotte is here now—another banner moment for today—and Aunt Charlotte means no cake. Just tons of lectures about keeping Gockey away from sugar because it might cause Alzheimer's.

And no way am I going home.

Not when I'm feeling this raw inside.

JUST PAST 7:30, Toot's kitchen still feels crowded even though it's empty. Pots and pans hang from the ceiling. Appliances stand ready. And the blue pilot light hisses from the big iron stove. It's also hot and humid in here. I open the refrigerator, savoring the rush of cold air that sends a delicious shiver down my back.

On the top shelf, a handwritten note has an arrow pointing up. *NOBODY TOUCH THIS FOOD.*

On tiptoes, I see two glass pans of red Jell-O with canned fruit trapped inside the gelatin.

Not to worry, I want to write back.

Since there's no sign on the next shelf, I start to lift a big bowl of egg salad, pushing aside a container of Brussels sprouts—*shudder.* And then—*jackpot!*—I find an entire platter of roasted ham and a loaf of white bread.

As a precaution, I pull out my phone, saliva already pooling in my mouth, and tap the familiar number.

Titus answers. "Now what."

"Your mom's fridge."

"What about it?"

"There's a lot of food in there."

"Some kinda crime?"

"I was just wondering, it's okay if I eat some of it?"

"Food's for eating."

"Even this platter of roasted ham in here?"

He hangs up.

Fine.

I stash the phone in my pocket and quickly wash my hands in the long stainless steel sink, then blot my forehead with a paper towel because, *man,* it's humid in here. And then comes the first step to making myself feel better—find the mayo. Then slather it on cushiony white bread, layer the roasted ham that's so tender it's falling off the bone, and finally—this is genius—I scoop the egg salad onto the ham and close with another mayo bread-cushion.

At last, I say grace.

Thank you for Toots.

Titus.

Karlene.

Please help Myra get well. And Wilma, too. Forgive me for acting like a brat. And help DeMott's crazy Uncle Cab.

And please—please—help me get Drew out of here, without taking a cat.

The first bite confirms my hunch. Egg salad belongs in this sandwich, the perfect creamy match for the salty meat. My throat hums as I chew and stare out the windows above the sink, watching the sapphire dusk turn into darkness. One perfect sandwich. It can make an otherwise bad day almost bearable.

But when I start wash my dishes and utensils, all the water backs up in the sink's basin. I shut off the faucet. Only the gunky gray water just sits there. *Great.* Toots will have my head for this mess.

Reaching down, I feel my way to the drain. And the garbage disposal. I yank out my hand. Garbage disposals scare me. I search for the switch and find it on the wall. I flip it.

CLUNK!

Clink-clack-clink-clack-clink-clack!

I flick off the switch, listening as the loud clatter slows then finally stops. But before I reach back in, I count to ten because if I have one excellent irrational fear, it's getting my fingers mangled in a garbage disposal—even if it's turned off. I push my hand through the rubber flaps and reach into the slime. My genius sandwich threatens to come back up, but I touch something solid.

Cold.

Hard.

I pull the thing out.

A couple inches wide, the metal is so solid that the disposal blades only nicked the sides. Even more amazing is that there is a red object stuck smack dab in the middle of this thing.

A gemstone.

A large ruby.

Lifting the gold ring higher, I speak the very words he predicted I'd say.

"Hey, that's Halvorsen's college ring."

21

WITH THE GOLD ring washed of all its sink goo, I run to the infirmary. The front desk sits empty, and there's no sign of Pink Nurse. I jog down the hall to Myra's Pythagorean prime room. But as I glance through the door's window, I see Drew leaning down to her grandmother, nodding and talking. Myra's awake, smiling at Drew. Even from here, I can feel their connection.

And I can feel how opening this door will suddenly shatter their moment.

I back away with Halvorsen's ring in my pocket.

I FEEL the need to tell somebody about this ring so I head for Karlene's office. Unfortunately, she's not there, probably still with Wilma. But since her office door is open, I place the ring inside her top desk drawer and leave a note on the calendar blotter which is covered with all her many duties to call people, help people, talk to people. I explain where I found the ring—again, not stolen—and tell her I'll be back as soon as possible to get Drew out of here.

Through the darkening night, I ride my bike home. A cool breeze whips the edge of my plaid skirt as I pedal past the silent brick warehouses in Scott's Addition, catching the Closed sign in Titus' window. I cross the railroad tracks, bike several more blocks past empty loading docks, then turn onto Monument Avenue. Another giant gust of wind grabs me as I pedal around Robert E. Lee and Traveller. With the landscape lights shining up on him, the somber general looks like he's coming home from battle.

I jiggle the carriage house lock and hang my bike on the wall hook. There's just enough light from the alley to catch my reflection in the mirror. The messy ponytail doesn't bother me. Or even the dark circles under my eyes. What gets me is that I look so...solitary. Just a face in a mirror, all by itself. And blackness all around.

I lock the carriage house, cross the cobblestone alley, and start walking across the patio when I notice the lights are on in the kitchen. From here, I can see my parents sitting side by side at the pine table. In front of them, a jigsaw puzzle is laid out. They are working the pieces together, their heads tilted toward each other, as if tied by invisible string.

For a long time, I stand there. I don't want to go inside, and that's not unusual. But it's always because bad trouble waits inside. Now?

Now it's like seeing that connection between Drew and Myra, knowing that by just opening the door, I'm going to destroy something invisible yet real. The quiet thing that knits people together, lets them know they are loved.

I pull my phone from my pocket and text my dad.

I'll be home soon.

I watch his head swivel away from the puzzle. He picks up the phone that lays on the table. After he reads my text, he turns to my mom and says something. She nods, softly smiles. My dad taps the screen.

Seconds later, his words pop up on my phone. **We miss you! See you soon!**

I stand in the shadows even longer, watching my parents on a

Friday night, acting perfectly normal. The wind swirls around my feet and the leaves in the trees whisper and flutter and clap their hands. The loneliness is almost unbearable.

22

MY SATURDAY MORNING ritual is to run before my parents get up. That way, whatever bad stuff comes hurtling down life's highway over the weekend, I've already sped my motor fast enough for my system to cope with it.

But this morning, I hesitate. Charcoal clouds smear across the early morning sky, leaking out only a slightly lighter gray light. All of it promises rain.

Speed, I decide.

Speed will take care of this problem.

Racing down Monument to The Boulevard, I sprint through Byrd Park, startling the ducks floating on the lakes reflecting that dark sky. I run and I run, and I keep running even as the churning clouds marble gray, blue, black. The wind gusts against my back, pushing me forward like invisible hands. I reach the Nickel Bridge and drop down-down-*down* to the dirt trail alongside the river. Running upstream, I watch as the wind flips tree leaves upside down. Air inversion. Drew's explained the physics to me, but all I remember is it means a serious storm is coming. I run faster.

The rain comes softly, at first. Like the drops are asking permission to fall. But just before I make it to the Huguenot Bridge, permission is granted. The sky unleashes curtains of slashing water, slamming into the soil like strafing bullets. I lose sight of the bridge, blink, and hear the sound of heaven clearing its throat. Two seconds later, yellow lightning slices the graphite clouds.

I hear another throat clearing and stumble over the tree roots on the trail. The sound cracks so close that the river flashes white. I dart into the trees and press my back to an ancient oak. The next rumble of thunder hammers my chest. I hold my breath and watch light spear the riverbank, the green canopy of trees blooming yellow then black. Another rumble. Even closer. Electricity crackles over the river like fireworks, heading straight for me. My heart bangs its fist, begging to flee, and an eerie tingle invades my scalp. Every strand of hair stands up. I press my back into the bark, close my eyes. *It's right here, right now—*

I open my eyes. Light blisters the air. The world disappears into a sea of white. I blink. Blood vessels shimmer on the backs of my eyelids. Another breath, and the rain begins pelting the leaves above my head. The next crack of lightning flashes, but it's behind me, shooting a spotlight onto the granite boulders in the river. The black rocks blaze with white crystals.

Three more lightning strikes and I see mist rising from the river rocks. Or is it smoke? I push myself from the tree, wipe the rain from my cheeks, and stand on the river's edge.

Inside the black granite rocks, the white quartz glows like ghosts. I yank off my running shoes and socks, wading into the silty soil that feels cool against my heated feet. I can smell the scorched minerals, a scent like rocks trapped in a fire pit. I reach inside the first boulder. Under the gray light, a strange pattern appears inside the quartz. Zigzags. Like the cartoon version of lightning bolts. I take hold of the largest prism and lean my full weight against it. Tingles of electricity race up my arms. When the quartz snaps, I hold the specimen up to the sky, staring at those jagged lines.

Two days ago, I collected this very same quartz for Teddy. These jagged lines were not there.

I carry the quartz back to the riverbank and wipe my feet on the soft grass. The tingling sensation electrifies my palm. I glance up at the sky. The dark clouds are tumbling toward downtown.

When I start my run again, rock in hand, it feels like I'm carrying something delivered to me from another world.

23

TEDDY CHASTAIN'S little brick house looks like the third one in the story about the three little pigs. The house that the wolf blew and blew at but the house didn't fall over. Probably because in this case, because the guy inside the house blasted right back at the wolf.

As the last drops of morning rain finish their show, I walk up the wooden wheelchair ramp that leads to Teddy's front door. The door still needs paint, and the window shutters hang by one hinge. But, interestingly, all the dead leaves that usually stay here after each autumn until they dissolve into a brown mulch on their own are gone. I lift my hand to knock on the door when I hear music. Hillbilly music. That weird stuff where the singer sounds like he's yodeling through mountain hollers. Like the missing dead leaves, music is new to this house.

I knock twice, but there's no response. I beat my fist against the peeling paint until a voice yells.

"I ain't turning it down! Shove them complaints where the sun don't—"

"It's me—Raleigh!"

The door opens, the music blares out. And Teddy's red hair flumes off his forehead like every single strand can hear his thoughts and is now screaming "GET OUT WHILE YOU CAN!" He runs his green-eyed gaze over me. "Nobody told ya running in the rain means ya get wet?"

I lift the zigzagged quartz.

Teddy reaches out, pinching the rock with his crimped fingers. With his other hand, he brushes back the left wheel of his chair, pivoting to make an opening for me.

My running shoes *squooze* with rainwater as I step inside. Teddy's living room holds as much clutter as his van—books, rocks, photos, random equipment.

He lifts his face, hollering over the yodeling music. "Dot, come take a gander."

A woman steps into the living room. Like the missing dead leaves and the music, I've never seen a woman in this house—ever. Even more startling, I recognize her. The red braids, the freckled face.

She smiles. "Hi, Raleigh."

"Uh..." I manage. "Hi."

My mind steps on its gas pedal, speeding through the possibilities, searching for some logical explanation to why Dorothee Fulbright is here instead of on Ocracoke Island in North Carolina. That's where I met her, when I was losing a science contest and Teddy told me to go talk to her for help.

But Dorothee Fulbright had acted like she hated Teddy.

"You need a towel," she says, leaving the room.

Teddy's still studying the rock when Dorothee comes back with a large white towel. She gives me a look that says, *He'd never think of a towel, would he?*

"Thanks." I wipe down my face, my arms where goose bumps have broken out.

Teddy looks up. "Spit it out."

"Spit what out?"

"Whatever's hunkerin' down in your brain."

Whole bunches of things are hunkering down in my brain. Like, *This woman acted like you were a nasty virus.* And, *You told me back then you broke her heart—now she's here?* But my running shoes are *squoozing* like sponges, and my goose-bumpy skin looks like a plucked chicken, and after dealing with Drew and Sunset Gardens, I do not have the energy to figure out whatever's going on here between these two. So I say the only thing that makes sense right now.

"I want to know what happened to that rock."

24

TEDDY'S FAVORITE SAYING?

"There's no teaching, only learning."

I hate it when he says it, because it means that instead of telling me what happened to this quartz, he heads for the back room in his house. Normal people would've used the room as a bedroom, but Teddy's got it stocked with all kinds of geology stuff, including the long table in the middle with four microscopes—four, so Teddy can keep projects going like a cook using every burner on the stove.

He starts barking out directions. Towel around my shoulders, I place the quartz in the table's vice grip and crank it tight. Teddy grabs the small circular saw. Whatever injury snapped his spinal cord also yanked his fingers half-closed. But he manages. Guiding the spinning blade into the crystal held by the vice grip, he slices off a thin specimen, flicks off the saw, and wipes mineral dust from his T-shirt. It says *Call Somebody Who Cares*. He tosses me the thin section. Dorothee comes into the room.

I place the sliver of quartz under one of the microscopes, focusing the light beam until it strikes those zigzag lines. I back away so Teddy can peer through the lens. His gnarled hands crank the focus knobs.

"Dot," he says. "Come take a gander."

When Dorothee bends down to the scope, her long red braids dangle on either side of her face like copper ropes threaded with gold. The yodeling music floats down the hallway, and I stare at her profile. Dorothee looks different than she did on Ocracoke. I'm not sure what the difference is, exactly, but when she looks up from the microscope, her freckled skin is bright. And her amber brown eyes are dancing.

She smiles at Teddy. "I know what it is."

"But I saw it before you saw it," he says.

"But I *knew* before you knew it."

"How ya reckon that?"

"Because you're dumber than a felt boot."

He grins. "Zat so?"

"Sew buttons on your shirt."

I stand there—*right there*—but apparently, I'm invisible as they continue this hillbilly fighting or flirting or whatever the heck they're doing. Right this second I could walk out the door and neither of them would notice I was gone. But now I realize why Dorothee looks different. Love. And after witnessing my parents' lovey-dovey stuff lately, this West Virginia mating dance makes me want to gag. The whole world has fallen in love—right when DeMott fell out of love with me.

"Hel-lo?"

They both look over at me.

"Oh, Raleigh," Dorothee says. "Why don't you take a look for yourself."

I lean into the microscope. Light floods the stone, streaming through the mineral. The geology word for it is translucent— one of those words that actually makes me grateful for all the Latin we're forced to learn at St. Cat's. *Trans* means "through," *lucere* means "to shine." The light shines right through the quartz. I adjust the focus knobs, zeroing in on the zigzag lines. My hunch was the lightning left burn marks on the outside of the rock. But these lines are *inside* the stone. Like there was a structural change to the mineral's atomic bonds. I still have no idea what happened here, but the sight of it is beautiful and haunting. Gazing through the scope's lens, I try to think of the best way to ask my next question—so Teddy will give me actual answers. But I hear giggling.

I look up.

Dorothee's tickling Teddy's ear. And he's giggling like an eight-year-old.

"Hello."

They keep flirting.

"Hey, over here?"

Teddy looks at me. "Hay's in the field."

"Hay's in the barn," she says.

I grit my teeth. "Just tell me what happened to this quartz."

He raises his eyebrows. They're like red caterpillars camping above the green leaves of his eyes. "How many times I got to say it?" he asks. "There's no teaching, only—"

"Don't—"

"—learning."

"And I am soaking wet. And I haven't had breakfast. And I almost got struck by lightning. And I want some answers. *Now.*"

He rolls back his chair. "Holy sidewindin' snakes. You're worse than ya were on Thursday."

"Can't you just tell me how those lines got there?"

"Oh, wait, hang on..." He raps his crimped hand, like he's knocking on a door. "Knock, knock. Who's there? Drewsky. Drewsky who? Drewsky who still won't behave. *That's* what climbed into your crankhouse. Am I right?"

"No."

He rolls to the table's vice grip, loosens the clamp, tosses the whole quartz crystal to me. When I catch it, that tingle shimmers up my wrist again. And Teddy's shaking out his arm.

I point. "You feel it, too. That tingle?"

His green eyes sparkle like emeralds. "Just 'cause I'm such a fine gentleman, I'm gonna give you one clue."

I hesitate. Sometimes Teddy tricks me with these offers. They seem like they're about one thing, but they're really about something else. "Is it a clue about this rock or about Drew?"

"You figure that out."

I glance at Dorothee, hoping she'll help. But she only smiles.

"Raleigh," she says. "You are so much stronger and so much smarter than you realize."

"Hey!" Teddy hollers. "Don't be givin' her fat head! I'll have to take back my two-fer."

I narrow my eyes at him. "Two for what?"

"Silica."

"What?"

"Silica."

"That's your clue?" I shake my head. Silica is one of the most common elements on earth. When it combines with oxygen, quartz is formed. Saying "silica" is like saying *water*. Or *air*. "Since you need silica to make quartz, that's not even a clue."

Teddy starts whistling.

"Are you—"

"Nope, done, over. Now you go tell Drewsky what you done saw this morning. Watch what happens."

I wait. There's got to be more. But they're just standing there, grinning at me. "Your big two-fer is *silica*?"

"Yerp."

Teddy pivots the wheelchair. He looks at Dorothee like she's an angel.

"Now, if you don't mind," he says, offering one of his damaged hands to Dorothee. "Me and my darlin' got a dance to finish."

25

BY THE TIME I get home from Teddy's, my dad's already up and making his Saturday morning pancakes. He doesn't say it, but I can tell he's been worried about my running in a thunderstorm. To make him feel better, after I shower and change clothes, I eat four pancakes. And no syrup needed—my mom comes to the table and the sweetness between them is like a gallon of maple syrup.

After breakfast, I go back upstairs and call Myra's apartment. Drew answers and I really want to blurt out about Halvorsen's ring. But that has to wait. First things first. I've to get her out of Sunset Gardens.

"Something weird happened this morning." I describe for her the lightning storm, how smoke rose from the quartz beds. How the zigzag lines are embedded in the stone, not scratched on the outside. "Drew, it's quartz but it turned into something else, just by lightning striking it. Like, it's a whole different mineral now."

She is silent.

"I'm going to the library to do some research."

"When?" she asks.

"Right now. I want to check the science archives in the basement."

The pause stretches out between us.

"I still have the blindfold," I add. "You could come with me."

The Richmond public library's basement archives are a private place for me. I've never invited Drew, just like she's never invited me to use the MIT geek knowledge library. We each have our sources. And it's better that way. But extreme times call for extreme measures.

And Teddy's right.

Ten minutes later, I'm pedaling for Sunset Gardens with the blindfold in one pocket, the zigzag stone in the other. Saturday morning traffic is thin and the morning storm has washed my city clean. The black pavement shines. The warehouse windows sparkle. And above me, the clear blue sky looks like the first Saturday morning ever created.

But just as I'm cruising down the long driveway to Sunset Gardens, I'm reminded how the universe operates on some kind of push-pull mechanics. It's always one step forward, one step back.

Take the good with the bad.

The Lord giveth, the Lord taketh away.

Because here on this hopeful and perfect Saturday morning when Drew Levinson is going to leave Sunset Gardens, DeMott Fielding is standing on the front porch—with Tinsley.

Sitting in rocking chair between them, Uncle Cab is grinning like some cat who ate a canary.

I climb off the bike, and return Uncle Cab's hello. The old man hoists a silver flask, like he's toasting this great day, and his voice sounds really happy—maybe too happy. He takes a long pull on the flask. His grin is lopsided. I'm pretty sure Karlene doesn't allow any alcohol inside the building, but it would be just like her to let Uncle Cab have a drink on the porch. Just like she lets Wilma keep a lock on her door and everybody can have cats. Like how she's letting Drew stay three days. Which is now down to one.

Tinsley moves toward the stairs just as I'm making my way to the front door. "My goodness, Raleigh."

I look over at her. "What."

"Your hair."

I reach up. My rainy running, combined with a fast shower,

followed by bike ride—so, okay, my hair's probably a total mess right now.

"Tinsley, don't judge. At least my hair is a natural color."

Uncle Cab hoots. "Keepin' it real." He raises the flask.

I step inside the front door—not even daring to glance at DeMott—and find Drew sitting in Mrs. Donner's chair. She looks as uncertain as the old woman who waits for the imaginary milkman. Taking the stone from my pocket, I offer it to her. "Check it out."

She rolls it between her thin hands. "What do I detect—a tingle?"

"Yes."

"And you think that's from the lightning?"

"Let's go find out." I dangle the blindfold. "Ready?"

She draws back.

"Drew, I promise, when you see the basement archives, you will not regret going."

"Raleigh, I'm Jewish. My DNA is full of regret."

I take the quartz, drop it into my pocket, and move around behind her, gently placing the blindfold over her eyes and tying the knot in a way that doesn't snag her crazy hair. Then I take her elbow.

"Six steps down." *Please, God.* "And I'm right here. You can trust me."

But we are only halfway across the porch when Uncle Cab calls out. "Are we playing Pin the Tail on the Donkey's Butt?"

Tinsley throws him a look, like he's a sub-moron. "Drew's agoraphobic."

"Ah-gore-ah-what?"

"She's afraid to go outside."

"Smart girl. World's full of crazies."

Tinsley sighs.

But DeMott—being DeMott—moves toward us, taking the stairs and facing Drew.

"Drew," he says. "It's me, DeMott."

"Oh. Hi."

"You're doing great."

"That's an exaggeration." She raises her blindfolded face. "And exaggeration is a form of lying."

He glances at me. My pulse hammers my skull. It doesn't help that I'm holding my breath, waiting for him to move, but he holds my gaze as he says to Drew, "Let me help you down the stairs."

She lifts her other skinny arm, waiting for him to take it. Standing on either side of her, we guide her to the bottom of the stairs and over to my bike. I let go and hop on the seat. "Okay, Drew, I'm ready."

DeMott says, "For what?"

"Drew gets on the handlebars."

He shakes his head. "No."

"*No?*"

"Raleigh, she's wearing a blindfold. You can't ride her on the handlebars."

"Why not?"

"It's dangerous."

So's dating a poisonous snake, but do I say anything about that?

"It's okay." Drew turns her blindfolded face toward DeMott. "That's how Raleigh brought me here."

"Wearing a blindfold—on her handlebars?"

"Yes."

"You're lucky to be alive."

"Raleigh doesn't believe in luck. Don't you remember?" Her face turns back and forth between us. "Although this seems like a good time to ask... do you think I'm going to die?"

"No!"

We both say it at the same time.

"Man." Uncle Cab lifts the flask. "This's even better than reality TV."

Tinsley sighs like seven hundred singed matches.

DeMott looks directly at me as he tells Drew, "I'll drive you wherever you need to go."

Tinsley lunges forward, so fast Uncle Cab's chair rocks into the wall.

"Drive her?" Tinsley storms toward us. "DeMott, you cannot be serious, we're supposed to be at my—"

He holds up a hand, silencing her, still looking at Drew.

"You remember my truck?" he asks Drew.

Drew nods, hair waving. "Your license plate number adds up to seventeen. Prime number."

"Good," he says. "Walk with me." Still holding her arm, he leads her toward his truck parked in the visitor's space near the stairs. "I'll take you wherever you want to go."

"Raleigh's coming, too. Right?"

He looks over at me. "Whatever she wants to do."

Grumbling under my breath, I mule kick the stand on my bike, and follow them to the truck.

26

I KNOW we're not supposed to enjoy other people's suffering. But we're also not supposed to lie. So here is the truth. I'm pretty darn happy when I hear DeMott tell Tinsley, "Wait here. I'll be back later."

The look in Tinsley's mean eyes is almost as delicious as my genius ham-and-egg sandwich. Uncle Cab, meanwhile, just rocks his chair and raises the silver flask for another toast. "Take your time," he tells DeMott. "We're not going anywhere."

I climb into the familiar truck. Even though I've ridden in it more times than I can count, suddenly it feels unfamiliar. When DeMott and I were dating, I always sat on the bench seat next to him. When Drew rode with us, she sat on the passenger side, usually staring out the window counting things. But now our positions are reversed. Drew's sitting next to DeMott. And I'm the one counting—counting the seconds until we reach the library downtown and I can jump out of this rig.

Ten million seconds later, I am pointing to the curb on East Franklin Street. "Right here, you can drop us off here."

But DeMott—being DeMott—takes his time parking in the library's side lot. Then he walks all the way around the front of the truck to open the passenger door. I hop out like the bench seat's on fire.

Drew doesn't budge.

Blindfolded, face positioned toward the windshield, she looks like someone who's been kidnapped.

"Drew." I smile so she doesn't hear my frantic feelings. "You can get out now."

She shakes her head.

DeMott leans inside the truck. "Want me to help you get inside the library?"

"No." I push my way in front of him. "I've got it. She's fine."

The words come out harsher than I intended. Even worse, I know why I'm sounding like this. After our breakup, I realized just how much I was depending on him. DeMott was always there, always ready to help. I got used to that. When he broke up with me, I made a vow. I'd never let myself feel that vulnerable again. "Thanks for the ride," I add, trying to take my tone down a notch. "But we're fine."

He takes my arm. "Can I talk to you for a second?"

Before I can answer, he's leading me away from the truck, his voice almost a low growl. "This isn't about you."

"I never said it was. But you can't just—"

He goes back to the truck, not even listening to me. He leans toward her again. "Drew, how about I carry you inside?"

I watch through the window as her shoulders sag with relief. Then I brace myself, expecting DeMott to give me a harsh look. *Told you so.* But he only reaches into the truck, all the while speaking in a soft tone to Drew, and slips an arm under her knees, the other around her shoulders.

"On the count of six," he says. "Ready?"

He lifts her barely-ninety pounds, backing away from the truck, swinging a leg out to slam the door.

"I could've done that," I point out.

He continues talking to her, reassuring her, telling her she's doing a really brave thing and that he's not exaggerating even one bit.

I take the library's front stairs by threes and get in front of them to punch the handicap button. The automatic glass door swings wide. I follow them inside. The air smells like old forgotten paper in books waiting for people to read them.

"And here you are." DeMott sets her down on the polished marble floor. "You made it, Drew. Safe and sound."

She reaches up, lifting an edge of the blindfold, and blinks at the bright overhead lights.

DeMott turns toward me. "How long will you be here?"

I try to read the expression in his eyes. And fail. "Why?"

"Should I stay here or come back?"

"Neither. We don't need you to—"

"Raleigh, if you want to run home, that's your problem. But Drew will need a ride."

"I know that." I sound defensive. So I go on the offensive. "Don't you think you should go check on your girlfriend?"

For a long moment, he stares. Then he turns to Drew.

"I'll be outside in my truck if you need me."

We watch him walk out the library's front door. Drew hands me the blindfold.

"Don't lose it," she says.

"I'm not going to lose it."

"I don't know about that," she says. "You managed to lose DeMott."

27

THE INTERNET IS A GREAT INVENTION. I really like it. But nothing compares to the basement archives at the Richmond public library.

"I must admit," says Nelson Heid, walking down the marble stairs with us. "Raleigh is the only patron who visits the basement anymore. I'm happy to see another visitor appreciate the artifacts."

Mr. Heid is the reference librarian. An all-around fact detective, he grew up in North Carolina which makes him very aware of etiquette, which is why he's moving down the stairs behind us— ladies first—and acting like it's perfectly normal that my best friend has taken each step forward like it might hit a landmine. She's also counting every stair, exclaiming on the sixes.

"And here we are," Mr. Heid says politely at the bottom of the stairs that nobody else uses. "Please enjoy your treasure hunt." He unlocks the steel door. "I'll check back on you two in an hour."

"Thank you!" I grab Drew's arm and pull her toward the far back sections labeled **Natural Earth Sciences and Physical Properties**.

In the old days, people used that kind of wording to describe science. We pass a floor-to-ceiling shelf marked **Cartographic and Geographical Studies of the Earth**. Nowadays, the sign would just say Maps. Or Geography.

"There!" Drew points.

Astronomical and Physical Phenomena.

She gazes at the section's antique cloth books like she's seeing a vision.

"I'll be over here." I keep moving until I reach **Geological and Mineralogical Sciences.**

"Hello, my friends," I tell the dusty books.

"Is someone else here?" she asks.

"No. Just us."

When I do a search on the Internet, the newest information will often pop up first. And that's good. But when I want to figure out something from scratch—because Teddy won't help—I start at the beginning of the information and work my way forward. It helps me see how other people figured something out. Kind of like what my dad says the really good lawyers do—they figure out what the other side is thinking, so they see their facts more clearly.

"Raleigh." Her voice is high, anxious.

I freeze. "Are you alright?"

"An entire bookcase is dedicated to Archimedes."

"Oh." I smile. "Great, isn't it?"

"Beyond great. Archimedes developed the law of buoyancy."

"Hey, whatever floats your boat."

She doesn't get it. "Archimedes also calculated the area under the arc of a parabola—"

I move down my aisle, reading the book titles, searching for what I need.

"—with the summation of an infinite series. He had a remarkably accurate approximation of pi."

"We should get some pie. I'm hungry."

"Has anyone else told you that you have a strange aversion to math?"

"It's what divides us."

She pauses. "Was that a joke?"

"Yes." I smile. "Good job, Drew."

We go back to our searches. Mine begins in the general mineralogy books, including some 1920s primers on chemical geology. The old volumes explain things in simple terms. I read over the basic information about silica. The chemical compound mostly appears as silicon dioxide or SiO_2. Also known as quartz. Which is the main component of sand. I turn the page and sneeze. Dust.

I lift my face. "Drew, when someone sneezes, what do you say?"

"'Cover your mouth'?"

"Yeah, okay. But before that. You're supposed to say, 'God bless you.'"

"I don't get that."

"I'll explain later."

I flip open a mid-1930s booklet titled *Ground Soil Deposits of Note.* Published by the U.S. Geological Survey during the Great Depression, it's focused on the economic deposits. I've learned a ton of geology from these 1930s projects. During the Depression, the federal government paid people to collect rocks and study the landscape. The Dust Bowl had wiped out a lot of farmers, and the government was searching for farmland with good soil. This little pamphlet gives a bunch of information about high silica levels in the soil. Sandy soil, with good drainage. Certain crops thrive in that soil. Crops like tobacco.

"Drew?"

"Mmm-hmm."

I don't say anything more. That's the sound she makes when she's deep in a book. Meaning, she's fine. More than fine. The hunt has caught her, too.

I move down the stacks. When World War II broke out in the 1940s, geology became even more important to the government. Something called the War Production Board hired geologists to write hundreds of pamphlets about certain minerals—especially minerals that could be used to kill an enemy, such as uranium and plutonium. Only problem is, the pamphlet only focused on a narrow topic and didn't create enough pages for a book spine. That means I have to carefully draw out each pamphlet and read the title on the cover. It takes patience, which I barely have, but finally I come across a faded blue paper book, the pages stapled together.

Silica Deposits of the Southeastern United States

"Getting warm," I say.

"Mmm-hmm," Drew says.

I flip open the cover, checking the table of contents. There's an entire section on "radio-grade" quartz. Back in WWII, radios were like the Internet—the fastest way for people to get news, including the news that Japan had bombed Pearl Harbor. With radios being so important, so were the minerals needed to build them. Like quartz.

Central Virginia, the paper reads, *offers some of the highest-grade usable quartz for radios.*

Richmond is in the middle of central Virginia.

"Getting way warmer," I say.

"Then open a window," Drew says.

Meaning, *Be quiet.*

I keep reading.

In some parts of central Virginia, quartz crystals can be found lying atop the weathered mantle foundation. In general, these crystals are larger than 200 grams—

I let out a groan—the metric system. Ugh. *Grams.*

"Drew."

"Is this important?"

"Yes. How many ounces is 200 grams?"

"Seven."

The human calculator. "Thanks."

Seven ounces is almost half a pound. That's a large specimen, way larger than the piece of quartz I found this morning. I scan the pamphlet's pages, flipping through sections about how silica can absorb moisture from the atmosphere like a sponge, how different colored sands get formed when other minerals contaminate the silica. Red sand usually means there's iron among the quartz. I take a deep breath. One problem with these archives is there's almost too much information.

But one word suddenly jumps from the page.

Piezoelectricity

Along with all our Latin classes, St. Cat's also drills Greek into us. I know *piezo*. It's a Greek root meaning "to squeeze or press." *Electric* —well, that one's obvious. But here is an entire section explaining how when quartz is placed under extreme pressure it can generate electricity— piezoelectricity. So back in the 1940s, the government geologists were studying quartz as an alternative energy source, not just for radios but radar equipment and clocks. All of it to help the war effort.

I lower the book and reach into my pocket. My fingertips tingle. I turn the quartz over in my hand.

"Drew?"

"Raleigh, not now. I just found a scientist who worked with Richard P. Feynman!"

Feynman. Her idol in physics.

"Just one question. Please?"

"Quickly."

"How does lightning work?"

"Lightning's caused by energy imbalances between the clouds and the ground. Sometimes an imbalance in the clouds themselves."

"And that energy can't be created or destroyed. It can only be transferred—"

"Or transformed. Raleigh, I already explained this."

"I know, but I'm wondering if lightning strikes a rock, can the rock turn electric?"

"That's a geology question," she says. "Can I go back to reading?"

I open my hand. Silica is the chemical that creates the mineral known as quartz. And according to this booklet, quartz can generate electricity if it's put under enough pressure.

The kind of pressure that comes from being struck by a lightning bolt.

I lift the stone to the overhead lights, feeling the tingle move all the way to my wrist. Even Teddy had to shake out his hand out after touching this rock, like something invisible clung to it. Because the energy in the lightning was transferred to the rock. And right here, on a dusty page from 1940, is the explanation.

"The transferred electrical charge sometimes produces a distinctive mark inside the piezoelectric quartz. The mark is a zigzag pattern—"

"That's it!" I cry. "I got it!"

"Raleigh," Drew says, "do you mind?"

28

BLINDFOLDED ONCE AGAIN and carried by DeMott to his truck that waited for us, Drew tells him about some of the interesting facts she discovered in the library's basement. While she talks, I silently point out the window, directing DeMott to the West End—to Drew's house. I'm convinced that if we can get to her house, she will stay there.

"At one point," she's saying, "scientists believed in the theory of contact electrification. That's what they thought produced all electrical charges." She faces the windshield as if the blindfold wasn't there and she is taking in the view of downtown Richmond. "And it's easy to see why they believed that. Right now, Raleigh's emitting electrostatic charges, in part because she used the Xerox machine in the library's basement."

I turn my head, taking in her narrow profile. It's true, I made Xerox copies of the pages explaining how silica changes, but... "What does the Xerox machine have to do with it?"

"Elementary physics," she says.

"I'm sorry?"

"Xerox machines use static electricity to attract the toner to the printing drum."

I could ask more questions, but I'm too busy pointing our way through downtown. Richmond has way too many one-way streets. DeMott is already making our third right—turning and turning— just to take one left and head west toward Drew's house.

"Contact electrification," she continues, as though I actually asked another question, "happens when two objects touch each other and become spontaneously charged."

"Good to know," DeMott says.

"One object develops a negative charge. The other object develops an equal but opposite positive charge. That's what validates the theory of contact electrification. Touch it, and it's electric. In the abstract, I would say that there's an electrostatic charge between you two."

The truck lurches.

"But that example is more metaphorical." She turns her blind-folded face to me. "See, Raleigh? Meta-phor-ical. Wait until I unleash that on Sandbag."

I nod, even though she can't see me.

"But scientists later moved away from the theory of contact elec-trification. They discovered other physical properties could produce electrification. Metals. The Volta effect. Triboelectricity..."

Part of me begs to ask her about these theories, especially since metals are geological. But another part of me is afraid she'll fling out another comment about some attraction between me and DeMott.

"—responsible for photocells, LED light, thermoelectric cells—"

DeMott hangs a right.

"And friction." Drew moves her head back and forth, her crazy brown hair brushing against my bare arm. "Notice how mild friction, combined with contact electrification, combined with Raleigh's elec-tric rock, makes my hair lift up."

I look over. Her hair is climbing up the truck's back window, sticking to the glass.

"Now imagine what kind of electricity would happen if I wasn't sitting between you two."

The quiet in the truck hangs heavier than a lead balloon.

"Raleigh, tell him about your silica discoveries."

"That's okay," DeMott says.

"No, tell him."

I gaze out the window. "Not much to tell. Silica's the main ingredient in quartz. Also known as sand."

I lean forward, pretending to adjust the tongue of my Converse All Stars while stealing a glance at DeMott. His face looks stern, almost angry. He glances over, catches me looking. I shove myself back, flames shooting up my neck as I press my entire spine into the bench seat. Drew's so skinny her body barely hides me.

"Tell him about the lightning quartz," she says. "Truly fascinating. And the whole thing happened right before her eyes this morning, on a run by the James River."

I roll down my window, ordering the wind to ice down my reddening face. But the warm humidity of May only brushes my cheeks as softly as—*no, not*—as DeMott's kiss. I close my eyes, willing my mind to think of something else.

"My dad's experimenting with windmills," DeMott says.

I open one eye. *Windmills? What do windmills have to do with anyth—*

"Speaking of electricity," he adds.

"You mean turbines," Drew says.

"I do?"

"Yes."

The Fielding estate stretches over three thousand acres along the James River. Plenty of room for windmills.

"The energy in the wind moves the windmill blades," she explains. "But those blades revolve around a rotor and the rotor is connected to a main shaft. The shaft spins the generator which transforms wind energy into electricity. It's the turbines that make the whole thing operate."

"How about that." DeMott sounds impressed. "Have you ever seen a windmill—in person?"

"No."

"Want to see one?"

There's no response.

We both turn, checking her face for signals, but our gazes lock. And something zigs and zags through my heart. Like lightning.

"I want to go back to Sunset Gardens," she says. "You're taking me back there, right?"

Our eyes lock again. Defeated, I nod.

"Yes," DeMott says. "Headed to Sunset Gardens right now."

Ten minutes later, my heart feeling so low it's on the ground, we ride down the long driveway to the white plantation house. On the front porch, Tinsley waits in a cute skirt and top, arms crossed and clearly annoyed. DeMott parks near the front steps and I jump out before he can open my door.

Tinsley looks down from the porch, baring her teeth at me. Nice teeth. Perfect for tearing things apart. "Have a good time?" she sneers.

"Electric." I tap Drew's arm, signaling her to get out, but DeMott's already moving around me, picking her up, then carrying her up the stairs.

He deposits her at the top of the porch and glances over at the rocking chairs. Uncle Cab's still there but he's snoozing now. Head back, mouth open.

"How long's he been sleeping?" DeMott asks Tinsley.

"I don't know." She fires back. "How long were you gone?"

DeMott watches his uncle. "Uncle Cab?"

Drew begins waving her arms like a blind person searching for any objects they might bump into. I take her hand, lead her to the front door. "One step up then we're inside."

Inside, Mrs. Donner is waiting. A little early today, but she's wearing her usual bathrobe, her gray hair once again plastered to the side of her worried face.

"Where's the milkman?" she demands.

"On his way," I tell her.

"I can't send the children to school without breakfast."

"The milkman will be here any minute now."

Drew takes off the blindfold, looking around the foyer. She smiles at Mrs. Donner, and sighs with relief. "It's good to be home," she says.

"It would be if we had milk for the children," Mrs. Donner says.

The screen door opens behind us. DeMott stands there, but doesn't step inside. And there's a strange look on his face, an urgency that makes my heart stutter. Even Mrs. Donner senses it. She reaches up, clutches the collar of her robe like a chill just blew into the room.

"DeMott, are you okay?" I ask.

"No." He points down the porch. "Call an ambulance."

29

THE OLD PEOPLE shuffle onto the porch.

What's going on, they want to know.

Why is the ambulance here again?

But as soon as they see the medical guy shining that penlight into Cabell Fielding's eyes—and Cabell isn't reacting—the questions dissolve into the warm air.

"Y'all should go back inside," Karlene tells them.

But a silence falls over the porch instead. It holds one more question.

Is he dead?

Only nobody wants to ask that question. As the old people shuffle back inside, Tinsley looks at her watch, sighing. To her right, Drew and DeMott focus on the medical guys, one of whom is now inserting an IV of clear fluids into Uncle Cab's limp arm.

He glances over at Karlene. "Status?"

She shakes her head. "He insisted on a DNR."

DNR. I know those letters from my dad's courtroom. It means Do Not Resuscitate. Someone would rather die than come back.

"Take him to MCV?" the medical guy asks.

MCV. Medical College of Virginia. The nearest hospital.

But Karlene shakes her head and her voice quivers like she might cry. "No."

A serious look flickers between the two medical guys. DeMott catches it.

"He needs to go to a hospital," DeMott says. "Take him to MCV."

"I agree he needs a hospital," Karlene says, trying to control her shaking voice. "But I can't let them."

"Why not?"

"Because your uncle drew up legal papers. He not only refused to be resuscitated, he refused to go to any hospital, ever. He made me promise."

"*What?*" DeMott spins toward her. "He did *what?*"

"It took me over a month to convince him that if, anything happened, he should go to the infirmary." She shakes her head. "Your uncle's an extremely strong-willed man."

The medical guys are already carrying Uncle Cab on a stretcher down the stairs. They slide him into the back of the ambulance wagon, its flashing lights punching at the afternoon sunshine. As the stretcher goes in, Uncle Cab's head jostles with the movement. But otherwise, he doesn't move. A chill runs down my back.

"No." DeMott's voice sounds desperate. "No. Tell them to take him to MCV. I'll call his doct—"

"I can't." Karlene reaches out, taking hold of arms, trying to calm him or herself, it's hard to tell. "Your uncle insisted. I can't defy his wishes. He made me sign papers."

The back door to the ambulance slams shut.

"You crazy old man," DeMott whispers hoarsely.

Karlene glances at me. She looks ready to cry. First Myra, then Wilma. And now, Uncle Cab.

DeMott watches the ambulance drive across the grounds. He drops his head. "It's all my fault."

"I told you," Tinsley says. "I told you not to give him that rum."

Karlene looks stricken, like she was just slapped. "DeMott, you gave him *rum?*"

Head still down, he nods.

"Why?" she asks. "Why would you do that? You know he's not well."

"He kept asking," DeMott sounds angry, defensive. "And I kept saying no but he told me he was unhappy and bored and nobody in my family comes to see him. I thought the rum would cheer him up." He stares down at the porch floor. "I was wrong."

Karlene's eyes redden. She blinks away the moisture. "He shouldn't have asked you."

DeMott looks over at her. His blue eyes are the color of the sky after a tornado rips away the clouds. "That's how he is."

She nods, touching his arm again.

"O-kay." Tinsley sighs. "Now he's going to be fine and we can all go home, right?"

The silence. The silence is exactly the kind you hear after somebody farts in public. I glance at Drew. But she looks confused. Another social cue she's missing.

But DeMott—being DeMott—remains polite. "Tinsley, I need to stay with my uncle."

"Can't you just drive me home? I've been here for *hours*."

"If you'll wait—"

I back away, not wanting any part of that argument. I take Drew's arm.

"His uncle has a cat," she whispers.

"I'm done with cats," I tell her, my voice rising before I can stop it. "I *hate* cats."

The silence.

The silence that follows my statement tells me I'm no better than Tinsley Teager.

"I'm sorry." My face feels really hot. "It's all for love, right?"

Karlene ignores my outburst. "DeMott, go be with your uncle. We'll take care of everything."

My mind continues its rant.

Not another cat.

But when I look at DeMott's face, there's enough sorrow to shut me up...forever.

30

DREW WALKS with DeMott to the infirmary, clinging to his arm, wanting to check on Myra.

I stand on the porch, apparently stuck with Tinsley.

"Here's the deal," I tell her. "You'd have to ride on my bike."

"Only losers ride bikes." She takes out her cell phone, sighing once again like a leaking tire, and taps in a phone number. I presume she's calling her closest friend—satan—but I'm wrong.

"Mom." She sighs one more time. "Come pick me up. I'm at that disgusting old people's home."

I walk inside, amazed that Tinsley couldn't even manage one sympathetic word about Uncle Cab. Then again, I griped about the man's cat. As I climb the stairs, the audience on the TV in the rec room applauds, as if hearing my plank-in-the-eye revelation.

Like all the third-floor apartments, Uncle Cab's place is big. But it's also a total bachelor pad and smells like mothballs. In the living room, I find a cat. It's curled up on an ugly brown couch, nesting on a bunch of newspapers. A matching coffee table—matching because it's also ugly and brown—displays chewed-up cigar butts, teetering on the table's edge. I don't smell cigar smoke so Uncle Cab must just chew these things. Which is its own special sort of grossness.

According to Karlene, the cat is named Fu Manchu. He's a Siamese but not the precious kind, like Wilma Kingsford's. Or Drew's. This Siamese's fawn-colored ears are dented and nicked up, like he's been in dozens of fights.

"Sorry, it's just me," I tell him. "Your dad will be back soon."

In the big kitchen, where dirty dishes fill the sink, I open the cupboards and find one plate. One bowl. Two glasses. All of them are brown. In the pantry, where ten million plastic grocery bags are stuffed into the shelves with more newspapers, I find a bag of generic brand dry cat food.

"Excellent choice."

Dry cat food has almost no smell.

I dump some food into the one remaining clean bowl. At the sound, Fu Manchu jumps off the couch and walks into the kitchen. He offers me a soft *mee-owww*.

"You're welcome."

Maybe it's my imagination, but he bows his head before eating. Like kitty grace.

"You're not so bad," I tell him. "For a cat."

He turns his small brown head, blinking his almond-shaped blue eyes at me. As if to say I'm not so bad...for a human.

Under the sink, I find dish soap and a bone-dry sponge that was probably last used seven months ago. I start scrubbing the dirty plates and bowls. The food's been stuck on these surfaces so long it's mineralized. But after a few minutes, the warm water and velvety suds bathe my hands like a bubble bath. My mind drifts. I think about Uncle Cab in that rocking chair, so alive one minute, out cold the next. And DeMott, the sorrow in his face. I rinse the glasses—*who buys brown glasses?*—and realize it wasn't just sorrow there. It was guilt. And shame. DeMott probably snuck that rum out of his dad's liquor cabinet. Which tells me how just much he loves his uncle. DeMott Fielding only breaks the rules under extreme circumstances.

Leaving the dishes to dry, I pick up the newspapers. A couple weeks' worth of the *Richmond Times-Dispatch* are randomly strewn around the apartment. On the walls, I straighten the shadow boxes that hold military medals and old Fielding heirlooms. Fu Manchu walks back into the living room. He gives me another nice meow.

"You're welcome, again."

I take a plastic bag from the pantry and—with a shiver—toss in the chewed-up cigar butts. Fu Manchu leaps on the couch, luxuriously turning a circle on the fabric which no longer is covered by newspapers. I find yet another chewed-up cigar butt inside a plastic bowl on the coffee table and toss that in the bag. There's also some prescription bottles in the same bowl, too. I pick up one bottle.

Fu Manchu flicks his tail.

"Wrong," I tell him. "I'm just being helpful."

I take another plastic bag from the pantry and start tossing in the prescription bottles. Only the child-proof caps are loose. The first bottle spills red-and-white capsules in the bag. I put the capsules back in the bottle, press down on the cap, and lock it in place.

The bottle's label reads:

Cabell Branch Fielding.

For symptoms associated with high blood pressure.

I look at Fu Manchu. He blinks at me.

"He might need this stuff."

The cap on the next prescription bottle is loose, too. I tighten it and read the label, something about diabetes. Third bottle—more diabetes medication—needs tightening too. As I'm locking the next cap in place, one word from the label leaps out at me.

Suppositories.

"Oh, gross!"

Fu Manchu gives another flick of his brown tail. Like he's saying, *Tell me about it.*

I know about suppositories. When Grandpa Harry got sick, he couldn't swallow pills and Gockey had to help him take suppositories. Which go in the butt. That image makes me turn the plastic bag into a glove before twisting the cap in place.

Fu Manchu lets out another good meow.

"I agree. Some things are too disgusting for words."

The last bottle, however, might be the worst. The label says, *For erectile dysfunction.*

I turn the label so the cat can read it, too.

"Are you kidding me?"

Fu Manchu yawns, as if to remind me he lives with this guy.

"Whatever." I toss that last prescription into the bag, give the cat a pet, and head for the infirmary, all the while telling myself—over and over and over—that this particular errand has *nothing* to do with seeing DeMott again.

31

DeMott stands beside Uncle Cab's bed. He watches the old man as if expecting the closed eyes to suddenly open.

I wait in the doorway. But DeMott doesn't notice me. He's traveled to another country. A place I know all too well. Unless something drags you back, your mind will stay there.

"Hey," I whisper.

He lifts his head, the comma of brown hair still dangling over his forehead.

"The nurse said I could come in." I lift the bag. "I brought some of his medications."

DeMott looks inside the bag, then begins taking out the bottles, one by one, and reading each label. I glance at Uncle Cab. His wrinkled skin is a pale gray hue, almost like cloudy quartz. Unlike Myra, he doesn't have any IVs with fluids flowing into his veins. And no heart monitor. Not even an oxygen mask. Do Not Resuscitate, and he meant it.

I head for the door. "I'll be around, if you need anything else."

"Raleigh."

I look back. All that sorrow remains in his face.

"Could you stay?" he asks.

THIRTEEN MINUTES LATER, a doctor walks into the room looking like he just got off the 18th hole. A white M.D. jacket has been thrown over a yellow polo shirt and green pants. A stethoscope dangles around his tan neck. He extends a hand to DeMott.

"I'm sorry," he says. "I got here as soon as I could."

"Thank you, Dr. Boatman."

The doctor offers me his hand, introducing himself. Dr. Robert Boatman.

"Raleigh Harmon," I say. His handshake is strong, a veteran golfer's grip.

"Are you family?" he asks.

"No, I'm just—"

"She's like family," DeMott says.

I look over at him, surprised. But he doesn't look back.

Dr. Boatman pops the stethoscope into his ears and slides the bell-shaped end beneath the collar of Uncle Cab's hospital gown. The old man doesn't even flinch. As he listens to the heart, Dr. Boatman glances up at DeMott. His hazel eyes are bright against his deep tan.

"When was the last time you spoke to your uncle?" he asks.

"Not long. A couple hours ago. We were with him on the front porch."

Dr. Boatman pulls the stethoscope from his ears and takes a clipboard hanging beside the bed. He writes something down, in penmanship nobody will be able to read. "How did he seem?"

"Like himself."

"Feisty?" Dr. Boatman almost smiles. "Full of fire?"

DeMott nods, and takes a deep, deep breath. "I also brought him a flask."

The doctor's pen halts, the tip hovering over the page. After a moment, he sets down the clipboard, carefully, and removes a penlight from the chest pocket of his white coat. Lifting one of Uncle Cab's eyelids, he shines the beam into the ashy blue eyes. The old man's gaze is so empty his eyes could be glass.

"How old are you, DeMott?"

"I'm not old enough to drink, if that's what you're asking."

"No." Dr. Boatman clicks off the penlight. "That's not what I'm asking."

"Seventeen."

"In other words, you're old enough to know that your uncle doesn't look after himself the way he should."

DeMott drops his head. "Yes, sir."

"And the last thing this man needed was alcohol. With his diabetes, it could've killed him."

DeMott nods, the comma of hair bouncing. But inside my chest something fierce rises.

"You're forgetting one thing." I hold my tone in check. I think. "DeMott didn't do this on purpose. His uncle begged him for that alcohol."

"Raleigh." DeMott raises his hand, signaling me to be quiet.

"No, DeMott. I just saw his apartment. It wasn't the rum. Your uncle chews on cigars and takes Viagra."

The doctor draws back, surprised. "Viagra?"

DeMott lifts the plastic bag, offering it to him.

Dr. Boatman takes out the battles, carefully reading the labels. He drops three bottles back into the bag but hands two others to DeMott. "I didn't prescribe these."

I lean closer, checking the bottles. The suppositories and the stuff for erectile dysfunction.

"These medications should be destroyed," the doctor says. "Can I trust you to take care of that?"

"Yes, sir."

"And no more alcohol," the doctor adds.

DeMott nods, takes the bottles, puts them in his pockets. "Is he going to be okay?"

"Your uncle's among my favorite patients." Dr. Boatman places a tan hand on Uncle Cab's forehead, like a father checking his child's temperature. "Unfortunately, he's severely limited what help I can offer him."

"Can't you do anything?"

"We will do everything possible. But we have to obey your uncle's orders. He was adamant about that."

Dr. Boatman reaches under his white coat and takes a leather wallet from the back pocket of his golf trousers. He hands DeMott a business card. "My cell phone number is on there. I've also alerted the staff. They're to call me immediately if anything changes."

DeMott's voice cracks as he says, "Thank you."

The doctor looks him in the eye. "DeMott, your friend Raleigh is right. This is not your fault."

The door to the room opens. A young nurse steps in, pushing a cart with medical supplies. She looks at Dr. Boatman.

"Should I come back?"

"No, Ellie. Please, take care of Mr. Fielding."

The nurse moves the cart next to the bed, Dr. Boatman says goodbye to DeMott and leaves, but I'm keeping an eye on the nurse's cart. There's a long clear tube connected to a disposable plastic bag. And a kidney-shaped bed pan. Cleaning swabs. Suppositories are bad enough, but a catheter for the bladder? I am so out of here.

"I'll be back later," I say, heading for the door.

The nurse gives DeMott an apologetic smile. "You might want to wait outside, too."

"How long do you need?" DeMott asks.

"Depends on how things go," she says. "But give me at least fifteen minutes."

32

STOMACH GROWLING, I open Toot's giant refrigerator and see that glorious platter of roasted ham is waiting for me. *Come to mama.*

"You just walk in here?" DeMott has followed me from the infirmary like a lost puppy. "Are you sure that's okay?"

He really doesn't like breaking rules. And the one time he does break a rule, his uncle ends up in the infirmary. I try to reassure him.

"I got permission." I place the ham platter on the stainless steel island, followed by the egg salad. But as I'm closing the fridge, another wave of inspiration strikes. Rolls.

"Who gave you permission," he asks, "Karlene?"

"No." I pull out my phone, tapping the familiar number.

Titus answers on the first ring. "Now what."

"There's a bag of potato rolls in your mom's refrigerator."

"You didn't listen last time."

"I did listen, but I'm wondering if it's okay to take—"

"Listen. Real close."

But for a long moment, I don't hear anything. I pull the phone away from my ear, checking the screen. It says, *Call Ended.* He hung up on me.

"Remember my friend Titus?"

"Your *friend*. Right. Raleigh, Titus Williams is a big deal in sports."

DeMott follows baseball. He can probably rattle off all of Titus' major league batting records but I really don't care about those because—*oh, man*—potato rolls. "His mom cooks all the meals here."

"You're kidding me."

I remove two rolls from the plastic bag, but they're small so —*listen*—I take out two more and tell DeMott about Toots. And about my attempts to get Drew back to real life. And about how Titus showed up yesterday with burgers. "But Drew doesn't want to leave this place. She's trying to move in."

"That makes sense."

"Why does that make sense?"

"Drew's obsessive-compulsive. Sunset Gardens runs on a tight schedule. That's probably comforting to her."

He walks to the far side of the room.

I place the rolls on two plates but one of those DO NOT EAT packets is stuck to the bottom of one roll. I peel it off but as I'm throwing it in the trash, I remember Toots threw a similar one into a jar by the stove, muttering about Do Not Eat. I add the packet to her growing collection and turn around. DeMott's taking the prescription bottles from his pocket, holding them over the trash can.

"Don't," I say.

He looks up. "Excuse me?"

"Your uncle's personal information is on those bottles. Somebody could steal his identity."

"But I promised to get rid of these things."

"Yes, the pills. We'll wash them down the sink."

"Why would we do that?"

"Because addicts go through landfills looking for drugs."

"Raleigh." He shakes his head. "You know the weirdest things." He lifts the prescription bottle for *erectile dysfunction*. "Do you think my uncle has a girlfriend?"

"It's probably Mrs. Donner. And she probably won't remember, even with the Viagra."

DeMott stares at me, shocked. Then throws his head back. And laughs.

The sound of his laughter—I hear surprise, relief, even some sort of joy—and it makes me feel like I'm running, that quick moment when the weary world rolls away and there is only here, now. So I stand there in Toots' kitchen, listening to DeMott laugh. But when my eyes start burning, I walk toward the sink, keeping my back to him.

I turn on the hot faucet, letting it get really warm. DeMott walks over, wiping tears from his eyes, and I hold out my hand for the prescriptions. Unscrewing the child-proof caps, I pour the pills into his hands. The Viagra ones are red-and-white capsules. The suppositories are little waxy footballs. *Yuck.*

"Hold them under the hot water, if you can. They should dissolve."

I carry the empty bottles over to a bulletin board where Toots keeps a Sharpie tied to a string. I black out the name *Cabell Branch Fielding* on the label. When I get back to the sink, the red-and-white capsules are dissolving but the little footballs seem to be coated with something water-resistant. *Ugh.* Suppositories. Shivering about where those things are supposed to go, I take some of them from DeMott and hold them under the warm water. And suppress a long sigh. I want to eat, not deal with this.

"Odd stuff," he says.

I nod, pinching my fingernails into one of the waxy footballs to speed things up. Inside there's a bunch of things that look like tiny clear beads. I watch them swirl into the water.

"I'm not looking forward to getting old," he says.

"Truth." I squeeze open another suppository, dumping the beads. "Does your uncle have another doctor?"

"Why?"

"Dr. Boatman says he didn't prescribe these things." I watch the beads. They're not dissolving. In fact, they're getting bigger. Expanding in the water. I reach down. Some of them are the size of pearls now. And they feel soft, like little gel balls.

"What's wrong?" he asks.

I squeeze the undissolved football. The beads inside are hard as sand. Weird. "Did your uncle seem any different lately?"

"How so?"

"I don't know. Not himself?"

"He was really tired. Thursday he called me because his chest hurt. I drove over, thinking he was having a heart attack. I took him to the infirmary and, well, you saw us."

I nod. "They checked him over?"

"Yes. No heart attack. Just really constipated."

I drop the suppositories into the sink.

"Yeah, I know." DeMott looks over at me. "But now do you see why I gave him that flask?"

"Yes." I watch the clear beads float on the water, like tiny bubbles of Jell-O. I pluck one of the unopened footballs from the water and slide it into my pocket.

"What're you doing?" DeMott asks.

"Nothing."

"Raleigh?"

"Nothing."

"Why are you taking—"

"I'm curious, that's all."

"Curious." He shakes his head. "This is how things always start with you."

Things.

Things that I do. Things that DeMott never liked me doing.

I reach into my pocket, take out the pill, offering it to him. "Fine. Toss it."

His blue eyes hold me for a long, long moment—a moment that just a couple months ago would've meant a really good kiss was coming.

Now?

Now the moment snaps like a dry twig.

Because I snap it.

"I need a sandwich," I tell him, turning around.

33

WITH HIS LAST bite of the ham-and-egg sandwich, DeMott pays me a huge compliment. "That might be the best version of ham-and-eggs I've ever tasted."

"I'm glad." Really glad. DeMott's finally looking a little less stressed. So it's now scientific fact: Comfort food works. I pick up our plates, carry them to the sink.

"Raleigh, I can wash my own plate."

"I've got it."

"But I invited myself over here," he says. "I should at least wash my own plate. And yours."

"DeMott, I've got it. I can wash plates."

And just like that, we're bickering again. Exactly like the end of our relationship. Is that what doomed it—arguing over stupid stuff? I take a deep breath, vowing to change. Vowing to help him. "How about you dry?"

"Good, thanks."

I start with the serving spoon I used for the egg salad. Wash, rinse, hand it to DeMott—and try not to think this is like my parents as he wipes it dry with a dish towel.

"Where does it go?" he asks.

"Over there." My hands are soapy so I chuck my chin toward the cutlery bins. He carries it over, and I resist the temptation to watch him go. DeMott's got a good back. Strong and straight. Instead, I stare down at the sink basin, watching the clear beads collecting in the corners. Some are even larger than pearls now. I reach down, pinching one. It pops like a zit. *Yuck.* I watch the clear goo oozing out.

"What's this doing here?" DeMott asks.

I glance over my shoulder.

He is standing by the storage shelves, holding up a large silver cup. Some kind of medieval chalice.

"What is that?" I ask.

He turns it upside down, pointing at something on the bottom. "This is from 1618."

"You mean, the year 1618?"

"Yes." His voice sounds tight, angry. "The year 1618—the date is stamped right there."

"Okay, cool..."

"Raleigh, this chalice has been in my family since 1618."

"Oh." I walk over, wiping my hands on my shorts. A bunch of scrolling monograms decorate the side of the cup, the engraved letters so ornate and entwined I can barely decipher the initials. M. D. F.

"MacKennas," he says. "DeMotts. Fieldings."

DeMott's named after his ancestors, like so many Southerners.

"Where did you find it?"

"Right there." He points angrily at the shelves above the cutlery bins. "It was just sitting there."

I try to remember when I found Gockey's cake knife—was the cup there, too? I didn't notice. But then, I wasn't looking for it. "So it belongs to your uncle?"

"It's a family heirloom. Uncle Cab inherited it from my great-grandfather."

"Then he probably brought it down here for dinner." I tell him about Gockey's cake knife, how she makes birthday cakes for people, and how we think she probably left the knife in the dining room after one of those celebrations. "Your uncle must've done the same thing."

But even as I'm saying it, my stomach tightens. *What about Mr. Halvorsen's ring?* "You know, stuff gets misplaced."

"Raleigh." DeMott lowers the chalice. "You're the last person I would expect to defend something like this."

"Something like—what?"

"Theft."

"You don't know that was stolen."

"I know Uncle Cab. He would never bring this chalice to dinner. It's worth a lot of money."

"But stealing? That's a really serious charge."

"Also, one of his war medals is missing."

"Wha-aat?"

"He earned a Purple Heart in Korea." DeMott's gaze searches my face. "Why don't you want to believe—"

"I just want to be fair."

"Fair?"

"Yes, fair. I don't want to accuse anyone unless there's solid proof. Remember what happened between me and Titus?"

Speak the name, the door opens, just like yesterday. Only this time, it's Toots who walks into the kitchen. She's wearing a wide-brimmed straw hat with her red glasses.

"You say somethin' about my Titus?" She heads for the thermostat on the wall, cranking down the dial to start the air conditioning. "What you say about my boy?"

DeMott lowers the chalice.

Since I don't know what to say, I grab my manners. "Toots, this is DeMott Fielding. His uncle, Cabell Fielding, lives here."

"Good ol' Cab." Toots removes the straw hat, using it to fan her face. Mist is gathering on her red glasses. "Cab's just the sweetest man. Sweet as cherry pie."

Sweet isn't a word I'd use to describe Uncle Cab, but Toots sounds like she means it. She hangs her hat on a wall hook, lifts a white apron, and ties the strings around her wide middle. "Y'all get some-thin' to eat?"

"Yes, ma'am. Titus said it was okay."

"Food's for eatin'." Toots opens the big fridge.

"Excuse me," DeMott says. "May I ask you a question?"

"You just did."

"A different question."

"Well, get to it." She hoists out the platter of ham, throwing me a significant look. "Hope it was good."

"Delicious, thank you."

"You heat it up?"

"No, ma'am. We ate it cold, topped with some egg salad. On the potato rolls."

She smacks her lips. "That sounds right tasty. Have to try that myself."

"Excuse me!" DeMott lifts the silver chalice, shaking it until it glitters under the ceiling lights like the Holy Grail of Virginia. "Did you steal this?"

My jaw drops so far open I could catch flies.

DeMott Fielding. He didn't just say that.

Toots squints at him over the rims of her red glasses. "What did you say to me?"

"This is a priceless family heirloom. It belongs to my family."

"Then get it outta my kitchen." She reaches to the fridge's top shelf, carefully sliding out the pan of red Jell-O and trapped canned fruit. "I don't need crap like that clutterin' up my kitchen.

"Crap? This is not crap. And I'd like to know what it's doing in here."

With one foot Toots closes the fridge. Slowly, she sets down the pan of Jell-O. Then her plump hands land on her round hips and the resemblance seeps into her dark brown eyes. This is the look Titus gave me last year, when he was glaring at me through the Plexiglas at the city jail. Seeing it once was enough. I close my eyes.

"You think I *stole* that thing?"

"I don't know. That's why I'm asking."

"You callin' me a thief."

"No, I was simply wondering if—"

"No, siree. Uh-uh."

I open my eyes. She's wagging her thick index finger back and forth.

"Don't you *dare* come into *my* kitchen, eat *my* food, then accuse *me* of being some kinda sticky-fingered *thief*."

"I didn't—"

"Now you gonna *lie* to my face?"

"I was just—"

"Don't you dare." She storms over to the stove, flicking a knob. The blue flames burst into the air.

"I'm simply asking," DeMott says. "This cup shouldn't be here."

"And I don't want it in here!"

I can feel another blast heading our way, just like I could sense this morning's storm was coming with thunder and lightning. I close my eyes again. Only the blast takes a sudden turn.

"Niko!"

I open my eyes.

Niko the waiter is wandering through the back door, bike helmet on his head, book in hand.

"NIKO!"

He lifts his amber eyes from the book. The cover shows a bloody knife. He gazes around the kitchen and seems to pause when he sees DeMott.

"Get yo-self out to my tables!" Toots hollers. "I got supper to put out!"

I grab DeMott's arm, pulling him and that heirloom out of her kitchen before we become the target again.

34

DeMott grips the silver chalice so tightly his knuckles are white. A half a step behind him, I follow upstairs.

"Did you see that kid Niko?" I ask.

He turns down the third-floor hall, heading for his uncle's apartment.

"Here's what's going on," I tell his good back. "Niko the waiter reads all the whole time, he's not paying attention. He picks stuff up in the dining room without actually seeing what it is."

DeMott walks into the apartment. I stay in the hallway. I know what his silence means—*I'm too polite to tell you to shut up.* Unfortunately, I understood that too late, always filling all the silences with my nervous chatter. Now, lesson learned, I keep my mouth shut and wait for the silver cup to go back where it belongs.

DeMott steps out. And we start walking for the stairs. But here comes Mr. Halvorsen, waving his hand.

"Hey, there!" He points to the gold-and-ruby ring. "Thanks for finding my ring."

DeMott halts, looks over.

"You're welcome," I choke out.

"Karlene says you found it in the kitchen."

DeMott's gaze on the side of my face feels like a hot iron.

"Any idea how my college ring ended up in the kitchen?"

Mr. Halvorsen waits for me to answer. I shake my head.

"I've never even been in that kitchen," he adds.

I turn toward DeMott, forcing a smile onto my face.

"We should check on your uncle, don't you think?"

◇

MORE SILENCE as we cross the grounds.

Inside the infirmary, the air smells like someone blew up a case of Lysol. At the nurses' desk—empty—DeMott turns toward Uncle Cab's room. I turn the other way, toward Myra's room. But at the last moment, I look back.

"DeMott."

He stops, but doesn't turn around. That great good back. Right now it looks like a brick wall.

"I hope your uncle gets better."

He glances over his shoulder. One long blue gaze from far, far away.

No words come with it.

◇

THERE'S a reason I don't believe in luck. Actually, a bunch of reasons, but the main reason is that after looking at hundreds of minerals and crystals, every single one showed some kind of structure. A design. Nothing random about them. Plus, for the last three years, Drew's lectured me about the laws of thermodynamics—laws. Not sometimes-this and sometimes-that. Laws that happen every single time, without fail. Which means there's order down to the last grain of sand—and how that grain of sand was created. Which also means nothing can be random.

Which is also why right now, as I move through the Lysol-stinking air toward Myra's room, there's a really bad feeling expanding inside me.

Things don't happen randomly.

That means the three objects—cake knife, college ring, family chalice—didn't just happen to fall into Toots' kitchen.

My three theories of how they got there?

One, the owners of those objects, like Gockey, took them into the dining room and forgot to take them back to their apartments. Niko the waiter picked them up while reading some horror novel and stuck them in the kitchen.

This is possible—old people forget things. And Niko is distracted.

But DeMott claims Uncle Cab would never bring that silver chalice to dinner. And Gockey doesn't remember taking her cake knife to the dining room. And Mr. Halvorsen's ring was in the garbage disposal—would Niko really drop it there?

My second theory.

Toots collects stuff in that kitchen, including, weirdly, those packets that say DO NOT EAT. Maybe she collected these things, too.

But if that's true, then she lied to us.

Third theory.

Somebody stole those things and hid them in the kitchen. Maybe they planned to come back and grab them later. The silver cup's an antique. So is Gockey's knife. And the ring is gold with a three-carat ruby. Big money.

But if that was the plan, why would the thief shove Mr. Halvorsen's ring into the garbage disposal where it got dinged by the blades?

I'm trying to come up with an answer as I turn down the hallway to room 137. But Drew steps out of the room, and she's smiling—her real smile, the one that makes her dark eyes crinkle until they're almost closed.

"Myra's better?" I ask.

"Tremendous forward momentum. What's going on with Uncle Cab?"

"I don't know."

"Did you check?" She starts down the hall, leaving me standing there. "Let's go see."

"Drew—no—hold on—"

She doesn't stop.

We pass the nurse's station, where the phone is ringing and ringing into the Lysol air. When we turn down the next hallway, I can see Uncle Cab's room. The door is wide open. And two nurses stand on either side of his bed.

Suddenly, Drew halts. I bump into her back.

"What's wrong?" I ask.

She doesn't answer.

I shift around her stiff body, moving closer to the room. DeMott is standing across from the bed, all the way against the far wall. His face looks as white as the blanket on the bed. I step into the room.

"When?" asks the nurse who was in here earlier, doing the bladder catheter. "When did you come back?"

DeMott only shakes his head more.

"You don't know?" She sounds impatient.

"Just now," I tell her. "He came back just now. Maybe five minutes ago."

She looks over at me, squinting like I'm lying.

"We went to get something to eat," I explain. "You said it'd be awhile and..."

DeMott is shaking his head. Shaking it so hard that comma of hair swings back and forth across his pale forehead. But the whole time, his gaze never leaves the white bed.

I look over at his uncle.

The white sheet has been pulled up, completely covering the old man's face.

35

When Karlene walks into Uncle Cab's infirmary room, my mind's running four hundred miles an hour. Drew's already hurried back to Myra's room. DeMott's a zombie. So when Karlene looks at me like I can explain, I can't.

Uncle Cab is dead.

He lays under the white sheet, the nurses staying by the bed as if guarding his body. The medical guys arrive—same ambulance guys who brought Uncle Cab to this building just ninety minutes ago. In silence, they hand Karlene some paperwork. She signs, and I hear them say something more about Uncle Cab's DNR order.

Karlene walks over to DeMott. Her voice sounds as soft as down feathers.

"Would you like me to call your family, let them know?"

DeMott doesn't seem to hear. He's in a trance. I nod at her for him. Then I wipe my clammy hands on my shorts, close my eyes, and pray. But it's one of those times when my prayers have no words. In the room, there's a sudden zippering sound—*brrr-zzzing*. I open my eyes, and the ham-and-egg sandwich curdles in my stomach. They have placed Uncle Cab's body in a black bag, zipped closed on a gurney. They wheel him into the hallway.

DeMott jumps. "Where are you taking him?"

The medical guys hesitate, glance at Karlene.

Her voice is still feather-soft. "The morgue. All sudden deaths have to go the morgue by law."

"I want to go with him."

"Oh, DeMott. You don't want to see—"

"Raleigh." He turns to me. "You'd go if this was your family. Wouldn't you?"

I open my mouth but before I can answer, he asks another question.

"Come with me?"

Whatever words I planned to say, only a stutter comes out.

IN THE BACK of the ambulance, DeMott looks at the black body bag the same way Drew stared at the infirmary while I interviewed Mr. Halvorsen about his missing ring. The gaze that could bend spoons, read minds, and force all kinds of things to happen just by thinking it —except bring someone back from the dead.

Sitting across from him, the gurney between us, my heart feels like it is literally cracking. I look away. Out the small back window, the ambulance seems to meander through Saturday afternoon traffic on Broad Street. No sirens blaring. No lights flashing. None of that's needed. Cabell Fielding is dead.

I squint into the late afternoon sun, wondering if Uncle Cab died while we were eating in Toots' kitchen. The thought makes my eyes sting. The view blurs until I can only see people-shaped figures, strolling down the sidewalk, all of them looking like their ordinary day will go on forever. But the memorized words roll forward in my head.

Tell me not, in mournful numbers,

Life is but an empty dream...

When the wagon swings left, the commercial district disappears, replaced by narrow brick houses on worn-down streets. Plywood covers some of the windows. The short stoops are missing their handrails. The wagon turns again. Out the window, I see an elderly black man sitting in a tattered deck chair. He's reading the newspaper but glances up as the ambulance passes, his deep dark eyes full of concern. The wagon stops and cold dread freezes my veins.

The rear door bursts open.

"Son," the older medical guy says to DeMott, "you might want to rethink this idea."

"No." DeMott moves off the metal bench, climbing out, almost pushing the man aside. "I'm not leaving him."

The older guy glances at his partner, who looks young but jaded. "What's the law?" he asks.

"I don't know. Nobody's ever asked before."

Lifting the gurney, they roll out the body in its bag. I climb out last, with my dread growing heavier by the second.

"Raleigh," DeMott says, "the law says this is okay. Right?"

Unable to speak, I pull out my phone, tapping the number for my dad's home office. I clear my throat—twice—and hope for once my dad says no.

"Hey, kiddo," he answers. "What's going on?"

Life. Death.

I step away from the wagon, away from DeMott, lowering my voice. "Promise not to get upset?"

"I'm listening," he says, without promising.

"Is it legal for a relative to go into the morgue with a dead body?"

The pause. It goes on. And on. At the street corner, the traffic light turns from green to yellow. Then red. The elderly black man in his deck chair watches us over the top of his newspaper as the medical guys roll the cart with the black body bag toward a set of steel garage doors. DeMott watches them. Watches me.

"Dad?"

"Why would you be asking this?"

"DeMott's great-uncle just passed away."

"Cabell?"

"Yes."

"I'm sorry to hear that." Another pause. "You're asking for DeMott?"

"Yes, sir." I drag the toe of my Chuck Taylors against the pebbly pavement, struggling for the right words. Why does death make even ordinary words sound odd? "He's asked me to go into the morgue with him."

Please tell me that's illegal.

"The most direct next-of-kin is Harrison Fielding." DeMott's dad, Harrison. "He should be the person taking care of this matter."

"Dad, that didn't answer my question."

One of the garage doors is lifted now and a Hispanic man wearing medical scrubs appears. Uncle Cab's body bag waits on the cart, like nothing more than groceries. I pull in a slow breath, hold it, counting like I'm Drew Levinson.

"Are you at the morgue now?" he asks.

"Yes, sir."

"Raleigh."

"Dad, I'm here. So that's done."

"The coroner will make the final decision," he says.

"So DeMott has a legal right to be there?"

"Unless his uncle had legal wishes stating otherwise."

"What about me?"

Another hesitation. "DeMott can request your presence."

The Hispanic guy hands a pen and clipboard to the ambulance guys. The older one takes it. The younger one glances back at DeMott. He's already walking toward the lifted garage door, looking so perfect and so totally wrecked. Like some marble statue of Adonis smashed on the ground.

"Raleigh," my dad is saying, "I don't think it's wise to go—"

"He asked for my help. I can't say no."

"Then be careful," he says. "The last look sometimes lasts forever."

36

THEY LEAD us into a cold and empty space, and tell us to wait there. I keep my gaze on the bare concrete floor, but the metal drain makes me imagine how things get hosed down in here. The air smells like rotting hamburger meat, disinfectant, and suffering. I shiver.

"Thanks for coming," DeMott says.

I nod.

The silent morgue workers in green scrubs have already taken Uncle Cab's body into another room, somewhere on the other side of the darkened Plexiglass which I'm pretty sure is some viewing area. I'm also pretty sure that if somebody flicks on the light in there, my stomach is going to lose all its contents.

From my dad's courtroom, I've heard medical examiners testifying about all kinds of violence. Assault. Battery. Gunshot wounds that make a human body look like it was there for target practice. The photos are hideous. And it upset my dad that I was seeing stuff like that. But I kept telling him the photos didn't freak me out. If anything, those images only made me want to stop the crimes from happening.

Real life, however, is different. Real life is seeing DeMott's sorrowful face and hearing Uncle Cab's voice in my ear just a couple hours ago.

"You're sure about this?" I ask.

There's a sound of a metal lock tumbling open. The heavy sealed door opens and a small woman steps into the room. I've seen her in my dad's courtroom. Wendy Walters, assistant medical examiner. But here she's wrapped her long blonde hair into a very large bun and wears plastic Crocs that match her green medical scrubs. In the courtroom, she's always seemed distant, with a cold attitude. But now I wonder if she carries the temperature of this room with her.

"You wanted to speak to someone?" she asks DeMott.

"Yes, I want to know what killed my uncle."

Wendy Walters looks annoyed by the statement. I've seen her this annoyed by certain lawyers, so, despite the odors flicking at my uvula, I manage to squeak out a polite question.

"When were you planning to do the autopsy?"

"Not now," she says. Her biting voice echoes in the empty room. "In case you haven't noticed, it's the weekend. We're rather busy, what with people killing each other for sport."

"Great," DeMott says. "But I need to know because I might've killed my uncle."

Wendy Walters hesitates to bark back. Maybe she thinks there's more to this confession. But DeMott's jaw is locked.

"His uncle had diabetes," I explain. "This morning he drank some alcohol and passed out, and then ..." My eyes start to burn. *And then we went into the kitchen and laughed like there was nothing wrong and ate sandwiches and Uncle Cab died, alone.* "Is there any way you could do something soon, like, the preliminary stuff?"

"Preliminary stuff?"

"You know, initial findings. Before the conclusive results of a full autopsy."

She studies me. "Where did you hear this, on television?"

DeMott glares at her. "Are you also dead?"

If the room had windows, I'd be checking for flying pigs. Or Hell freezing over. Because DeMott Fielding just lost all his manners.

"Can't you understand?" His voice sounds hoarse. "My uncle's not coming back and I probably killed him. Doesn't that bother you —at all?"

For a long looooong moment, Wendy Walters watches him. I could be wrong, but her big blonde bun seems to vibrate with annoyance. Or fury. But one thing's for sure. In the silence, the marble-cold air is melting.

~

THE LAW—*THANK you, God*—says we can't be in the autopsy room itself. Sudden deaths all become law enforcement cases, until the coroner clears them of foul play. And in another hint that she's not a freezing witch, Wendy Walters says we can wait in her office.

Her office. It looks decorated by an eleven-year-old girl. Pink everywhere. Pink curtains on the window that faces the grim street below. Pink rug over the chilly brown tile flooring. And pink chairs next to the tidy desk which offers a small blue jar of Vicks VapoRub. I unscrew the lid and smear some under my nose, breathing in the menthol scent. I offer the jar to DeMott. He looks at the goo smeared on my upper lip. And shakes his head.

"How long does this thing take?" he asks.

I could explain why pathology reports can take weeks, but it will only annoy him even more. The Fieldings live in a time-warp bubble. Their gigantic estate is a world of their own making. Meanwhile, in hot and humid Richmond, murder keeps a constant appointment with the morgue because nobody else has that privilege. As I stand there, one of the Longfellow lines creeps into my head. About how our hearts, *like muffled drums, are beating funeral marches to the grave.*

"It's only been twenty minutes," I tell him. "Be patient."

He throws me a look.

"Okay," I admit. "I have the patience of gnat on fire. But *you* can do it."

He rolls his eyes.

Wow. Another rude gesture from Mr. Manners?

Eight minutes later, Wendy Walters and her big blonde bun walk into the office. She's changed her clothes. Sitting down in the also-pink chair facing us, she places a small white binder on the desk and flips it open. No niceties, no greetings, she just starts reading some of the preliminary findings about Cabell Branch Fielding. Age. Height. Weight. The basics. I know what this is—nothing, really. The full autopsy takes much longer, including sending tissue samples to the lab.

"I know all this," DeMott says. "What are you holding back?"

She leans back in the chair. "A number of factors contribute to expiration in old age—"

"He didn't *expire*. Milk expires. He *died*. Now tell me why."

"I could only hazard a guess."

"Then guess."

She closes the binder. "His skin and organs showed signs of acute dehydration. Kidneys, liver, bladder, they're all affected by that. But only the full report can confirm what—"

"He was thirsty?" DeMott says. "You're telling me he was thirsty?"

"Probably not."

"But you just said—"

"With severe dehydration, the signal for thirst is unreliable."

The tension in here is making my stomach tighten again. I take a deep breath of menthol and stare at this woman's forehead. Perspiration dots her skin, like those clear shiny beads we washed down the drain. There's also a fresh dent near her hairline, probably from the face shields that protect these people from all kinds of disgusting medical stuff.

"The human body doesn't always recognize thirst," she explains. "If your uncle was suffering from acute dehydration, and I believe he was, then he would likely lose all sense of thirst. You would only be able to detect the problem by visible symptoms."

"Which are?"

"Lethargy. Confusion." She shrugs. "But those conditions are already chronic problems for the elderly. It's one reason dehydration is so difficult to diagnose."

"So he was thirsty—for a really long time." DeMott's voice cracks. "That's what you're telling me?"

Each time DeMott gets more emotional, this woman does the exact opposite and now she's starting to sound like a car mechanic who lifted a hood to inspect an engine. I glance around her office. The same gap-toothed girl is in all the pink-framed photographs. Wendy has a life. A heart. Doesn't she?

I clear my throat, swallowing menthol. "Are you saying this isn't his fault?"

"That's one way of viewing it."

I lift my eyebrows, trying to signal her. *Just tell him it's not his fault.* But she misinterprets what I'm doing.

"It is worrying," she says. "You should alert the other people."

I lean forward. "Alert—who?'

"Mr. Fieldling lived at Sunset Gardens. Correct?"

"Yes."

"You should alert the other people living there."

"About what?"

"Dehydration." She says it like I'm a total idiot. "I'm trying to convey to your friend that dehydration is a very serious problem among the elderly. Once the human body becomes deficient in fluids, it's very difficult to rehydrate the system." She taps a white folder on her desk. "Mr. Fielding is not the first case we've seen."

I think of Myra, how she fainted from dehydration. Maybe that was Wilma's problem, too. And if Uncle Cab was dehydrated, the alcohol combined with diabetes doomed him. *That's* why this woman won't come out and say DeMott isn't at fault. I glance over at him. Head down, comma of hair dangling, he seems to know it, too.

The assistant coroner watches him. Her hard shell begins to crack, just a little.

"I'll send the blood and tissue samples to the pathology lab," she says, in a slightly softer tone. "When those results come back, we'll have more definitive answers."

DeMott turns his face away.

"Can he get a copy of the report?" I ask.

She doesn't even look at me. Her gaze is zeroed in on something. I follow it. And see the tear at the moment it falls from his chin.

37

THE HISPANIC ASSISTANT escorts us out a different way, through what he calls the "reception area." DeMott crosses the room in a beeline, heading straight for the front door that faces the sidewalk outside. But I stop. In one of the plastic chairs, the tallest man in town is reading *Sports Illustrated*. He looks up.

"Raleigh?" he says.

"Hi, Detective Holmgren."

He glances at DeMott, heading out the door. Just one quick look, but I'm sure Holmgren could close his eyes right now and describe DeMott down to his white shoelaces. That's the kind of detective he is. "I'm almost afraid to ask," he says. "What are you doing here?"

I tell him that my friend's uncle just died. He seems about to ask another question but the door swings open again. DeMott stands there, impatient for me to leave.

"Take care," Detective Holmgren says. "And say hello to Drew."

Outside, a drowsy haze of sunlight tips the afternoon toward evening. The black man across the street in his deck chair is still reading his newspaper but also watches DeMott, who looks dazed. Lost.

I pull out my phone and call my dad. We need a ride. In mere minutes, he shows up, driving the old black Mercedes that belonged to Gockey until she gave up driving. My mom's not with him, and I feel guilty because I'm glad.

DeMott climbs into the back seat. I take the passenger seat up front, adjusting my side mirror so I can see him. I also roll down my window all the way because despite the sharp menthol lingering on my upper lip, the stink of death clings to us. My dad doesn't so much as wrinkle his nose. Still parked at the curb, he turns all the way around. DeMott's cheeks are lined with trails of dried salt.

"I'm so very sorry for your loss, DeMott," he says. "Your uncle was a wonderful and unique man. He will be missed."

DeMott's eyes redden. "Do you think he's in heaven?"

In the old car, with the odors of death and disinfectant radiating off us, I hold my breath. Not for the smells.

"God loves us," my dad says. "Each and every one of us. He loved your uncle, and he will fight to the bitter end for his soul."

DeMott looks out the window. The black man looks back. As we pass, I can barely hear DeMott's whisper. But it's enough. "Thank you."

My dad drives away from the morgue, casting a weighty glance my way. When we reach Broad Street, my dad looks into the rearview mirror. "Would you like me to call your mom and dad?"

"Karlene already called them."

I look over at my dad. "Can I stay with Gockey tonight?"

"I'm sure she'd appreciate that." He glances once more into the rearview mirror. My dad has always liked DeMott, except for when DeMott broke up with me because of how much time I spent helping Drew. Since my dad spends all his free time taking care of my mom, it struck a nerve.

When the car stops at the front porch of Sunset Gardens, my dad once again offers his condolences. DeMott thanks him, gets out, and heads for the stairs.

"Thanks for the ride," I tell him.

He reaches over, taking my hand. I'm expecting one of his *did I ever tell you what so-and-so said* moments. But he just holds my hand, looks into my eyes, and says in an odd voice, "I really *really* love you, kiddo."

38

DINNER IS over at Sunset Gardens, but all the white-haired people are still ringed around the dining tables, listening to the skinny girl in purple standing on her chair. I move into the doorway.

"Two atoms are walking down the road," Drew is saying. "One of them says, 'I think I lost an electron!' The other one asks, 'Are you sure?' And the first one says, 'I'm absolutely positive!'"

The old people chuckle.

"Here's why that's even funnier than you realize," she explains.

Even Gockey is listening, almost beaming as Drew tells them how atoms function and why they're so fascinating. From personal experience, I know this lecture will turn into a passionate defense of physics, which Drew claims is the greatest science on earth. These people digesting their dinner have nowhere else to be. But I've heard this lecture so many times before, I turn away.

And bump into DeMott.

"Sorry." My face feels suddenly hot. "I didn't realize you were..."

But he doesn't notice me. All his attention is on Drew.

"Okay, a neutron walks into a bar," she's saying. "He asks, 'How much for a drink?' The bartender replies, 'For you? No charge!'"

The crowd laughs until it coughs.

"Now you get it!" She smiles. "Let's keep going."

DeMott looks down at me, his blue eyes full of pain and wonder. "She seems like her old self."

I swallow all the emotions crowding my throat, and open my mouth, praying something half-intelligent will come out. Instead, I say, "Cat."

"Pardon?"

"Your uncle. He has a cat."

His eyes glisten again. "Yeah."

I look up into those stormy eyes. "Want some help with it?"

SINCE MOST EVERYONE is in the dining room listening to Professor Levinson, the third-floor hallway feels even emptier. Like it's reminding us Uncle Cab isn't coming back.

DeMott stops outside the apartment door.

"You want me to go in there?" I ask.

"No," DeMott says. "But thank you."

"For what?"

"The morgue. And I know how you feel about cats."

"This isn't a bad cat. I actually kind of like him."

But the moment we walk into the apartment, my opinion changes.

DeMott halts. "What the—"

Broken brown glass sparkles from the kitchen floor. In the living room, shredded paper litters the brown couch, two books torn into a mean confetti. And the brown curtains look like somebody took a knife to them.

"What happened?" he asks.

"I don't know. It didn't look like this when I left."

On the kitchen counter, Fu Manchu hunches near the dishes that I washed. Half of them have been knocked to the floor.

"What's wrong with you?" I ask.

He arches his back, opens his sharp-toothed mouth. And vomits.

Wonderful.

I step over the broken glass and yank out plastic bags from the pantry. Fu Manchu staggers across the counter. When he reaches the sink, he starts making that hacking sound Drew's cat makes when a nice wet hairball's about to appear.

DeMott picks up a toppled lamp in the living room. He moves slowly, mournfully.

I open one of the plastic bags and use it like a glove to scoop up the cat vomit. Never mind morgue stink. Forget canned cat food. Nothing is as gross as mushy stomach gunk reeking of hydrochloric acid. I step back, gagging, as my shoe slides across the floor.

I glare at Fu Manchu. "There's more?"

He weaves into the living room, once again making that hacking sound.

"What's wrong with him?" DeMott asks.

"He's a cat."

"Raleigh."

"I don't know, he was fine earlier."

Fu Manchu makes his way across the room like an inch-worm— his back arching then straightening out, arching, straightening—until he barfs. I grab more plastic bags and wipe up the puddle of yuck. The cat staggers into the next room. I follow, muttering under my breath. In the bedroom, a brown comforter heaped on the floor spews its white polyester filling.

"You tore this up too?" I ask, low enough that DeMott can't hear. "Don't freak out. Someone will take care of you. Not me. But someone with—"

The cat pukes on the carpet.

I sigh. "Go ahead, get it all out."

I swab up the mess. It's just clear liquid now—no food left—but it's thick, clinging to the plastic bag. Some kind of colorless paste. I lean closer. The clear beads. The things we washed down the sink. They're floating in the paste. I sniff but there's no smell. Not even the sour bite of hydrochloric acid. I lean in closer, my face inches from the vomit.

"What're you doing?" DeMott stands in the doorway, looking horrified.

"Something's not right."

"Because it's *vomit*?"

"Yeah, but, look." I stand up, holding the plastic bag so he can see the stuff. "Those beads, that's what we washed down the sink."

Fu Manchu is hacking again. I hand that bag to DeMott with a couple of the fresh ones. "You get this pile."

I follow the cat as he swerves into the bathroom. Wobbly, he leaps on top of a small trash can, knocking the thing over on his way to the counter.

"Nice move."

I start picking up the spilled trash when a bottle of cologne slides off the counter, smashing on the ceramic tiles.

"Are you alright?" DeMott asks.

"Yes." But the musky scent flooding the air fills me with sadness. It's like Uncle Cab is suddenly here, only as a ghost. I pluck the pieces of broken glass, tossing them in the trash can, while Fu Manchu arches his back again. When I look up, he seems ready to jump off the counter—right into the broken glass that will slice his paws.

"No—" I lunge. "Don't!"

He vaults over the broken glass, hits the floor, and leaps into the bedroom.

DeMott calls his name.

I restrain a heavy groan and start picking up the rest of the broken glass. But the cologne's spreading across the floor, under the counter. More trash is down there, too. I grab a towel, sopping up the fluid, and pick up a tube of denture cream. Pair of nail clippers. And a black comb, white hair weaving through the plastic teeth. Like the cologne, the hair fills me with sadness.

"Raleigh?"

"I'm fine." I toss the comb into the trash before DeMott can see it. Then reach for the other stuff that's spilled. My fingers find some red-and-white capsules, and an orange prescription bottle. Empty. Cap gone. The label reads, *Cabell Branch Fielding. For symptoms of insomnia.*

No doctor listed.

I look up, catching my reflection in the mirror above the sink. My brown hair's doing its usual escape-the-ponytail routine. But a deep frown creases my forehead.

"Whoa." DeMott stops at the door, waving a hand in front of his face. "Is that his cologne?"

I stare into the mirror, watching his face.

"What's wrong?" he asks.

I hold out the empty prescription bottle. "I think the cat ate your uncle's medicine."

DeMott takes the bottle. "Where's the cap?"

"Probably fell off." I tell him how the caps on those other bottles needed tightening. "The caps are child-proof. But with no kids around, why tighten them?"

"The cat ate all those pills?"

"No, but enough to make him sick. And he's so small, it wouldn't take much."

"So he..."

We rush to the bedroom where Fu Manchu splays himself across the clawed-up comforter, eyes cloudy as ash.

"He needs help," I say. "Take him to Karlene, she'll know what to do."

Gently, DeMott picks him up. The cat drops his small head on DeMott's arm, mewing pitifully.

"I'll stay and clean up," I say, avoiding half of the truth.

39

As soon as the apartment door closes, I race to the kitchen.

In my pocket, I still have the waxy little football we were going to dump down Toots' sink. I find a knife in a drawer and carefully cut open one end. The clear beads roll out. Pinching one, I dig my fingernails into its sides. But I can't dent it. I can't even make a scratch.

I walk over to the garbage can—and suppressing a gag—and check the plastic bags of cat vomit. There are clear beads floating in all of it, like miniature jellyfish. I dig my fingernails into the hard bead again. Why won't it scratch—

Scratch.

I throw open the cupboards and find a brown drinking glass. Holding it up to the light, I drag the hard bead across the surface. There's no mark. Not even a gray smudge I'd expect from something like medicine—something that's supposed to dissolve inside a person's body.

I go back to the garbage can. As I'm staring at those pearls, one of them bursts.

"Gross!"

A clear gel oozes out.

My lip curls.

"That's disgusting."

"What's disgusting?"

DeMott, once again, stands in the doorway. Beige cat hair clings to his shirt.

"I didn't hear you come in."

"Raleigh?"

I point at the garbage. "Vomit. It's disgusting."

"You mean, that same cat vomit you were sniffing?"

"I was *looking*." I point. "See for yourself."

"No thanks."

"DeMott, I'm serious. Something's wrong."

"And your first clue was half-digested cat food inches from your face?"

"Please. Look." I lift the opened capsule. "These things are hard as rocks. But they touch liquid, and magically turn into gel. It's like they're absorbing all the moist ..."

My voice trails off.

"Absorbing what?"

"Moisture." I'm looking right at him, but his face disappears. Reaching into my pocket, I yank out the tightly folded pages from the library's Xerox machine. I scan the words, the descriptions. On the second page, the list describes silica's many uses, including "absorbs moisture."

When I first read that, I imagined minerals. A mineral sponge, quartz absorbing rust, making sand red.

I look up at him. "Silica."

"What?"

"Silica, it's a mineral. Sand, quartz, all made of silica." I pinch the bead. It's like a grain of sand. Only it's not. "Silica in its purest form absorbs moisture. Like, if it's made pure. By some manufacturer."

"Okay..."

I shake the capsule, capturing another glassy bead, and rub it on the drinking glass. No mark. No, of course not. Silica, glass. Same hardness. One won't scratch the other.

"Oh, wow." I look at DeMott. He's coming back into focus. Handsome. Wounded. Confused.

I turn around, opening the cabinets, rifling through cans of Bush's baked beans and Campbell's chicken soup. Spam. All the bachelor foods.

"What're you looking for?" DeMott asks.

"Bread. Rice. Crackers. Anything like that."

He reaches over my head, opening a top cupboard. One box of saltine crackers. One box of dried mashed potato flakes.

"I don't see any bread or rice," he says.

"Hand me the potatoes. And a big bowl."

He finds a large bowl—brown, of course—and places it on the counter. I dump in the entire box of potatoes, watching the flakes flutter like snow. And then, *plop.* I reach in, plucking out the square packet. The cover reads: DO NOT EAT.

I hold it up. DeMott still looks concerned.

"What is that?"

"I think it's what killed your uncle."

40

TITUS ANSWERS on the third ring.

He says, "Again."

But I can barely hear him because there's a ton of noise in the background. I glance over at DeMott. He's standing by that bowl of potato flakes, holding the packet that says DO NOT EAT.

"I can barely hear you," I say. "Where are you?"

"Church."

"It's Saturday night."

He says nothing.

"Where's the church?" I ask.

"Why?"

"I need to talk to you."

"Now?"

I glance over at DeMott. Titus' tone is making me feel queasy and I could very easily be persuaded to say, *No, not now, let's talk when you don't sound like you're going to yell at me.* But the look on DeMott's face changes everything. It's a haunted sadness.

"Yes," I tell Titus. "Now."

∾

IN THE DUSKY sapphire light of evening, DeMott drives us across the Mayo Bridge over the James River. The big granite boulders punch at the water like black fists, the late sunlight making the white quartz sparkle like diamond rings.

"You talked to your dad yet?" I ask.

No answer. I look over. Grief seems to hang off him, invisible, yet so real I could touch it.

"DeMott?"

"My dad always knows what to say."

"What did he say?"

"He said he was sorry Uncle Cab died. But I know the truth. He's actually glad. He was embarrassed by Uncle Cab. Never invited him to family gatherings. He really didn't exist in my dad's eyes."

I want to say something, but every possible sentence sounds wrong compared to what he's feeling. So I wait. I wait until the simple truth stumbles forward and finds my tongue. "Then your dad lost out. Big time."

He looks over. Eyes red as the sunset.

I let the quiet hover as we drive deeper into Southside, up Hull Street where Saturday evening starts to feel like some moody tyrant just waking up. Neon light glows from convenience stores, iron bars covering the windows. Women with too-fancy hairstyles stand in a cloud of cigarette smoke outside nail salons. DeMott hangs a right. I see an empty beer bottle clogging the gutter drain. On either side, we pass cars that look nothing like the cars parked outside our schools. These are older, boxier, the metallic paints fading to pastels from too much Southern sun.

DeMott pulls up to a building that looks like an eroding Greek temple.

"Let me come in with you," he says.

I shake my head, staring at the cracked white columns. I can't risk DeMott blowing up again. "Better if I go in alone, I think."

He gets out, walks around the truck, opens my door. "I'll be right here."

The wide marble stairs lead to double doors, where a thin black man waits. He has a pencil mustache and a pinstripe suit that's almost purple.

"Can I help you?" he asks.

"I'm here to see someone."

He gives me a curious look.

"They're inside," I add.

He glances over my shoulder, watching DeMott's truck.

"It'll just take a second." I don't offer Titus' name because I don't want to cause any more trouble. "My friend's going to wait for me."

The man opens the door. Noise rushes out, like water from a firehose.

"You'll find a seat in the back," he says.

I see an ocean of ladies' hats flow over a dozen wooden pews. Some are blue as winter skies, others red as fresh blood. Yellow as spring daisies. Above them, three paddle fans swirl the moist air. As I walk forward, an organ cries through a hymn about Jesus. I find an open spot in the pew furthest from the stage. As I sit down, I realize I'm the only woman in here without a hat. And the only white girl.

"You hear that?" asks the preacher on stage. He wears a long black robe like my dad's courtroom robe, only with an amethyst scarf embroidered with gold crosses. I lean to one side, searching among the hats for a man the size of an oak tree.

"You hear that?" the preacher asks again.

There's a murmur of response.

"Excuse me?" The preacher glares. "The good Lord brought you to church tonight—alive—and all you can do is mumble at me? Try that again. HEAR me?"

"AMEN!"

"Better." The preacher smooths down the gold crosses on his scarf. "Now hear me and hear me good."

I keep searching. The preacher talks about a camel passing through the eye of a needle. "Greed! Hear me?"

"Preach it!"

"Jesus says that camel's got a better chance of moving through the eye of a needle than a rich man getting into heaven."

"That's right!"

"But Jesus wasn't talking 'bout money. Because being poor ain't getting you into heaven either. Jesus was talking about the heart." The preacher opens his arms and the robe gives him wings. "The heart. Because that's where greed lives—in the heart."

"Preach it, brother!"

"Yeah, you hear me now. *Greed!* Don't give into it. Greed's a trap set by our enemy."

The organ cries out again. And I hear thunder. Only it's actually everyone jumping to their feet, clapping—clapping like they want this roof to collapse. But now that everyone is standing, the hats can't hide the man who is head and shoulders above the crowd.

I get up and move down the far wall. The stained glass windows are boarded up on the outside, in case somebody chucks a rock at the disciples. For several moments I stand behind Titus, getting my courage up. His suit pulls tight across his shoulders with every clap. When I touch his arm, it feels solid as slate. He glances over, a flicker of surprise in his onyx eyes.

He didn't think I'd come.

WE STAND in the steamy foyer, the service continuing behind us. Titus looks like a stranger to me in that suit.

"Problem?" he asks.

"Uh, can we go outside?"

His dark eyes glower. "We ain't like you white folk."

Not off to a good start. And it's about to get worse.

"So, in your mom's kitchen…"

"Eat. She don't care."

"Not that." I lick my lips. "I found some things that shouldn't be there."

"Things."

"Yes, and, well, these things belong to other people."

I've seen video footage of Titus at bat. Right before he swung, he'd lower his chin, daring the pitcher to throw something nasty. And that's what he's doing right now.

"Titus, I'm not accusing anyone of anything I say."

"Get to it."

"What?"

His iron face turns sideways, like my words are some wild pitch that almost hit him. I can't blame him. Last October, my words sent him to jail.

"I'm really trying to be careful here," I tell him. "I don't want your mom to get in trouble if she's not responsible."

"*If.*"

"I don't know!"

The organ smothers my cry.

"Look, I'm just trying to figure out what happened. That's all."

"She paid back every dime."

"What?"

"Listen. Listen good." His dark eyes drill into me. "Spring of my junior year. I got sick. Couldn't afford no doctor. But the college scouts were coming to my games. Toots walked down to Walgreens and took some cough syrup." He closes his mouth, but his lips twist. "And vitamins."

"I didn't know."

"She paid back every dime."

"I'm sorry."

"Are you?"

"Yes."

"Tell her yourself," he says. "Wait here."

41

My ears burn. From embarrassment. From the preaching. From the organ that sounds like it's dying—or giving birth. I step outside the church where it is fully night now. The white columns glow.

The man in the pinstripe suit steps out from behind one of them. He looks like he's about to ask something, but Toots steps out. She's wearing a gold lamé hat the size of a pot roast. One look at her face and the man in the suit moves down to the very last white column, disappearing.

"You light my kitchen on fire?" she asks.

"No, ma'am."

"Break somethin'?"

I shake my head.

"But you still pull me outta church?"

"I found—" My voice spikes so high I sound four years old. I lick my dry lips, try again. "My grandmother's cake knife was in your kitchen. And Mr. Halvorsen's ring, in the garbage disposal. And you saw that silver chalice—"

"*Chalice?*" She shakes her head, the gold hat glimmering in the dark. "You mean that cup your boyfriend had?"

Not my boyfriend. But no way on God's green earth will I correct her. "Yes, ma'am."

She glares through those red eyeglasses, taking in DeMott's truck at the curb. "Y'all must just play games at them fancy schools."

"Pardon?"

"You think it's some game. I steal things and leave 'em in my kitchen."

Which is why I wanted to talk to Titus before talking to Toots, because I can't figure out this part. Who would do that? But saying that sounds bad—this whole thing sounds bad. And getting worse by the second. "Also, those silica packets."

"Say *what?*"

"You know, those square packets. Do Not Eat—they're in the rice."

"What about 'em?"

"You collect them in that jar by the stove."

Her frown's like a cyclone heading straight for me. "You got a problem with *that,* too?"

"It's just—I mean—why do you collect them?"

"You blind?"

"P-pardon?"

"Are. You. Blind."

"No, ma'am."

"So you see those words. Do Not Eat. Means the stuff's poison."

"Right. So why not just throw them out?"

"Niko."

"Niko?"

"Yeah, my no-good waiter. Niko. He told me they'd pollute my water."

"I'm not following—"

"My water comes from a well. In the ground. You following me?"

"I don't know."

"City landfill's down the way from my place. Niko says that stuff drips into the water and then I drink it. No thanks. That's why I don't throw them out anymore."

The man in the pinstripe suit peers around the column, giving me a look like I'm the person polluting Toots' well.

"Okay. But after you put them in the jar, where do they go?"

She harrumphs. "You still think I'm lying."

"No, ma'am, I—"

"I can hear it even if you don't move your mouth."

The red glasses burn like embers. The gold hat. The large eyes hard as obsidian. Toots looks like the wrath of God bundled into one short woman.

My voice squeaks again.

"But you have to take them somewhere."

"Yeah, medical."

"Sorry?"

"You should be sorry, but you ain't." She reaches up, adjusting the hat. "The poison goes with the medical trash. Needles, bandages, all that stuff. Niko says they burn it."

Niko. Again.

"And how often does—"

She wags that finger at me. "Uh-uh."

She grabs the door, throwing it open. The organ lets out a wail.

"You ain't keeping me from the Lord any longer," she says.

I watch the door close. And listen to my heart beat, beating so hard every pulse taps my lips.

42

When I wake up Sunday morning, I decide there is no way I can listen to another church sermon. Not after the hellfire at Titus' church last night—complete with brimstone from Toots.

And yet, here I am. Sitting in our antique box pew at St. John's Church between my dad and my grandmother. My mom's on the end, holding my dad's hand. My sister Helen isn't here. Years ago, she declared herself an atheist and nobody was surprised.

St. John's is almost as old as Richmond itself. We have an organ, like Titus' church, only this shiny beast covers an entire wall, floor to ceiling, and every note bellows like God has a bad cold. While the opening hymn is winding to a wheezing close, I weigh my chances of getting in a nap during the sermon.

But Reverend Burkhardt surprises me.

Climbing into the high pulpit that hangs over us like a ship's prow, he says, "Cabell Branch Fielding went to be with the Lord."

I sit up.

There wasn't even a "Good morning" with that.

And Uncle Cab never came to church, not that I saw. On the other hand, the Fieldings have been members of St. John's since before Patrick Henry stood up in here and shouted about liberty or death.

Maybe that means your black sheep get memorialized during the Sunday service, too.

But that's not it either.

Reaching into his white robe, Reverend Burkhardt takes out a piece of paper, slowly unfolding it.

"Over the years, by God's providence, St. John's Church has been greatly blessed. In particular, we've had one anonymous donor who paid for many of our programs. College tuition for orphans. After-school programs for inner-city kids. Even repairs on the pipe organ. Many of you have asked me about the identity of this anonymous donor." Reverend Burkhardt runs his hand over the paper, flattening out the folds. "Today I'm going to tell you. That anonymous donor was Cabell Branch Fielding."

I glance over at my dad. He's smiling—no, *beaming*—like this is the best news he's heard in a long, long time. He glances over and winks at me.

"In addition to helping St. John's whenever a need arose," Reverend Burkhardt continues, "Cabell also funded many charities throughout Richmond." He lifts the page and begins reading off a list that includes everything from new trees for city parks to animal shelters to historic renovations of Edgar Allen Poe's house. "All of it was done anonymously."

For several moments, Reverend Burkhardt doesn't say another word. Beneath the sunlight streaming through the wood-frame windows, his white robe glows like a candle.

"And he never came to church."

He waits.

"That's what you're thinking. Isn't it? Cabell Fielding never came to church."

The silence. My ears ring.

"And he drank alcohol. Loved his cigars. Never married, never had children. In fact, you pitied the man."

The silence deepens.

"But you're wrong. Cabell Fielding was a better Christian than most of you sitting here today."

I lean to the side, trying to see the Fieldings' box pew. It's up front —where all the important people sit—and I can just barely see DeMott's face, lifted to Reverend Burkhardt. Meanwhile, his dad, Harrison Fielding, is giving Reverend Burkhardt the stink-eye.

"In Second Corinthians," Reverend Burkhardt continues, "God says that everything we see is temporary. Our houses. Our cars. Our status in the world. These things won't matter in the end. But the invisible—everything we can't see—will last forever. Love. Compassion. Honor. Integrity. These things matter. And Cabell paid attention to them—to the invisible. He saw the plight of the poor. He saw the needs of the destitute. And he always stepped in to help." Reverend Burkhardt takes a moment. "How about you?"

People are squirming.

"When Cabell's health started to fail, he didn't ask for any help." Reverend Burkhardt stares down at Harrison Fielding, the man who owns half of the city. "But one person faithfully visited him. That person was his grand-nephew, DeMott. Cabell told me those visits reminded him of the passage in the book of Matthew. 'For I was hungry and you gave me something to eat, I was thirsty and you gave me something to drink.'"

Gockey reaches over, squeezing my hand.

"My prayer for each of you is that you would reflect on the generous nature of your brother in Christ, Cabell Branch Fielding. And that you, too, would focus on the invisible. Because when we step into eternity, the invisible is what will matter."

Reverend Burkhardt abruptly steps down from the pulpit. The woman who plays the organ seems a little startled. She starts pumping the pedals and pressing the keys and soon the brass pipes are moaning like the beginning of time.

I lean forward, searching for DeMott again, but there's a flash of light to my left. I look over. Tinsley. Her family sits up front, too, and she's flicking her platinum hair, apparently trying to get DeMott's attention.

But DeMott's head is down.

And his shoulders are shaking.

43

IN GOOD WEATHER—BEFORE the summer heat melts us with humidity —our church gathers in the courtyard after the service. It's all very nice and proper. It's also one big schmooze-fest of Who's Who in Richmond. But today there's also some kind of receiving line. The picture-perfect Fielding family stands in a row, while men in seersucker suits and women wearing the finest linen come to offer condolences and act like they all cared about Uncle Cab.

My family gets in line, too. And suddenly more of those Longfellow lines slip into my mind.

For the soul is dead that slumbers,
and things are not what they seem.

When my parents reach the front of the line, Harrison Fielding shakes my dad's hand and glances at my mom. It is 10:35 on a warm Sunday morning in May, and my mom's wearing a wool sweater dress with a red velvet cape thrown over her shoulders. Like it's Christmas. Mr. Fielding's frozen smile greets Judge Harmon's crazy wife. I look down the line.

DeMott stands at the end, next to his two sisters. And Tinsley. Her arm is snaked through his bent elbow like a bike lock. I warn my heart to obey, but it skips a beat anyway.

"Deepest condolences," my dad is saying.

"Thank you, David, I appreciate that," Harrison Fielding says. "We'll be hosting a reception today at three o'clock." He glances at my mom again. "Perhaps you can come?"

My dad answers. "Thank you for the invitation. Unfortunately, we have a prior engagement."

My dad guides my mom to the next person, Mrs. Fielding.

Gockey is up next.

Harrison Fielding smiles at my grandmother. "Lovely to see you, Frances, even under these circumstances."

Gockey offers condolences, moves to shake Mrs. Fielding's hand, and now it is my turn and Mr. Fielding glares at me with an expression that says it's all my fault. Everything. Anything. I am a constant source of trouble in his eyes. The two of us don't even bother to shake. His hand moves to the next person behind me. *Okay by me.*

I finally reach DeMott. His eyes are red and swollen. But, man, he still looks great. "Ready to go?" he asks.

I nod.

"Excuse me." Tinsley's icicle-green eyes stab my skull. "Did I miss something?"

"Raleigh and I need to run an errand," he says. "It won't take long. I'll see you at the reception."

In one split second of vanity, she decides not to make a scene in public.

"See you then." She uncoils her arm, the same way I remove my bike lock, and rises on her high strappy sandals to kiss DeMott's cheek. "I'll be waiting for you."

We cross the courtyard, walking toward his truck parked in the side lot. Tinsley's cold stare grips my back. She's also probably laughing at my wardrobe since I stayed at Gockey's last night. I'm wearing some old clothes I keep in her apartment at Sunset Gardens. And my Chuck Taylors. "Maybe you should stay here," I suggest.

"No," DeMott says.

"But you've got—"

"My uncle's dead, Raleigh. Don't argue with me."

~

INSIDE DEMOTT'S TRUCK, I text my dad. Earlier this morning I told him I'd be taking off after church. But that sweater dress my mom's wearing tells me that my dad—once again—has his hands full and will probably forget what I said.

When I look up from the phone, DeMott's stopped at the bottom of Church Hill, waiting for the light to turn green.

"How long have you known that kid Niko?" I ask.

He looks over. "What makes you think I know him?"

"When he saw you in Toots' kitchen, he hesitated."

The light turns green. We pass through Shockoe Bottom, moving through the narrow old streets built originally built for horse carts.

"Invisible things," he says.

"What?"

"Reverend Burkhardt talked about invisible things. You know what came to mind?"

"Your uncle."

"Yes. And you."

I stare out the windshield. Downtown passes in a blur. A bead of sweat curls its way down my spine.

"Don't you want to know why?" he asks.

No.

Yes.

"I don't need to know."

"Raleigh, you make a big deal out of things that don't matter."

Oh, great. Here's the stuff we argued about. I turn my face to the passenger window. The buildings flicker past, all their windows like eyes.

"And I could never understand what was wrong," he continues, like we're having a conversation. "And then, when I didn't understand, you'd get even more upset."

Another bead of sweat rolls down my back. I press my spine into the bench seat. "About Niko—"

"That's what I'm talking about. Did I tell you I knew that kid?"

"No."

"Right. But in his one small hesitation, you realized something. People don't usually see that stuff, Raleigh. It's invisible to them. But you see it."

The sunlight burns my eyes.

"I'm sorry." He looks over. "That's what I'm trying to say, I'm sorry."

"For what?"

"A lot of things. But mostly for how I acted about Drew. She was getting better. I couldn't see that. But you could. You saw what she needed. It was invisible to everyone else."

Right. And if I don't get Drew out of Sunset Gardens by tomorrow afternoon, they'll lose their insurance. I look away.

"Raleigh?"

"Thanks. Really."

West of town now, we turn into the neighborhood of Windsor Farms. Wide roads weave between regal estate houses on grassy lawns. A lot of my classmates live here because, like Monument Avenue, it's one of Richmond's high-regard neighborhoods.

DeMott leans over the steering wheel as we pass the houses, checking the addresses.

"Don't ever lose your gift for the invisible," he says. "Especially now."

44

DeMott parks in front of a red brick house.

I lean forward, checking out the place. "You're sure this is where he lives?"

Unlike the rest of Windsor Farms, this house looks like it was once horse stables. Only now the arched animal entrances are covered with bricks more orange than red. In the dead-grass front yard, a staked sign advertises *For Sale By Owner*.

"That's what the school directory says." He looks down at the paper. "Niko Baruffi. 114 Windsor Steeples Lane."

I stare at the strange stable-house, waiting for Mr. Manners to walk around the front of the truck and open my door.

"How does his family afford St. Christopher's?" I ask.

"Full scholarship."

"So you do know him."

"*Everyone* at school knows Niko. Or knows of him. You'll see."

He closes the truck door behind me. But I don't move. I have a bad feeling about this "errand."

"Come on," he says. "I need to get home soon."

The family estate. Tinsley is waiting.

"Right." I walk down the uneven brick path. The front door is narrow, like it was once a feeding bay for horses. I should start preparing to ask Niko Baruffi some questions, but my mind keeps sabotaging me, reminding me of *Tinsley*. Waiting for DeMott. Tinsley. The girlfriend approved by Harrison Fielding. The good girlfriend.

"My dad," DeMott says, as though reading my thoughts. "He avoids Uncle Cab his whole life. But now that the man's gone? Full memorial service. Because it's the proper thing to do."

A woman answers the door. She looks as though she just woke up. Or maybe never went to sleep. Red-rimmed eyes peer at us from under frizzy brown hair.

"Yes, what, can I help you?" Her voice is nasal, as if she's got a cold. "You need something?"

DeMott introduces himself. Then says, "I'm looking for Niko Baruffi."

"You're friends with Niko?" She says this with suspicion.

"Classmates," DeMott says. "At St. Christopher's."

"Oh. *That* place." She wrinkles her nose and points at the side of the house. "Go through the hedge. Into the garden." She starts to shut the door, then pops out her frizzy head. "Watch out."

By the corner of the house, a tall green hedge rises, unclipped and frizzy as the woman's hair. Some kind of opening's been cut into the middle. We walk toward it. Something stinks.

DeMott sniffs the air. "You smell that?"

Rotten eggs. That's what it smells like. I wrinkle my nose, like the woman at the door. "Sulfur."

Sulfur shows up in minerals as bright yellow. It's the chemical compound that makes matches flare up and volcanos erupt and when the Bible says "brimstone," it means sulfur. As we pass through the hedge, the rotten-egg stink gets so powerful that I wonder if hot springs are bubbling under Windsor Farms—sulfur being the source of the underground heat. But as we turn the corner, I hear a *putt-putt-putt* engine noise. And a high metallic whine, like a leaf blower.

And there is Niko Baruffi.

DeMott and I both stop and stare.

Niko stands inside an extra-large metal garbage can. It's placed in the middle of a dirt yard that only a realtor would call "the garden." He holds a leaf blower in one hand, pointed into the bottom of an extremely large blue balloon. The balloon is expanding over the trash can and tied to the sides with nylon ropes.

DeMott calls out, but Niko doesn't seem to notice us.

I lift the collar of my shirt, pressing it over my nose, and watch a green garden hose snaking from a weathered garden shed to the leaf blower. My guess is that's the source of the stink.

DeMott waves his arms.

Niko looks over, his face that same blank expression I saw in Toots' kitchen.

DeMott yells, "Shut that thing off!"

Niko stays in the trash can, not moving an inch. He also doesn't look the least bit surprised to see us here. My radar starts quivering.

DeMott yells again, and slowly, as if thinking over something else, Niko reaches down and flicks off the small engine sitting on the ground next to the trash can. The leaf blower dies with it. The big balloon sags. Niko looks over at us.

"I am not an alchemist," he says.

"Excuse me?" DeMott asks.

"I cannot conduct alchemical experiments."

"What?"

"You seem to think I can somehow manifest silver cups." Niko lifts himself out of the trash can, negotiating his legs over the four sandbags that anchor the thing to the ground. "And don't judge."

"I don't even know what it is."

"This." He turns like a game show host. "This amazing contraption is my ride to school."

Niko walks across the dirt yard, following the green hose to the old shed. DeMott slides his eyes toward me. I breathe through my shirt and shrug.

Pushing open the shed's crooked door, Niko twists a lever on the hose.

"You'll get over the odor," he says, "once you realize I've made free fuel. Courtesy of Sunset Gardens."

I smash my nose into my shirt, glancing at DeMott, my eyes watering. But Mr. Manners is pretending there's just fresh air around here. And now I know why the woman at the door sounded nasally. My voice sounds the same way when I ask, "Care to explain?"

"Bio-waste," he says. "All that food gets thrown out at Sunset Gardens. I bring it home. Free fuel."

I glance at DeMott. Those manners are powerful—more powerful than this stench. DeMott hasn't even flinched.

"What about the sulfur?" I ask.

"Sulfur dioxide," he says, correcting me. "And I know it's not the most environmentally friendly option. But it's working."

"Let me get this straight," I say through my shirt. "You're going to fly that balloon to school—attached to a trash can?"

"I told you not to judge."

"I'm not judging. I'm trying to get the facts."

"Being a waiter at Sunset Gardens isn't exactly remunerative," he says.

Remunerative. That word popped up on the SAT vocabulary test. *Financially rewarding.* I could keep discussing this crazy balloon idea but DeMott's impatience is palpable—another SAT word.

"You told Toots not to throw out those Do Not Eat packets."

"Naturally." He eyes me. "She lives two-tenths of a mile from the city landfill. Her water well is in her backyard. Anything in that land-fill will—"

"Seep into the water table and pollute her well." I've studied the geology of groundwater for years, another of Teddy's missions. "So what happens to the packets after they're in the jar?"

"I take them to the infirmary."

"You do?"

"Yes."

That matches what Toots said.

"What does the infirmary do with them?"

"Sends them away with the medical waste."

"What does that mean?"

"How would I know?"

Because you're like Drew. Brilliant. Extremely intelligent. The kind that figures out how to turn decomposing food into biofuel. Obsessive. Niko's mind will demand to know every detail. But he's holding back.

"Why won't you tell me what happens to the packets?"

He pushes the shed door closed, leaning his body against it. "If you must know, a medical collection company comes to the infirmary and collects the waste. They collect weekly. And they incinerate the waste, and, yes, I realize air pollution is no better than ground water pollution, but at this moment in time, incineration is the most sterile form of dealing with—"

"You've never taken any packets?"

Niko gives me that blank look. Which I now realize is like a mask. When the wheels are spinning inside that big brain, his face goes blank. Drew does this, too.

I walk over to the metal trash can. Inside, there's a bottle of soda. A bike helmet—lot of good that'll do if he crashes this contraption. One box of crackers. And a book. Of course, a book. I reach down, flipping it over to see the cover. Skull and crossbones. The title has the word "death" in it.

"What are you doing?" he asks.

I lift the book. "Interesting stuff you read."

Niko turns toward DeMott, standing by the house. "Your uncle."

DeMott waits. "What about my uncle?"

"That's why you're here. Isn't it? The cup must be incidental. Something happened to your uncle."

"He passed away." DeMott's mouth tightens. "Yesterday."

"Doesn't surprise me."

DeMott's jaw drops, speechless.

I step forward. "Say that again."

"I'm not surprised." He shrugs. "Cabell wasn't doing well."

"And you know...because?"

"Because I'm the one who scrapes the plates after dinner, remember? I know who's eating, who isn't eating, who's hoarding food." He nods at the shed. "I pay attention, for good reasons."

"Let's go back to those Do Not Eat packets," I say.

"Let's not," he says.

"When did you start collectin—"

The back door whips open. The frizzy-haired woman sticks her head out. "Niko!"

Everyone must yell at this guy.

"You promised to clip the hedge," she says in that nasally voice.

"I'll get to it, Mother."

"I want it done now. A realtor just called. He wants to bring someone to look at the house." She starts to close the door, then opens it again. "And get rid of that smell!"

She slams the door.

Niko's blank expression is making my radar quiver. He's a genius who reads horror novels. He knows sulfur dioxide combined with decomposing biomatter can create gas. He knows things.

"Tell me what you know about silica," I say.

"Didn't you hear my mother? You need to leave. I have work to do."

DeMott clenches his fists, holding them at his sides. "Did you poison my uncle?"

"Did I poison your uncle?" Niko repeats calmly. Almost as if he was expecting the question. "Why would I poison your uncle?"

DeMott steps toward him. "If you so much as—"

I grab his arm, pulling him back.

Niko stares at him. "You're trespassing," he says. "I'm offering you ten seconds to get off my property. After that, I'm calling the cops."

45

DeMott drives away from Niko's house, slowly. A stunned silence fills the truck's cab.

"Would he?" DeMott asks.

"Would he—what, poison people?"

"He works in the kitchen."

"You think he's putting those silica packets in people's food?"

DeMott's hands grip the steering wheel, like he's going to strangle it. "It's possible."

"Anything's possible. But all those people are old. And that silica is hard as a rock. Niko would have to soak the silica first, and turn it into that gross gel."

"It's still possible."

"Yes. But what's his motive? Why would he do that?"

DeMott takes a right turn at Stonewall Jackson. But he's still driving so slowly we might be riding in a horse carriage over these cobblestones.

"Raleigh, you saw his house. It's for sale—by owner. And he's on full scholarship. *And* he's turning garbage into gas so can get to school on something other than his bike."

"Money." I stare at his profile. "You think his motive is money."

"It makes sense. He's also stealing those things and stashing them in the kitchen. Probably waiting until he can find a buyer."

And Toots wouldn't notice. Gockey's cake knife. Halvorsen's ring. The Fielding family chalice. She didn't notice any of those things. It would be easy for Niko to hide stolen goods in that kitchen.

But something's bothering me about this scenario. Maybe it's just that my radar's been out of whack lately. Wrong about the big surprise for Drew and Myra. Wrong about Toots. Wrong about DeMott wanting me as his girlfriend. So how can I be sure about Niko? At the back of my mind, I feel an itch that I can't scratch.

"Strange," DeMott says.

"And brilliant. He's obviously a genius, like Drew."

"No, not Niko. *This.* You and me. *This* is strange."

My heart pins itself to my ribcage and flutters like a trapped butterfly. "How is this strange?"

"You're always the suspicious one. I'm always saying people could be innocent. We've reversed roles."

I turn my face to the open window. My city flows past like a river. Everything in its place. I watch one couple walking hand in hand down the sidewalk, enjoying an ordinary Sunday in May, instead of thinking about death and deception and—

"Now I understand," DeMott says.

His voice.

Something in it convinces me not to look over at him right now. I keep watching the storied Monument Avenue mansions, their porch flags waving in the breeze.

"I get it," he says.

"Get what?"

"Why you got upset. You said people deserve justice. Especially the dead. I get it now. I want justice, too."

His tone. I've heard that tone from people in my dad's courtroom. Wounded people who want revenge. Victims who really do deserve justice. And I've felt that emotion myself. But each time I got like this, my dad's warned me. *Seek justice,* he always said, *but walk humbly. And remember mercy.*

"DeMott, I'm not always right about these things. And lately, I've been wrong. About everything."

He doesn't reply.

I look over. His face is stone.

"I don't want to jump to conclusions with Niko."

He stares out the windshield, knuckles white on the steering wheel. "Tonight our family lawyer is coming out to read Uncle Cab's will."

Money. I look away again, dropping my hand into the breeze, cupping the warm air like I can hold it. The Fieldings are so different from my family. With them, everything revolves around money. Maybe because when people have that much money, the world does actually seem to move around it. I pull in a deep breath, tell my voice to stay calm, and say, "Your uncle probably left most of his money to those charities."

"Yes." He hisses out the word. "But if I find out he left even one dime to Niko, would that change your mind?"

I hold my tongue. DeMott stops at the curb in front of my house and I pull the door handle, skipping the whole chivalry thing. Right now, I'm not in the mood for his manners. I glance over before getting out.

His blue eyes look like a shattered window framing the sky.

"DeMott, you told me to look for the invisible. That's what I'm doing."

"Sure thing," he says. "I'll let you know about the will."

Standing on the curb, I watch him drive away. And wonder if seeing this side of him is going to change how I see him... forever.

It's just past one o'clock when I step through our front door. In the grand foyer, our grandfather clock *tick...tock...ticks*. And three stories away, I can hear my sister's music, some kind of Indie rock that sounds like dying birds. But the loudest thing in here right now is the familiar Sunday stillness. It makes me want to run out the door.

Forcing myself down the hallway, I walk to my dad's office. It's a large room that was once the men's parlor, back when Harmons could afford live-in servants and all of Richmond's important politicians came here to talk about Reconstruction, city politics, where to put those Civil War statues on the avenue. To this day, I can smell the bitter odor of cured tobacco. Like it seeped into the woodwork. And comes out to remind us of what used to be.

My dad looks up from his desk. It's covered with papers. "Hey there, Kiddo."

I can tell he's been working awhile because that mark is on the bridge of his nose, the line from his reading glasses. "Hi."

"Not going to the Cabell Fielding memorial?" he asks.

"Are you?"

He lays the reading glasses on the papers in front of him. White court documents. Yellow legal pads. Red leather books crammed with Virginia's laws, the pages open like tongues covered with too many words. He smiles.

"Raleigh, you would make a wonderful attorney. And I hope you never do."

"You didn't answer my question."

"You just proved my point." He smiles even wider, but it looks strained. "No, I'm not attending the memorial. Your mother wanted a nap."

He acts like her nap doesn't bother him. But it bothers me. At her worst, my mom always retreated into solitary confinement after social events—like church. Alone with herself and her voices. Maybe the new meds can't help with that.

"I thought you'd be going," he says, "because you left church with DeMott."

I don't mention Harrison Fielding. Or Tinsley. Or the Stillman family who will be there, too. Last December, my classmate Sloane Stillman committed suicide. Only Drew didn't believe it and my trying to decipher what really happened drove the first major wedge between me and DeMott. "It just seemed better if I'm not there. DeMott's got a lot going on."

"Of course."

My dad's watching me.

"What?"

"Pardon," he corrects.

"Pardon—why are you looking at me like that?"

"Are you two dating again?"

"Dad."

"I'm just asking."

"We're friends. That's all. So you can stop asking."

"Got it." He nods. "Homework done?"

"Oh, crap."

"Raleigh..."

"Sorry." That Longfellow poem, I forgot. It's due tomorrow. And Drew needs to memorize it, too—along with getting out of Sunset Gardens before the deadline—and a groan the size of Canada croaks up my dry throat.

"That bad?" he asks.

"It's this Longfellow poem. Sandbag—"

"Mister *Sandberg*?"

"*Sandberg* wants us to memorize the entire thing by tomorrow."

"Let me guess. *Paul Revere's Ride*?"

"No."

"*Evangeline*?"

"Dad."

"Then it must be *A Psalm of Life.*"

My dad majored in English at the University of Virginia. It turned him into a quote machine.

"You win." I sigh. "Go ahead."

"Just one line."

"Fine."

"It's one of my favorite lines."

"Don't let me stop you."

"'Let us, then, be up and doing, with a heart for any fate.' "

"Okay, great, thanks. But I'm not at that point yet."

His smile widens. "I think you've been at that point for some time."

My dad's smile is really great. Easy, natural, nothing forced. But it's his eyes that always catch my heart. They're this brilliant blue, a kind of infinity. An endless sea of love for me.

"I should get started," I say.

He picks up the reading glasses. "Here if you need me, Kiddo."

46

IN MY UPSTAIRS bedroom that was once the servant quarters, I sit on my bed and try to memorize the Longfellow poem. But I can't concentrate. For one thing, Helen's music burbles out of the next room, wrecking the poem's rhythm. Finally, I grab my phone and call Myra's apartment. Drew answers, but she sounds out of breath.

"Are you okay?" I ask.

"Just finished dance lessons."

"Excuse me?"

"I'm learning the cha-cha."

I stare out my window, pleading with Robert E. Lee to ride over to Sunset Gardens and kidnap her. "Have you looked at the Longfellow poem?"

"No."

"Drew."

"Raleigh."

"I'll come over. We can bike back to your house and get the whole thing memorized by tonight."

The pause between us goes on forever.

"Hello?"

"I'm not leaving."

She hangs up.

Great.

I yank my Latin homework from my pack and see that the assignment is about conjugating some deadly verbs. Like *corporo*—meaning, to make a corpse. I try, but my mind drifts again.

This time to Niko.

On the page with all the weird conjugations, I write down Niko's name. Then I draw three columns underneath it and label them:

Opportunity

Means

Motive

Cops want to know those three things. Because when you have all three, lawyers can prosecute.

Under **Opportunity**, I write, "Niko had access to the food at Sunset Gardens."

So does Toots.

They both have the opportunity to sneak into the apartments since the doors aren't locked—except Wilma's. During dinner, everyone's in the dining room. Toots could leave the kitchen. And Niko could run upstairs, too, grab something, run back, and still seem like he was the waiter. Toots called him "no good" as a waiter. Maybe he disappears sometimes?

I tap my pencil on the page, thinking back. When Wilma collapsed, Drew ran right into her apartment. Her door wasn't locked. Does Wilma only lock her door at night? And what if Niko was taking people's prescription medicines, replacing the capsules with other capsules, full of those silica beads? Toots could do that, too. There's no doctor listed on those bottles in Uncle Cab's apartment. But who reads the labels once they start taking something? A bottle could be switched out. But when I try to imagine this whole scenario, it seems like a lot of work. Then again, Niko is making biofuel from food scraps.

Under **Means**, I write, "silica packets."

If Niko or Toots was putting silica beads in the food, they'd first need to soak them in water. Otherwise, somebody would break a tooth.

I circle the words "prescription bottles." If the medicine was replaced, then the beads wouldn't need to be soaked. They're swallowed in capsules. Or—shudder—taken as suppositories.

Finally, **Motive.**

I tap my pencil again. That itch creeps into my mind again. I wrote down "money." DeMott thinks the motive is money. When we were talking to the assistant coroner, she said dehydration was a serious problem, and that Uncle Cab wasn't the first case from Sunset Gardens. I tap the pen. What if the people dying were leaving money in their will to Niko—their brilliant but poor waiter? Or Toots. Their nice cook.

I check my watch. 1:55 p.m. I check my phone. Full charge. Changing into shorts and a shirt, I tiptoe down the back stairs. Kitchen is clear, no sign of my mom. I move down the hall.

"Dad?"

He looks up from his work.

"I'm going for a bike ride. Just to clear my head."

"Be careful," he says.

~

I PEDAL SO FAST my thighs burn. Outside the public library, I lock my bike to the rack and sprint up the stairs, hanging a right for the reference desk. Nelson Heid is reading.

"Quartz again?" he asks.

I shake my head. "Obituaries."

"What sort of obituary?"

"There's different kinds?"

"There *are*," he says, correcting my grammar. "When did the person pass away?"

"It's more than one person. And it could be a whole year."

Laying a tasseled bookmark on the page he was reading, he picks up his desk phone.

"Are you busy?" he asks the person on the other end.

The question must prompt some long response because Mr. Heid lifts his gaze to the ceiling, looking like someone pleading with God.

"Not one iota of that matters to me," he says. "I'm sending over a young lady named Raleigh Harmon. I expect you to help her."

Another extended stare at the ceiling.

"You will help her," Mr. Heid says, "or you will be cut off from my archives."

47

Mr. Heid gives me instructions. Go down East Franklin one block to the rectangular gray building marked Richmond Newspapers, Inc.

Inside the glass-fronted lobby, a guard wearing a blue uniform watches some grainy security videos. Sunday afternoon seems boring.

"Hi," I say. "I'm here to see Paul Wasson."

The guard tells me to log in my Name, Time, and Reason for Visit in the binder on the counter. Under the last category, I write, Obituaries. He hands me a clip-on badge.

"Second floor, turn left. Go *all* the way to the back. You'll hear him before you see him."

The second floor turns out to be one large space. It seems both crowded and vacant all at once. Only a handful of people are here, but they're sitting at desks smothered with weird stuff. Stacks of newspapers. Styrofoam food cartons. A football helmet for the Washington Redskins. A giant foam finger. I turn left, passing computer after computer. I can hear a sound like static electricity—socks pulling apart and crackling—and it gets louder as I move to the far corner. I stand at a tall partition. The crackling now sounds like horses galloping over concrete. I lean around a partition and see a man with long gray hair. His back is to me but I can see he's on the phone. The galloping horses are coming from his keyboard. He's typing—hard. I step closer.

"Yeah, right, thanks, good-bye." A beefy hand slams down the phone. "You lying sack of manure."

I'm really-really hoping this guy is not Paul Wasson.

"Paul Wasson?" I ask.

He doesn't turn around. "Go away."

"Nelson Heid sent me. From the library?"

"You can wait."

"Yes, sir."

"Sir-sir-*sir*." His fingers pound the keyboard even harder with each syllable. "Rich creeps, can't stand 'em."

I want to leave. But Mr Heid's already called, and leaving would insult him. It might even make this guy angrier than he already is. I stand there, listening to his furious typing, his muttering. Then I do all the things that calm me down when my mom's having a crazy episode. Clench fists. Inhale. Release fists. Exhale. Take another breath. Hold it. *One one-thousand, two one-thousand*...all the way to *seven one-thousand*. Release the breath, feel my pulse drop.

"Done!" The guy slams his finger into the Return key and yells, "FRESH OBIT IN THE Q!"

Somewhere on the other side of the partition, someone yells back. "Got it!"

The chair swivels around. Fierce gray eyes stab me. "What d'ya want?"

"Uh, I was looking for obituaries."

"No kidding, Sherlock. Who died?"

"I don't know."

"Oh, my God." He shakes his head, his long shaggy hair flipping over his collar like a dog coming out of a lake. "I am going to kill Nelson—is this some school assignment? Do *not* tell me this is some school assignment."

"This is not some school assignment."

"Like I'd believe you." He sucks air between his yellow teeth. "Don't expect me to hold your hand."

I shake my head, thinking, *No. Way.*

He gets up—a snorting bull—and walks to the next desk, slamming his fingers into the keyboard. Above the monitor, a note reads, *Do Not Touch This Computer. Violators will receive 40 lashings with a dangling participle.*

"Editors." Wasson crumples note in his hand and flings it at an overflowing trash can. "You're logged in. Don't ask me any dumb questions."

He lumbers back to his desk, landing hard in the chair like he was dropped from the sky.

Carefully, I set myself in the editor's chair. A blinking cursor on the screen hovers inside a rectangular box. *Enter Search Items.*

I type **Sunset Gardens.**

Hundreds and hundreds of stories pop up. They're listed by headline and reporter and what looks like the first line of the story. I scroll through them. Wasson's phone rings.

"Wasson—what?"

I scroll to the next page.

"She's here and I'm busy."

Wilma Kingsford has written most of these stories. Everything from the health benefits of "chair aerobics" to why old people need flu shots. She also profiled two residents who celebrated 100-year birthdays on the same day. I check the date. Two years ago.

A voice thunders behind me. "What's the deal with Sunset Gardens?"

I whip around.

Wasson stands directly behind me, holding an unlit cigarette and a red can of the greatest drink on God's green earth—Coca-Cola. He notices where my attention goes, and lifts the can. "Want one?"

He walks over to a filing cabinet and yanks open the bottom drawer. Inside there's a six-pack of Coke. And a bottle of booze with a one-eyed pirate on the label.

"Just wondering." He throws me a can. "Nelson hates kids almost as much as I do. But that's his second call today. Ordering me to help you."

His gray eyes burrow.

Carefully, I pull the can's tab, slowly releasing the *ppfffzzz* so the thing doesn't explode.

"Back to my question," he says. "What's your big interest in Sunset Gardens?"

My dad used to be the city's prosecuting attorney. Reporters called our house all the time. They'd quiz whoever answered the phone—including my mom, which created even more paranoia. My dad finally unlisted our number.

"Reporters are greedy for information," my dad explained. "Any information. Even if it's wrong."

I lift the Coke and stare into a pair of greedy gray eyes. "Do you write the obituaries?"

"Kid, don't waste my time. What're you looking for?"

"Cabell Fielding's obituary."

"Slugged it for tomorrow."

"*Slugged?*"

"Scheduled. It runs in tomorrow's paper. I just turned it in." He slides the unlit cigarette behind his ear. "That was his nephew on the phone. I need some quotes."

"DeMott?"

"Who?" He shakes his head. "I was talking to Harrison Fielding."

Oh. Right. *Lying sack of manure.* I want to smile, but this guy's too scary.

"Now it gets more interesting," he says. "Cabell Fielding's barely cold and you're looking up Sunset Gardens. And Nelson calls—twice —forcing me to help you. Level with me. What are you looking for?"

"Obits."

"Plural now." He nods. "Keep going."

It's a gamble. But I need his help. "I'd like to find all the obituaries of people who died at Sunset Gardens this year."

Wasson plunks the Coke can down on his desk and punishes the keyboard. Text flashes on his monitor, he slaps the Return button.

"Nine people." He reads the results, eyes brightening. "Actually, ten. Fielding isn't in the system yet."

Ten people dying sounds like a lot, especially for not even five months this year.

Wasson's typing again. Then he snatches a pencil from his desk, scribbling on a random piece of paper.

Dread creeps over me. "What are you doing?"

"Finding out if that number's unusual." He types again, more text pops up. "Last year, four people died." He types, scanning the next results. "Five the year before that..." Type, type, type. "Six the year prior." He swivels toward me. "What're you onto, kid?"

"Nothing." I shrug. "Old people die."

"Uh-huh." He narrows those eyes. "You know something."

Back when our phone was unlisted, a reporter actually hid behind a tree on Monument Avenue and when my dad went for his nightly walk, the reporter jumped out. My dad told me and Helen to warn us. He also said he was considering a restraining order, but didn't think it would work. "Why not?" I asked.

"Because saying no to a reporter only throws gasoline on their fire."

In the end, my dad made a deal with that reporter. If the guy left us alone, he would get an exclusive interview with my dad later. "You have to make them think they're getting something special. They like something called 'exclusives.' "

I look into the grasping gray eyes and say, "I'll make you a deal."

He laughs. "What're you, fourteen?"

"I'm almost sixteen."

"But *you're* making *me* a deal?"

"That's right." I hold his gaze, watching that need-to-know hunger turn his eyes into stainless steel. "Take it or leave it."

"What kind of deal?"

"When I have all the facts, I'll tell you."

"No." He leans in, glaring at me. "Tell me now."

"I can't." I don't even blink. "I don't have all the information."

He pinches the unlit cigarette behind his ear, drawing it out. "What sort of information do you need?"

"All ten obituaries for the people who died at Sunset Gardens this year."

His face twitches.

I hold my ground.

Finally he turns to his computer, slapping the keyboard into submission, and moments later I hear that particular *bz-zzt-tt* of a printer spitting out paper.

I also hear Paul Wasson, muttering under his breath.

"I really hate kids," he says.

48

WITH THE OBITUARY pages folded into my pocket, I bike to Sunset Gardens. Inside the front door, Mrs. Donner rises from her chair. We do the milkman routine then I walk down the hall and find the two brainiacs focused on their remaining silver pieces on the black-and-white chessboard.

"Hey," I say.

Drew looks up.

Bill Goddeau slides a Bible-toting bishop across the board. And smiles. "Checkmate, Levinson."

"Again?" Drew scans the chessboard. "Bill, you're on a roll."

He draws an arthritic hand over that unruly white hair. "Play another round?"

"Uh, Drew." I wave my hand. "We need to memorize that poem." *And get you out of here.* "How about we work on it now?"

"Not now." She rearranges the pieces. "I have to break Bill's winning streak."

Bill chuckles, then starts coughing. And coughing. Finally he recovers. But I watch him, wondering.

Drew waves a rook at me.

"One hour," she says. "Meet me in Bubbie's apartment in

one hour."

ON SUNDAYS, the dining room's closed and most people go to eat with their families. That hasn't worked out for us, with my mom's paranoia, so Gockey's almost always around here. I knock on her door.

"Enter if you dare!"

She stands at her little stove, wearing a bright green apron. With her long arms and bent elbows, she kind of looks like a grasshopper.

"Just in time," she says.

The apartment smells of maple. I close the door. "Time for what?"

"Your Aunt Charlotte says I need to start eating healthier food."

Oh, no. My aunt. She has all the money in the world and could eat anything but instead thinks the Food Pyramid should be built with tofu. I force a smile. "What did you make?"

"Chocolate chip waffles."

I laugh.

She flips the waffle iron, releasing two golden squares. "Have a seat, we'll get healthy together."

My mouth waters.

"Protein?" she asks, pointing a can of whipped cream at the waffles. "Don't say 'When'."

She layers the waffles until they're wearing white hoop skirts of whipped cream. Then she holds up a jar of chocolate sprinkles. "Condiments." She dusts the swooping white valleys and carries the two plates over to the table.

"We have all the important food groups here," she says. "Eggs, wheat, cream, and chocolate."

We say grace, and I silently thank God for sending me this grandmother.

My first bite launches a thousand hums—crispy waffle, cool whipped cream, chocolate dots.

"And what about that adorable Fielding boy?" she asks.

My fork halts. I look up. Her eyes are so much like my dad's—an eternity of blue, full of love. And full of insight.

"Everything alright?" she asks.

"Oh, yeah, we just ... ran an errand." Not a lie. We ran an errand—to find out if Niko Baruffi is poisoning people here at Sunset Gardens. I want to tell her all that, but it sounds too scary. So I stare at the deflating whipped cream.

"Raleigh?"

I sigh. "Does it seem like a lot of people are dying around here?"

"One person is too many." She swipes her finger across the edge of her plate, polishing off the whipped cream. "You're thinking of Cabell?"

I hesitate. Because I've been wrong. "Remember how I found your cake knife?"

"I will never forget."

"Well, turns out, even more stuff was in that kitchen."

"What kind of 'stuff'?"

"Mr. Halvorsen's college ring. I found it in the garbage disposal."

"How very odd."

"And the Fieldings, they have this ancient silver chalice. That was in the kitchen too. DeMott thinks it was stolen."

"Stolen?" Gockey looks concerned. "You don't suspect Toots? She seems like such a lovely person."

"I don't know what I think." I tell her about how I went to talk to Titus last night, and wound up asking Toots instead.

Gockey holds up her hand, stopping me. "You and DeMott Fielding drove to Southside—on a Saturday night?"

"To a church."

"On Southside."

"Yes, and Toots got upset. But that doesn't really tell me anything because guilty people act upset, too. They try to throw people off their trail."

She shakes her head. "That's quite the tutorial you're getting in your father's courtroom."

"If someone came in here, in your apartment, and took something like your cake knife, would you notice?"

Gockey does another finger-swipe of whipped cream, and contemplates the question. "I didn't notice my knife was gone until I needed it. If you're suggesting Toots is the thief, she could come in during dinner. I'd be in the dining room with everyone else." She licks her finger again. "But I have a *very* hard time believing Toots would do such a thing."

"I know."

I pick up my fork, finishing my waffle, but only to make Gockey feel better.

My appetite has flown far, far away.

WHEN I WALK into Myra's apartment, Moses is still perched on his carpeted Mount Sinai. But Whitney has apparently wandered across the apartment like the Hebrew exiles. As I close the door clumps of white cat fur roll across the floor like tumbleweeds.

"Drew?"

"Over here."

Sprawled on the floral couch, she holds a green washcloth over her eyes.

"You okay?" I set down the plate Gockey gave me—a waffle for Drew. "What's wrong?"

"I've been letting Bill win at chess."

"What? You *never* let anyone win."

"Exactly. It creates false data."

"So why—"

"Because." She sits up. The rag slides off her narrow face. "Yesterday I mentioned one of Kasparov's winning moves. Do know what Bill said?"

"Who's Kasparov?"

"That's what Bill said!"

"Raleigh." She grips the washcloth. "Garry Kasparov is the greatest chess player of all time."

"Wonderful. But what does he have to do with—"

"Don't you see?" She shakes her head, the wild hair floating on the disturbed air. "Bill Goddeau *knows* who Kasparov is. He wouldn't forget."

"These people are getting old..."

Her dark eyes narrow. "Speaking of which, Larry Siegel wants his service revolver back."

"Right."

"You are looking for the thief, aren't you?"

"Sort of."

"In math terms, that means no."

I want to tell her about Toots and Niko but—in Drew's language —that information might create false data. "Remember what Richard P. Feynman said about having answers?"

"That it's better to have no answers than wrong answers?"

"Right. So until I have all the facts, I'd rather not say anything about the missing stuff."

She flops back on the couch, tossing the rag over her eyes again. "Instead, you're going to make me memorize that poem."

I sit down beside her and pick up the homework that's still on the coffee table—untouched—since Friday. I scan the lines, reading about our hearts acting like muffled drums. "Ready?"

Drew mumbles from under the washcloth. "Go get my notebook."

"Where is it?"

"The bedroom."

I walk to the guest bedroom where two twin beds are aligned parallel to each other, each one looking so perfect it's like nobody has ever slept in them. Very Drew. But I don't see her notebook anywhere.

"Where?" I call out.

"Other bedroom!"

In Myra's bedroom, Whitney lays snoozing between the two king-sized pillows, her white fur almost blending with the white pillowcases. On the nightstand, Drew's notebook sits next to several precisely placed black pencils.

"Pardon me," I tell the cat, reaching for the notebook.

But as I'm picking it up, I notice the prescription bottle sitting in the corner.

I lift it, reading the label.

Myra Levinson.

For symptoms associated with emphysema.

Emphysema. That's Myra's lung disease from smoking, the reason she uses the oxygen machine. But the label shows no doctor's name.

I twist the child-proof cap. Inside, a couple dozen red-and-white capsules are jumbled together. I shake out one and pry apart the shell.

A cold sensation spreads across my chest as the tiny clear beads roll out.

"Raleigh?" Drew calls from the living room. "What's taking so long?"

Myra fainted from dehydration. She seems to be getting better in the infirmary—because she's not taking this prescription anymore?

"Raleigh?"

I recap the bottle, and carry it into the living room.

"Drew," I tell her. "We need to talk."

49

"Ten since January."

I am sitting next to Drew on the couch, holding the obituaries and telling her everything that's happened while she's been in here. The visit with the assistant coroner. Finding Mr. Halvorsen's ring. The Fielding family chalice. Confronting Toots. Confronting Niko the waiter. And finally, all about the obituary writer at the *Times-Dispatch*.

"He said that, on average, five people die at Sunset Gardens each year."

"That's equivalent to one death every 73 days, on average." Drew frowns, deep and dark and brooding. "But we're not even to June and the average is already 13.2."

"What?"

"You said ten people have died here since January first."

"Right ... so?"

"So from January first to today is 132 days. Ten people, 132 days. That's one death every 13.2 days, on average. Raleigh, the ratio went from one death every 73 days to one death every 13.2 days? That is not normal."

I know what's going on in her brain. Whenever Drew's stressed, she tries to turn chaos into order. And everything becomes a math problem.

"I know this is hard to hear," I tell her. "But if Myra was taking those same pills, then you need to know what's going on."

She reaches over, taking the obituaries, smoothing her hand over the folds. Uncle Cab's obituary sits on top. The headline reads, *Scion of Fielding Enterprises Passes.* Above that, Paul Wasson's scrawled, *Strictly Embargoed!* I asked him what "embargoed" meant, he said, "It means nobody prints this before me." Like my dad told me, reporters need to feel exclusive.

"I want to see if anything ties these obituaries together. It might be a way to figure out what's really going on."

"You mean, common denominators."

Math.

"Okay, common denominators." But I notice the pages are shaking. She's scared. My heart does a horse-kick to the chest. "Myra's getting better?"

"The forward momentum continues."

"Good."

She gives a small nod, barely moving her head.

"Drew, you don't need to read these with me, I just wanted you to know about—"

"I can do this," she says. "I'm already letting Bill win."

"Letting Bill win isn't a bad thing. It's called being nice."

"*Is* it nice?" She looks over, her brown eyes full of pain. "Is it really nice to lower expectations, especially for a highly intelligent person?"

I can't answer that, so I just hand her the notebook with one of her black pencils. "How about I read the obituaries out loud, and you can write down any clues. You know, the common denominators."

"Hang on." She gets up, walks to the kitchen, and rummages through many drawers. When she comes back, she's holding a handful of long white candles.

"Shiva candles." She stands them up in the ashtrays. "It's the Jewish remembrance of the dead."

~

TWENTY MINUTES LATER, nine candles are lit and Drew's turned out the overhead lights.

I squint at the words, flicking under the candlelight. "George Yeamans."

Drew lights the tenth candle. I look up. Moses is watching from his perch, cat eyes glittering above that gray beard.

"Eighty-five years old," I continue. "Korean war veteran. Worked for DuPont for forty-six years. Came to live at Sunset Gardens nine years ago. He died April 28."

Drew writes in her notebook. "Cause of death?"

"Natural causes."

Eight people died of "natural causes," including Uncle Cab. Cancer killed the other two.

"Other common denominators?" I ask.

"Would you like to know the least common denominators or greatest common denominators?"

"Drew."

"Raleigh, there's a difference. And sometimes the least common denominator is also greatest common denominator."

The candles flicker on the coffee table.

"How about all common denominators?"

"Fine, be that way." She checks her notebook. "Each person was over eighty years old. Each one was unmarried at the time of death. Seventy percent were widowed. Three were bachelors their whole lives, including Uncle Cab. And while eighty percent died of natural causes and twenty percent from cancer, I would argue that cancer is a natural cause of death. You get cancer, eventually you die, naturally."

"We still don't have a smoking gun. So to speak."

She places the notebook on the couch between us and gathers her skinny knees to her chest. "How many murder trials have you watched in your dad's courtroom?"

"A lot."

"Raleigh—"

"Drew, I don't do numbers. Many. A lot. More than ten."

She hugs her knees. "So you must have some theories about why people kill each other."

I do, sadly. "Money's a big reason. And anger. Even love, weirdly enough."

"Place that in a centrifuge and give me the precipitate. One main reason."

I think about it, spinning the cases through my mind like a centrifuge machine. "People want something they can't have."

"Explain."

"There was this one cheating husband. He wanted to marry his mistress, but he didn't want to pay for a divorce or alimony. So he killed his wife."

"Subtraction in order to reach addition."

"Even murder turns into a math equation?"

"Absolutely. Math is the language of clear reasoning."

"If only they'd lose all those numbers..."

She stares at the shimmering candle flames. "When Rusty and Jayne were married, I thought they'd kill each other."

Rusty and Jayne, Drew's parents. Very possibly the least-qualified parents on planet earth.

"Their fights were scary. But instead of murder, they got divorced. Which, I suppose, is another form of subtraction. Only neither of them has found any addition through it."

I'm Drew's best friend, but she's barely ever talked about her parents' divorce. Maybe some little comments here and there, but that's it. I've never pushed her about it because I thought she just didn't want to say anything. But now, seeing the pain on her face, I realize it was the opposite—Drew cared about that divorce so much she *couldn't* talk about it. I watch as she clutches her knees, rocking softly back and forth, the candlelight throwing shadows under her hollow cheekbones. My best friend looks so fragile. Just as fragile as our friendship.

"I'm sorry, Drew. For everything."

"Hate," she says.

"What?"

"Hate." She turns her face toward me. "Hate could be a common denominator. Hate makes people kill."

"Sure. But one person hating all ten people? That seems like a stretch."

"Bubbie's got a saying. It's Yiddish. 'An enemy you get for nothing, a friend you have to buy.' " She glances over. "Not you, however. You're the one friend I didn't have to buy."

My heart squeezes, so hard the words barely escape my mouth. "Right back at you."

For a long moment, we stare at the candles. Reading these obituaries has been one of the worst things. Each one seemed to fill the room with more sorrow. But it's also been strangely good. We are talking, thinking, coming up with theories. Like we used to do, science nerds of geology and physics—sisters of stone and spark. I close my eyes and feel something inside my heart opening up, giving thanks for something I never expected. But what pops into my head? That poem—*things are not what they seem.*

"Money," I say.

"What about it?"

"DeMott thinks somebody might've killed Uncle Cab for money."

"Well, he could be right. The Fieldings have a lot of money. And people kill for money. Correct?"

"Yes." I pick up the obituaries, sifting the pages for Uncle Cab's obituary. Instead of flowers for his funeral, he asked people to donate to their favorite charity. I wonder, Could Niko Baruffi be one of those charities? Niko knew all ten victims...

Drew leans over. "What are you thinking?"

"Personal question for you."

"How personal?"

"About money."

She rolls her eyes. "Raleigh, money is just math with dollars."

"Okay, fine. Is Myra leaving you money in her will?"

"Of course. She's leaving all her money to me. She already has a trust set up."

"Wow."

"I can't touch any of it until I'm forty years old."

"*Forty?*"

"Bubbie says it's a precaution—I think she means a precaution for Jayne who is terrible with money. And there's a clause about 'medical needs.' Like if Jayne goes to rehab for her drinking, I could pay for that before I'm forty."

Most nights, Drew's mother drinks herself into a wine-coma. No wonder Drew likes staying here. I lick my lips, tempted to bring up the exit-strategy for tomorrow, but Drew continues.

"In the meantime, the bank holds my inheritance."

"Can I ask how much?"

"Four million dollars."

"*What?*"

"The funds are in a trust. The bank oversees it and they get an annual fee."

"How much is the fee?"

"Two percent a year."

"That's all?"

She releases her knees, turning toward me, the dark eyebrows coming down in a serious frown. "Raleigh, has nobody ever explained compound interest to you?"

Uh oh.

She flips to a fresh page in her notebook and writes:

$4 MILLION x .02 = $80,000

"THAT's the bank's fee for the first year. But let's say the bank watches that money for fifteen years—may God grant Bubbie that much time."

"And more," I say.

"Amen."

She writes:

$$\$80,000 \times 15 = \$1,200,000$$

SHE CIRCLES THE BOTTOM FIGURE. "That's how money compounds. And that number could be even larger, since it doesn't factor in annual interest on the principal."

"Principal—like, at school?"

Another deep-deep frown. "You don't know what the *principal* is?"

"Drew, I'm an Episcopal—we *never* talk about money. What's a principal?"

"*The* principal is your base amount, the money you have before annual interest gets added. On this principal, interest might be somewhere between five to eight percent. Over fifteen years, that interest could double the money. That's the power of compounding interest. It grows and grows and—"

"That's incredible."

"Yes. Einstein was thought to have said compounding interest was the most powerful force in the universe."

Nobody at Sunset Gardens is poor. Myra, Wilma, Uncle Cab, and Mr. Halvorsen—he worked as an accountant for big corporations. They all have money. Gockey has some money, too, just not that much. I grab the obituaries, searching those sections that mention survivors.

"Make a note," I tell her.

George Yeamans was survived by one daughter, who lives in Wyoming. Someone else had a cousin in Maryland. Another had a single niece. Another, a sister in Florida. Somebody else a brother-in-law in Georgia.

"None of these people had big families," I say. "That's another common denominator."

"Division," she says, looking excited. "With a small family, any money left behind wouldn't get divided many times. But—wait—what about DeMott? There are a lot of Fieldings."

"True."

"Uncle Cab could be an anomaly," she says. "Like the people who might've died naturally."

We watch the Shiva candles melt into waxy puddles, a white stream creeping toward the untouched pages of *A Psalm of Life*. We still haven't memorized the poem but it delivers to me a line about time fleeting, and those funeral marches within our hearts. Ten people died. And almost nobody was left to mourn them.

Drew looks over. In the soft candlelight, her eyes are polished agate stones.

"Are you thinking the same thing I'm thinking?" I ask.

"Another Yiddish saying." She picks up Myra's prescription bottle, shaking the capsules inside. " 'At the end of the game, the king and the pawn go into the same box.' "

Box. Like a coffin.

My throat aches. "You should go stay with her."

She gazes at the dimming candles. "What about you?"

"I'll stay with Gockey." I swallow the pain in my throat. "But don't leave Myra alone, okay?"

50

WALKING DOWNSTAIRS, I text my dad and ask to spend the night—again. When I walk into Gockey's apartment, I immediately start telling her she needs to drink more water—this dehydration stuff is scary—but she throws her long arms into the air.

"Not you, too," she says.

"Me, too—what?"

"Your Aunt Charlotte's already nagged me about it. And don't try to get me to take that medicine either."

A cold finger touches the back of my neck. "What medicine?"

She raises her index finger the same way lawyers do in my dad's courtroom when they're making an objection. She crosses the apartment, and I hear the medicine cabinet creaking open in the small bathroom.

She steps out holding a prescription bottle. "Tell your aunt I do not have a memory problem—I remembered *exactly* where I put this silly medicine."

I hold out my hand. The label on the bottle reads, *Frances Harmon.*

Nothing else.

I press down on the child-proof cap. More red-and-white capsules. I pry one apart. The clear beads roll out.

Gockey leans down to see them better. "Sort of like sprinkles. But don't get any ideas. I'm still not taking it."

"Don't. Don't ever take this."

"I'm glad you're on my side. Your aunt, she—"

Gockey continues telling me how Aunt Charlotte always looks for what's wrong, how she might be a little nuts, but I'm barely listening. I walk into her little kitchen and find the box of waffle mix. I dump the contents into a mixing bowl and pluck out the little square packet that says, Do Not Eat.

I tear it open, and lift my hand so Gockey can see those same clear beads.

"How *very* odd," she says.

"Myra has medicine with these same things. And Uncle Cab. Where did this stuff come from?"

"Well, your aunt, a few weeks back, she demanded I go see the doctor and he said—"

My stomach tightens into a knot.

"What doctor?"

51

THE NEXT MORNING, Gockey calls the attendance office at St. Catherine's.

"Watch out for Parsnip," I whisper. "She suspects everything."

Gockey nods, winks, holds the phone to her ear. "Hello, Miz Parsons?"

Parsnip, our school secretary, sucks ten lemons for breakfast.

"This is Frances Harmon. My granddaughter Raleigh will not be in school today."

Gockey listens for a moment, then gives me another wink.

"Thank you for your concern, Mrs. Parsons, but Raleigh is fine. She's taking me to the doctor today."

Parsnip is still talking when Gockey hangs up.

"There," she says. "And if your dad asks, you can say we didn't lie."

We eat breakfast—more waffles— and practice our routine that we went over last night, too. Then we watch the clock until 10:30. Gockey finds one of Grandpa Harry's old canes, strings her reading glasses around her neck on a beaded chain, and hands me her purse. We ride the elevator downstairs and walk across the courtyard, moving at a snail's pace. Gockey acts like she needs the cane.

"I think we'll get an appointment," she says as we approach the infirmary.

Dr. Boatman sees patients here every Monday until noon. Then he goes to his other office. It's downtown somewhere.

"He's always seemed like such a dear man," she says for the umpteenth time. "I just don't see how he could be involved in something so awful."

"He keeps two offices."

"Only because we don't have enough people for full time work."

I have my doubts about that.

Inside the infirmary, we turn down a different hallway than the patient rooms. The cool air starts to smell like vitamins and the walls are yellow instead of white. At a reception desk, Gockey dings a bell and—*oh, no*—Pink Nurse appears. She gives me a weird look, like she's been on the phone with Parsnip.

"Can I help you?" she asks Gockey.

"I need to see Dr. Boatman. I'm not feeling well." Gockey lists the symptoms we memorized last night instead of the Longfellow poem. "I feel dizzy. I have lost my appetite. I have nausea." She stops. "I know there's more but I can't remember what else."

"She's been forgetting a lot of stuff," I say.

Pink Nurse gives a sympathetic nod. "Let's get you an appointment right away."

Gockey leans on the cane. Her reading glasses swing from her stooped shoulders. "I brought my granddaughter. I can't remember what else."

I glance at Pink Nurse, raising my eyebrows to say, *See?*

"I can't remember," Gockey says, again. "So I'd like my granddaughter to stay in the room. I won't remember what Dr. Boatman tells me."

"Don't you worry, Mrs. Harmon." Pink Nurse reaches out, touching Gockey's arm. "Dr. Boatman will take good care of you."

∼

FIVE MINUTES LATER, we're in an exam room with posters of old people. They're all working on crossword puzzles or petting cats or strolling in sunny parks. Like being old is the greatest thing ever.

Pink Nurse asks Gockey to change into a gown and leaves. I check the drawers for supplies, and the cabinet under the sink but it's crammed with plumbing pipes.

"Rats," I whisper.

Pink Nurse knocks on the door. "All set?" she asks.

"Yes," Gockey says.

Pink Nurse comes back in and wraps a blood pressure cuff around Gockey's long arm. She pumps it up. Then pumps it some more because Gockey's so skinny. Finally, the wall dial starts dropping through the numbers.

"Your blood pressure's low. Is that normal?"

"I don't remember."

Pink Nurse frowns at me, tears off the cuff, and opens Gockey's medical file. She reads something, then writes something down, and takes Gockey's temperature—it's normal. She tells us Dr. Boatman is with another patient but he'll see Gockey as soon as possible.

The door closes behind her.

I motion for Gockey to climb off the exam table. I hop up, standing on the tissue paper, and lean into the air vent. The metal grate is about two feet wide.

"What are you thinking?" Gockey whispers.

There's a knock at the door.

"Frances?"

I hop off the table. Gockey climbs back up, the tissue paper crinkling.

"Yes?"

"It's Dr. Boatman. May I come in?"

Dr. Boatman comes in wearing his white lab coat. The golf clothes are gone, replaced by regular slacks and a white dress shirt. Even with all that white, his tan looks a little weird. Almost yellow like the walls.

"I hear you're not feeling well," he says.

Gockey looks at me. "Am I not feeling well?"

"Yes." She's pouring it on a bit thick, but Dr. Boatman only holds out his tan hand to me.

"I've met you before," he says. "Haven't I?"

"Saturday. I was with DeMott, Cabell Fielding's nephew."

"Ah, yes, of course." The doctor's stare suddenly seems distant, like he's watching something over my shoulder. "Tragic what happened to Cabell."

"Sure was."

He nods—he nods a long time, like he's thinking about something. Then he picks up the medical file on the counter, lifting the first pages as if searching. When he puts the file back down, he stands in front of Gockey and presses his fingers into her long thin neck. "Does that hurt?"

"I can't remember."

I tell my eyes not to roll—she's going overboard—and it's a good thing my eyes obey because Dr. Boatman suddenly turns to me.

"How long has she been like this?" he asks.

"Couple days. But it got really bad last night." Not a lie. Last night when we practiced this stuff, Gockey turned out to be a horrible bad actress. "She keeps saying she's thirsty."

The doctor frowns. "Does diabetes run in the family?"

"Probably."

"Excuse me?"

"She eats a lot of cake."

He smiles.

My blood runs cold.

He scribbles something inside the file, closes the cover, and holds the information tight to his chest. "Frances, I'd like to take a blood sample. Do you feel strong enough for that?"

"Will you give me a cookie?"

"You won't need a cookie." He pats her hand. "I'll have the nurse come in."

Dr. Boatman leaves and Pink Nurse comes back in. She stabs a needle into Gockey's arm, filling a vial with blood, then places a cotton ball in the crook of her bony elbow.

"Don't get up until you're ready," Pink Nurse says.

"I do feel *very* woozy."

Pink Nurse looks over at me. "Can you watch her? I've got some other patients to take care of."

"Absolutely."

The door closes.

I count to five—too impatient for ten—then lock the door. I pick up Gockey's glasses and shove them under the exam table.

She smiles and whispers. "Stage one complete."

52

WHILE GOCKEY GETS DRESSED, I climb on the exam table and try to keep my Chuck Taylors from making too much noise on the crinkly tissue paper. I run my hands over the vent cover.

Rats.

"It's screwed into the wall."

Behind me, I hear a metallic snap. Glancing over my shoulder, I see Gockey removing something from her purse.

The cake knife.

"I take it with me now," she whispers. "So I never lose it again."

Using the knife's tip, I unscrew the vent cover and find a metal channel behind it. It stretches back about ten feet, then turns, probably to join the rest of the air system.

"Raleigh, maybe you shouldn't—"

"I'll be fine." I listen to the whoosh of the air conditioning, and wonder if I'm right. "But how do I get the cover back on, once I'm inside?"

"I'll put it back on."

God bless my grandmother.

"Then how will I get out?"

"Oh," she says.

"Check that drawer by the sink," I whisper. "I saw some First Aid tape."

She hands me the white roll, and I give her the vent cover. Then I pull myself into the metal tunnel. It's a tight fit but with enough room that I can belly-crawl backward and get inside.

I whisper, "Now hand me the—"

The knock on the door startles us both.

"Mrs. Harmon?"

Pink Nurse.

We freeze.

"Is everything alright?"

"Yes," Gockey calls out. "I'm just getting dressed."

We wait, because it doesn't sound like Pink Nurse is leaving.

"It could take awhile," Gockey says. "I'm not as fast as I used to be."

"Sure, take your time."

The footsteps fade away. I reach down, stretching out my arms for the vent cover, and lift it over the opening. I hold it in place.

"Press on it," I whisper.

While Gockey presses on the other side, I tear strands of tape and stick them around the edges. "Okay. Let go."

The vent stays in place.

I lean my mouth into the metal slats, whispering. "You can go now."

Gockey whispers back. "Phase Two begins."

Laying on my stomach, staring through the slats, I watch Gockey leave the exam room. After five minutes, nobody else comes in so I carefully inch my way deeper into the shaft, keeping my ankles lifted because the rubber toes of my Chuck Taylors want to squeak against the metal.

At the corner turn, a shaft of light falls into the darkness. I pull myself toward it and find another slotted vent. I move closer, ankles raised, my hamstrings shaking from the effort, and see an old man sitting on an exam table. He wears a paper gown. But I can't see his face. I tilt my head to the side and—gasp.

Bill Goddeau.

He suddenly turns his white-haired head toward the air vent, as if he heard something. I hold still. Hold my breath. Hold a silent prayer for help because his face looks painfully sad. A moment later, I hear something dripping.

Plop, plop.

I shift my face again.

Bill's head is bowed, hands clasped in his lap. And tears. They slide down his cheeks, landing on the paper gown.

Plop.

I hear the door open. Bill looks up, wipes his face with the back of his hand.

"What about Binomial?" Bill asks.

"I'm sorry, Bi—?"

It's Dr. Boatman's voice. I lean to the left and see a white coat, tan hands gripping a medical file.

"Binomial," Bill says. "My cat."

"Ah." Dr. Boatman's voice sounds soft. "I promise you, Bill. We will find Binomial a good home."

Bill wipes his cheek again.

I want to run away. At least plug my ears. It feels so wrong to hear this conversation. But any move will make noise. I can only hold still.

Dr. Boatman is saying, "Is there anything I can do for you? Anything. Just ask."

"No, thank you." Bill sniffs.

Dr. Boatman places a tan hand on his shoulder. "Please don't worry about your cat, Bill. Promise me that?"

Bill nods.

"Good." Dr. Boatman removes his hand. "I'll be right back with your prescription."

53

BILL GODDEAU RISES SLOWLY from the exam table.

I hang my head, squeeze my eyes shut. The air system kicks up a fresh whirr and I decide it's loud enough to cover my movements. Moving away from the vent, rubber toes still lifted, I feel like my heart stays in that room with Drew's best chess buddy.

Further down the channel, there's another stream of light. I pull myself toward it and peer through another vent cover. An empty bathroom. I back away and notice that the fan's whirring sounds louder, almost drowning out my own thoughts. The temperature is dropping, too. Goosebumps break out on my arms. At the next vent cover, I peer into a dimly lighted room.

And see the back of a white lab coat.

Dr. Boatman turns around.

I pull back.

He's holding a cell phone several inches from his mouth. And his lips are moving. But I can't hear anything over the fan blowing inside this metal channel. When Dr. Boatman turns around again, I press my ear against the metal slats. His voice is a low murmur, but the words are lost.

I turn my head the other way, and see shelves along the room's walls. And one table. It holds a computer. And a printer, its blue light blinking. Dr. Boatman's voice is getting louder, he's shaking his head. With a sneer, he slides his finger over the screen and drops the phone into his coat pocket.

For a long time he just stands there.

I crane my neck again but can't see what he's looking at. Finally, he walks over to the shelves and reaches inside a white box.

He takes out a plastic prescription bottle.

Unscrews the child-proof cap.

I feel nauseous as he reaches into a different box. His hand comes out clutching red-and-white capsules.

My stomach lurches.

He funnels the capsules into the prescription bottle, twists the child-proof cap back in place, and walks over to the printer. A small piece of white paper is waiting in the tray. He peels off the back of the paper, leaving the label sticking to one fingertip.

My pulse hammers my neck.

He presses the label against the curved surface, then runs his tan hand over it, smoothing out all the wrinkles.

54

I CRAWL past the vents and see Pink Nurse going in and out of every room, closing up for the day. I'm worried that she'll hear me so I move very slowly through the channel. By the time I get back to Gockey's exam room, it's almost 12:30 p.m.

The room is still empty. But I wait a couple minutes before peeling off the First Aid tape. Holding the vent cover by its corners, I lower it to the exam table and pull myself out of the metal tunnel. I take four screws from my pocket, pinching the tops, and twist them back into place so the vent looks normal again.

Quietly, I climb off the exam table and reach under the base, feeling around until I find Gockey's glasses. With my T-shirt, I wipe dust off the lenses. There's also a fine white dust on my shirt. I check myself in the mirror over the sink. Dust on my brown hair, too. I yank out my ponytail, finger-comb my hair and wipe my face with a paper towel.

When I open the door, checking the yellow hallway both ways before stepping out, it's 12:40 p.m. I pass several exam rooms, doors closed, and continue down the hall following the basic direction of the ventilation system. Up ahead, I see an unmarked door. I jiggle the knob. It's locked.

"What are you doing?"

I jump.

Pink Nurse stands at the turn in the hallway, holding a small plastic box. And a mean scowl. "What do you think you're doing?"

I lift my hand, displaying the item. "My grandmother forgot her glasses."

"She wasn't in that room."

"I know. I was looking for the exit. But somehow I got turned around."

She waits for a better excuse.

There isn't one.

There is only my heart, thrashing inside my chest.

I smile. "The exit must be the other way, huh?"

Pink Nurse doesn't smile back.

HEART GALLOPING like I've swallowed the Pony Express, I hurry across the courtyard and pull out my cell phone. Gockey answers before the first ring ends.

"Are you alright?" she asks.

"Fine. But I saw something." I tell her about the room with the bottles and the pills and the printer. "I saw those same red-and-white capsules. And he put a label on the bottle. I think it was for Bill Goddeau."

"Call your dad," she says. "He'll know what to do next."

But even after we hang up, I hold the phone, resisting a call to my dad.

First of all, he won't be thrilled about me skipping school. Second, he might get mad that I spied on people during their doctor's appointments. And third, my heart's pounding like somebody is yelling in my ear—*now! now! now!*—and my dad is going to want to slow down, be cautious, wait for more information. He's a judge, he's always skeptical. And I don't think we've got that kind of time. Somebody else could die.

I lift the phone, tapping the numbers.

~

IN THE MAIN PARLOR, Karlene stands in front of a bunch of people sitting in chairs. Regular chairs, wheelchairs, armchairs. Some of them have cats in their laps, too.

"Now we lift our right leg and roll those ankles!" Karlene lifts her own foot, demonstrating the move. "Mrs. Landry, good work—orthopedic shoes are *heavy*!"

Mrs. Landry's wrinkled face lights up, and my heart plunges even further.

Chair aerobics is only fifteen minutes long, so I wait outside the door. But Karlene stays behind to thank each person for coming. They shuffle into the hallway. Walkers, wheelchairs, orthopedic shoes, the exit process takes forever.

"Mrs. Denny," Karlene says to the last old woman, who's holding a drooping black cat. "Keep up the good work. I'll see you Wednesday."

Mrs. Denny lifts the cat's right paw, waving it at Karlene. They laugh.

I can't even smile.

Once everyone's gone, I step into the room.

"Oh, hi, Raleigh," Karlene says. "Come to pick up Drew?"

"There's a problem."

Karlene's shoulders sag. "Don't tell me. She's still not leaving?"

"This is a different problem. And we better talk about it in your office."

~

KARLENE NEVER CLOSES her office door but now she practically slams it because these words are coming out of my mouth:

"Dr. Boatman's poisoning people."

Her mouth hangs open in shock. "What are you saying?"

"Dr. Boatman is killing people."

"What—how—I don't get it, where did this come from?"

I tell her about Uncle Cab's medicine. And how DeMott and I washed it down the kitchen sink. "Dr. Boatman said he didn't prescribe that stuff." Then I tell her about Fu Manchu throwing up, how those same weird beads were floating in his vomit. "DeMott brought you that cat, you saw how sick he was." Finally, I tell her about the Do Not Eat packets Toots is saving in the kitchen.

"Toots?" She closes her eyes, shaking her head like she can't follow all this. "What does Toots have to do with it?"

"Niko the waiter told her—"

"Niko? Now you're saying *Niko's* involved?" She pushes herself away the door. "Raleigh, this sounds like something Drew made up. Like all that stolen property."

"No, this is real. Dr. Boatman's prescribing bad medicine. There's a reason the packets say Do Not Eat—there's silica inside. It's a mineral and it dehydrates people. Remember how Myra collapsed? She was dehydrated. And I found those same capsules in her prescription in her apartment."

Karlene moves slowly toward her desk and almost collapses into the chair. "This can't be happening."

I move in front of her desk, making sure she's focusing on me. "Silica absorbs moisture. That's why food companies put them in packages, so stuff like rice and bread doesn't go bad. And according to the assistant coroner, Uncle Cab died of acute dehydration."

When she looks up at me, her face so pained it's like I just shot an arrow into her heart. "But who—who would do such a thing?"

"I keep telling you, Dr. Boatman. Toots is saving all those packets from the food, and Niko takes them over to the infirmary so they get disposed with the medical waste. I think Dr. Boatman is taking them before the medical waste people get there. He's putting that stuff in the capsules. And then the silica dehydrates people. But it doesn't leave any trace behind. It's like calcium, or magnesium. All anyone would see is a person who's tired or forgetful. The assistant coroner probably wouldn't even think of testing for silica."

"The...coroner?"

"Assistant coroner. And she said Uncle Cabell wasn't the first death by dehydration at Sunset Gardens. You should call her."

Karlene looks baffled. "What—who—?"

I tell her about going to the morgue with DeMott.

"You went *inside* the morgue?" she asks, shocked.

"DeMott felt guilty because he brought that flask of alcohol. But now it turns out that's not what killed his uncle. 'Severe dehydration.' You see what I'm saying? It's Dr. Boatman, he's poisoning his patients."

"Oh, my God." Karlene leans forward, head dropping into her hands. "Raleigh, are you sure?"

"Yes."

"*Very* sure?"

"Yes, I am."

"How can you be so sure?"

I hesitate. Like my dad, Karlene will freak out if she hears I crawled through the infirmary's ventilation system *and* spied on people during doctor's visits. And with Drew not leaving today, I'm already standing on thin ice.

"Like I told you, I saw the prescription bottles and the capsules inside. Myra had one, Uncle Cab had a bunch. Even Gockey's got one. You want me to show you?"

"And Dr. Boatman's name is on those prescriptions?"

"Well. No."

"Then how can you—"

"His name's not on any of them," I protest. "That's the point. He's hiding it and if—"

"So his name's not on any bottles?" She holds up one hand, signaling *Stop*. "Where's your evidence he's connected to this?"

I have an eyewitness report. But it came from trespassing, breaking and entering, violating doctor-patient confidentiality—which might even be breaking federal law. Which would mean felony charges. Which, if convicted, I would lose my right to vote and all kind of other things. Plus, I made my eighty-year-old grandmother an accessory to these crimes.

Terrific.

"I can show you the prescription bottles," I say.

"That's a start." She leans back in the chair, thinking. "But we need to be very careful. We can't risk panic among the residents. For now, we'll keep this between ourselves."

"Uh..." I look down at my Chuck Taylors, unable to meet her gaze. "There's just one problem with that."

"Yes?"

"I already called the police."

55

ELEVEN ENDLESS MINUTES LATER, I'm fidgeting on the front porch when a slick black Camaro shimmers down the long driveway and parks next to Karlene's gray Honda.

The driver gets out, unfolding his six-foot-eight-inch frame like one of those origami paper cranes. He throws on a schlumpy sports coat and sticks a small spiral-bound notebook in the chest pocket. His jeans are so worn out they're barely blue.

Detective Holmgren walks up the stairs. "Raleigh, have you ever considered having a normal teenage life?"

I wave my hand in front of my face. The breeze is blowing a powerful scent off his clothing. "Having you ever considered quitting clove cigarettes?"

"No." He sighs. "And probably for the same reason as you —I can't."

He gazes around the porch, that visual-broom sweep of all good cops gathering information.

Behind me, the screen door opens. Karlene steps outside. She still looks shaken from our conversation. And Holmgren's so tall she has to tilt her head all the way back to see his face. "Hello, I'm Karlene."

"Detective Mike Holmgren." He shakes her hand. "Richmond Police."

"Homicide," I add.

Karlene whispers. "Raleigh, we agreed to keep this—"

"Okay, fine, but Cabell Fielding was *poisoned* to death."

Karlene glances over her shoulder through the screen door. It's too early for Mrs. Donner, but now I'm wondering if Mrs. Donner actually has dementia or if she's been taking all that silica.

"I'm a little lost," Holmgren admits. "Can you bring me up to speed?"

"Yes," I say. "And I'll show you the proof."

We walk around the building to the infirmary because Karlene's worried Holmgren will cause a disturbance inside. She has a point. The guy's almost seven feet tall and walks the way sharks swim—pretending they're not on the prowl.

"Detective," she says as we head across the courtyard. "You have to understand. Dr. Boatman is adored by all our residents. That's what makes this accusation seem..."

Holmgren cuts his eyes toward me. He has deep-set eyes but even so, I can see the unspoken threat—*you'd better be telling me the truth.*

He turns back to Karlene. "Doctor's first name?"

"Robert," she says. "Dr. Robert Boatman."

"Is he here now?"

She checks her watch. We're passing that big tree where Whitney got stuck and my aunt called the fire department.

"No, he left for the day. He's only here certain mornings. And if we have an emergency."

"Right," I add. "Emergencies like somebody passing out because he poisoned them."

Karlene gives Detective Holmgren a pained expression. "Dr. Boatman's a highly esteemed physician. I checked his references."

Holmgren's gaze sweeps the infirmary's entrance. The front desk sits empty—thank God, no Pink Nurse—but I glance down the hallway to my left, hoping to catch a glimpse of Drew. But the hall's empty. To the right, in the yellow hallway, the lights are dimmed, doors closed. Business hours are over for the day.

"Follow me." I walk through the hall to the unmarked door. "The evidence is right in there."

Karlene tries the knob. The door's locked.

Holmgren shifts his deep gaze to me again. It feels like a cold shadow.

"If the door's locked," he says, "how do you know what's in there?"

The silence could crack my bones.

I reach out, trying the doorknob for myself. Of course it's still locked but I'm buying time, trying to think of an excuse. "I thought detectives always carried lock picks."

"And I thought you knew the laws," he replies. "Including the law that says in order for me to enter that room, I need a search warrant."

"Not if Karlene gives you permission."

He looks at her.

She starts typing on her phone. "I'll text maintenance. They can bring a key."

We wait. I pace the hall. Karlene and Holmgren start talking.

"Tell me more about Dr. Boatman," he says.

"Well, I can tell you he seems like a wonderful doctor." She picks up the charm dangling on her necklace and moves it back and forth. "Our last physician retired, and I searched a long time for a replacement. Not everyone wants to work with the elderly. Dr. Boatman came highly recommended. Board certified. Excellent bedside manner. And best of all, the residents adore him. That was very important, obviously. It takes a special person to work with the elderly."

"Someone like you," Holmgren says.

Karlene blushes.

I sigh, and pace faster.

"You said his credentials are good?"

"The best. He's also on the state advisory board for the aging."

I look over my shoulder at her. "Maybe he advises the state on how to add silica to people's diets."

Holmgren throws me a glance. *Settle down.*

Karlene asks him, "How long have you been a detective?"

"Seven years."

"It must keep you very busy."

"I don't mind." He shrugs. "It's not like I have a wife to go home to."

"Oh, that's too bad."

I narrow my eyes. Karlene's zinging that necklace charm really fast on its chain. And she's kind of smiling at him.

No. Way.

They're *flirting?*

My eyes roll back so fast they almost crack my skull. *Excuse me?* We're here to talk about *poison.* Felony crimes. *Murder.* And they're flirting?

"Detective—"

"You can call me Mike."

"Mike. That's a nice name."

First my mom and dad. Then Teddy and Dorothee. Even DeMott and Tinsley. What am I? Some kind of tragic love magnet—where everyone else finds romance except me?

"Mike, I just don't want to accuse him if we don't know for sure."

"I agree," he says. "I'm here because Raleigh called. And it sounded serious. But that's all."

I focus all my attention on Holmgren. But he's staring at Karlene like she's some shiny new car.

"I just can't imagine Dr. Boatman. He wouldn't do *anything* to harm his patients."

They both look over at me.

"You wait," I tell them. "You'll see."

Sometime in the next million years, a bulky maintenance guy shows up with a key. His blue overalls droop and leave grass cuttings on the vinyl floor. He runs his tired gaze up-up-up and down-down-down Holmgren. Then, without a word, he unlocks the door and walks away, leaving more grass on the floor.

Karlene steps into the room, Holmgren goes next. I follow, forcing myself not to look at the air vent.

"In there." I point to the shelves.

Holmgren glances at Karlene for permission.

She nods.

"Thanks for your cooperation," he says, walking over to the boxes. "It makes things much easier."

"Of course."

He takes a capped pen from his pocket and lifts the box top, peering inside. Then lifts the next box top. And the next. "Raleigh, what am I looking for?"

"Prescription bottles. Capsules." I step closer. "Red-and-white capsules."

He moves away so I can see inside the box.

It's empty.

I point to the next shelf. "Try up there."

He lifts those box tops. "Paper?"

"They're labels, right?"

He takes out a sheet. Plain white computer paper.

My hands start going numb. Holmgren looks inside the last box, and even tilts it so I can see the prescription pads. The kind that Drew used to write out her list of stolen objects.

I spin around. "There!"

One box sits in the corner on the floor. Holmgren strides over, looks inside. "Prescription bottles."

"Yes!"

He reaches in. "And they're empty."

"Right. Because Dr. Boatman fills them with the silica pills. Then he prints the label that looks like a real pharmacy prescription. See that printer?" I point.

But the machine's power cord dangles to the floor, unplugged.

"Raleigh?"

I know what I saw—in this same room.

But how can I say that?

Holmgren will ask *how* I saw it. Then I'll be guilty of trespassing, privacy violations...

"Raleigh."

I don't dare look at Holmgren. Or Karlene. Gazing up at the ceiling, eyes burning, I plead, beg, grovel for help. *Please.*

"Raleigh, I think we'd better go over this again."

I lift my arm, pointing. "Look."

Directly above the air vent cover, high on the wall, a small round lens glints its eye at us.

Video camera.

I glance over my shoulder, almost smiling, even though Holmgren's eyes have narrowed to slits of suspicion.

56

WE WALK BACK to the main building, with me following way behind Holmgren and Karlene. They're doing that small talk stuff again that's really about finding out personal information.

He asks, *So you live here?*

No, she says.

Right. Because your husband would miss you.

No husband.

Oh, really?

My eyes could roll like marbles but my mind is staying focused on that camera. Karlene says there's digital footage and we can watch it in her office.

We climb the front steps.

"Do you have cameras in all the rooms?" he asks.

"No." She walks inside, turns, leading us to her office. "We're careful to protect people's privacy. But we installed some cameras in select locations for insurance reasons. I don't like the idea, but as I've told Raleigh, you can't argue with insurance companies."

"Tell me about it," he says.

In her office, she turns on the computer. "But now I'm glad we have these cameras."

"You'll be very glad," I tell her. "Watch."

But ten minutes later, my face is burning with embarrassment.

"Check it again," I say.

We're going through the digital feed—three times—taking in the views of the infirmary's main entrance, the front desk, and—yes, there I am leading Gockey into the exam room. And then, we see Gockey leaving—without me.

"Where are you?" Karlene asks, moving the mouse. "I don't see you leaving with your grandmother."

Holmgren leans down. "You stayed behind?"

"Raleigh?" Karlene sounds a little ticked off. "What's really going on?"

"People are dying." My voice—my pathetic, whiny voice. "That's what you should be worried about!"

"I am!"

Holmgren straightens to his full towering height. "If you snooped around that medical office, you broke more laws than you know."

Karlene gently touches my arm. "It's about Drew, isn't it? You're protecting her."

"Drew?" Holmgren swivels toward me. "Drew's here?"

Karlene gazes up at him. "You know Drew?"

"Oh, yeah." He nods, seriously. "I know Drew."

"Look." I point at the computer screen. "The doctor is taking prescription bottles and putting fresh labels on them."

"How could you see that?" Holmgren says. "It's not on the tape. Unless...were you hiding in there?"

I don't answer.

"You'd need to be somewhere with a view of that room," he says.

"I wasn't spying." I stare at the image on the computer.

It shows that same storage room. Shelves, boxes, table. And the time stamp is correct for when I was watching Dr. Boatman in there. But on the screen, the room is empty.

"Speed it up," I say.

"What?"

"Speed up the tape."

Karlene clicks and clicks. Shelves, boxes, printer—nothing changes until the door swings open and there's Karlene, Holmgren, and me, stepping into the room.

My heart, it can't sink any lower.

"Alright, Raleigh," Holmgren says. "We've been over this before. You can't go around accusing people of crimes. You know that better than anyone else."

My temper snaps. "I have a prescription bottle with the silica in the capsules."

Holmgren just stares at me. "But no doctor's name on the label."

Karlene is rubbing her forehead, sighing. "I shouldn't have put so much pressure on you. Maybe I should just let Drew live her."

"Wait—Drew's *living* here?" Holmgren throws up his hands. "Now I understand."

"No, you *don't* understand." I stamp my foot. "Cabell Fielding died of acute dehydration. That's exactly what the assistant coroner said. And it totally fits with those silica pellets. Plus that bottle with Myra Levinson's name. And she fainted from dehydration. Karlene saw it."

"Levinson," he says. "As in, *Drew* Levinson."

Karlene sighs. "Drew's grandmother. And yes, Raleigh's right about the dehydration. That's a constant problem around here. Elderly people don't drink enough water. And Cabell, he had diabetes, and his nephew brought him a flask of rum which—"

"That rum did *not* kill Uncle Cab."

Holmgren's already putting that little notebook into his chest pocket.

"I think we're done here," he says.

57

I RUN OFF THE PORCH, sprint down the stairs, and grab my bike. I pedal so fast death could be chasing me. When I reach the carriage house, my lungs are on fire. I hang my bike on its hook then walk back and forth through the dark space until my hands stop shaking.

I need to appear calm.

In the kitchen, my mom is dusting breadcrumbs over a casserole.

"Hi." I close the door behind me.

She doesn't look over. "Where's your school uniform?"

I glance down. Shorts, T-shirt. "I, uh, changed after school." This is true because I changed after school—on Friday.

"Where's your backpack?" she asks.

One word pulses in my brain.

Busted, busted, busted.

"I didn't need my pack today. No homework." There's no homework because I didn't go to school.

She presses her hand onto the bread topping, pushing.

"Is Dad around?" I ask.

She pushes so hard on the crumb topping that it starts climbing up the sides of the pan.

"David came home early, too," she says.

David. Not *your father.* Which tells me I'm once again not her real daughter. On invisible stilts, I walk down the hallway to my dad's office. He stands at the bookcase. Just standing there. Staring at the books. Like they're some crowd of people.

"Dad?"

He jumps. "Oh, hey, kiddo." He tries to smile. "Come on in, I wanted to talk to you. Close the door."

Dark doom settles across my shoulders. I close the door.

"St. Catherine's called." He moves to his desk, resting on the edge that faces me. "They said something about your grandmother, she needed you to take her to the doctor?"

Sometimes it's like I can see into the future. Like right now, I know what my dad's going to look like as an old man. Creases across his forehead. Circles darker under his eyes. And way too much pain in his blue eyes.

"Gockey needed some help."

He frowns. "She didn't say anything to me."

"She didn't want you to worry. And it turned out to be nothing serious." Truth, according to Holmgren. "Gockey just wasn't feeling like herself."

The creases deepen on his forehead. I swallow and toss out a new topic before the judge can pursue this particular line of questioning.

"Mom seems a little tense."

He tries another smile. "She's also not feeling like herself."

I nod, like this is all perfectly normal that we are now among People Who Do Not Feel Like Themselves. That whole idea is so painful I change the subject again.

"Can I ask you something?"

"Only every single time."

"If somebody's doing something wrong—like, illegal—and you can't prove it, what do you do?"

Another deep frown. "You'll have to be more specific."

"I guess—" *Careful, careful.* "I'm wondering how you build a case. You know, so the crime is obvious to other people."

"Raleigh, is someone doing something illegal?"

I try to shrug.

"Raleigh..."

"I don't know—for sure. And I don't want to accuse someone and be wrong. So how do I find out for sure?"

He walks around the desk, settles into his chair, and evaluates me like a witness in his courtroom. I drop my gaze to my Chucks. For any number of guilt-ridden reasons, the rubber toes remind me of crawling through that metal vent, feet lifted. *Spying on people.* "Dad?"

"Let me ask you something." He leans forward, elbows on the desk. "Are you wondering how one proves criminality?"

I look up. "Exactly."

"Always start with the facts."

"The facts."

"Yes, because the facts are like fence posts. They create a boundary. When I was a lawyer, I would comb through the facts again and again. And then again. I wanted to know exactly what happened—not what someone claims happened, or what another person's opinion is about what happened. That speculation is..." His gaze seems to drift to the closed door. "That sort of thinking just isn't productive."

Paranoia, he means. Conspiracies. My mom's way of thinking.

"Okay, facts. Then what?"

"Then the case usually opens up. You'll start to see the larger truth."

"The larger truth?"

He taps his finger on the desk's paperwork. "*Why* something happened. *Why* someone chose to break the law." He stops, evaluating me. "Is this answering your question?"

I force a smile. "Thanks."

He nods, leaning back again. "Home for dinner?"

"Yes, sir."

There's the flash of some emotion on his face. Not joy, exactly. But maybe gratitude.

I stand up, turn for the door.

"Did I ever tell you what Einstein said?" he asks.

I turn around. "You mean, E equals MC squared?"

"Einstein did write that. He also said the world wasn't going to be destroyed by evil but by the people who witnessed evil and did nothing about it."

I stare at him a long moment. My heart is squeezing itself to death. "Thanks, Dad."

"Anytime, Kiddo."

58

My mom's dinner casserole tastes like it only contains breadcrumbs. But I choke it down. So does my dad. Even my sister Helen cleans her plate for the first time in years.

We all know what's happening.

The meds aren't working.

Stuffed with baked breadcrumbs, I carry our dishes into the kitchen. Helen stomps upstairs. My mom runs water into the sink, watching the suds grow. And my dad takes a dish towel from the drawer and starts singing about blue skies shining on me.

"Come on, Raleigh," he says. "Sing along."

"Thanks, but I need to get some homework done."

My mom spins toward me. "You said you didn't have any homework."

Fear bolts me to the floor. I glance at my dad, trembling as the numb feeling creeps up my arms. Facts? Yes. She's looking for facts, too. "I forgot."

She smiles, coldly. "You forgot?"

My dad nods. "She had a really busy day."

"Is that so?" My mom plunges her hands into the soap bubbles. "She didn't have her backpack when she came home."

My dad looks at me, waiting for a lifeline.

"I left my homework at Drew's house." That Longfellow poem, in Myra's apartment. Drew's new home. "I'll ride my bike over and get it."

My dad leans toward the kitchen window, checking the sky outside the window. "It's getting dark."

"I'll ride really fast."

He weighs that option. Weighs it for such a long time that my mom washes an entire plate and my whole body goes numb. I swallow the fear. My dad knows—like a sixth sense—something's not right.

"Helen can drive you over," he says.

HELEN'S VW BUG barely seems like a car. The motor rattles. The body shakes. The muffler backfires like a defective rifle.

"Your homework is downtown?" she asks, as we make our way down East Franklin Street—the opposite direction of Drew's house.

"Turn here." I point. "You can park in the lot."

"Where is this?"

"The newspaper. I need to see the obituary writer."

"Obituaries, like, dead people?" She parks the wreck in the visitor's space. "Can I come with you?"

IF BILL WASSON is surprised to see me, he doesn't show it. His greedy gaze lands on Helen and that's it. He immediately stops typing, stands up, and extends his hand to her.

"Bill Wasson," he says.

"Helen Harmon," she says.

He pulls the empty editor's chair from the next desk and offers it to her.

I clear my throat. "I need to talk you."

He's still paying attention to Helen. "People say, Let the past bury its dead. But I say, Not before I get all the juicy details about them."

Helen laughs.

She's wearing one of her flumey-hippie skirts like she raided Aunt Charlotte's closet. Only on Helen, this clothing looks like Snow White got turned into some forest nymph. Even in Birkenstocks and a torn red T-shirt with a fist on the front, Helen is drop-dead gorgeous. "Drop-dead" being ideal for an obituary writer.

"Hello?" I try again.

He keeps his gaze on Helen. "You two are sisters?"

I can hear the disbelief in his voice. "Can you reprint those obituaries, the ones you gave me yesterday?"

Now he looks at me. "You lost 'em?" He sounds ticked.

"No." I left them in Myra's apartment and there's no way I'm going back to Sunset Gardens now. Karlene doesn't want to see me. "But I need another set."

I'm expecting Wasson to pitch a fit, but he just smiles his Coke-stained teeth at Helen.

"You want copies, too?" he asks.

"No." Helen looks around. "But I'd like a smoke."

Bill laughs. "I hear you."

My eyes—my eyes are going to dislocate from their sockets from all the rolling. *Not more flirting.*

"Helen," I say, trying to be patient, "why don't you go downstairs and have a smoke. I'll be done in a minute."

"I'll go with her." Wasson spins around, slaps the keyboard like it talked back to him, and says. "Pages are printing, don't worry. We'll be right back."

We.

Because everyone is a *we* now. Except me.

I stand there, alone, simmering for a good sixty seconds before I realize the invisible gift. Peering over the partition, I check the newsroom. One balding man with thick eyeglasses peers at his computer screen. Behind him, a woman with purple hair is shaking her head and typing.

I glance at Wasson's computer.

It's 7:26 p.m.

And Wasson didn't log out.

I sit down in his chair and type into the search bar.

Dr. Boatman

The search results come back—more than 400 stories in the system. I clear the search bar and type his full name.

Dr. Robert Boatman

I scan the headlines. Civic awards. Charity work. More charity work. Bunch of stuff about "elder care." Lots of stories written by Wilma Kingsford.

Dr. Boatman—Mr. Good Guy.

I clear the search bar and type, **Offices of Dr. Robert Boatman**

Two addresses appear. I recognize one as Sunset Gardens. The other office is on St. James Street. I take out my phone, typing the address into my maps app. Jackson Ward, south of downtown. Not too far from here. I'm just about to clear the search bar when Helen's giggle floats over the partition.

I jump up. The chair topples to the floor. Wasson comes around the partition. And halts.

His yellow teeth are exposed in another big smile but as soon as he sees me, the chair on the floor, and his computer, the smile turns wolfish. And the greedy gray eyes dart to the monitor.

He walks closer, reading the screen. "Who's Dr. Boatman?"

"Nobody."

"Gimme the story, kid."

"I can't give it to you."

"Then no obituaries." He looks at Helen. "Sorry."

She shrugs. "You do what you gotta do."

I stare into his hungry eyes. "We had a deal—I would tell you something only after I knew it for sure. Not before."

"You know something now." He lifts the chair, setting it back on its legs. "So either tell me, or you get nothing from me."

59

I GOT NOTHING.

No obituary pages in my hands, I sit in Helen's trash-car still parked outside the newspaper building. And I try to explain.

Everything.

"You biked Drew to Sunset Gardens?" Helen asks, baffled by my choice.

I explain the whole agoraphobia thing. How Drew then found stuff was missing, and I found out people were being poisoned. And Gockey helped me catch the doctor. But the plan backfired.

"Now Karlene thinks I'm making stuff up, so I have to start over. I've got to get all the facts so I can nail that doctor."

Helen yanks out the car's rusting lighter, holding it to her cigarette, puffing until the cancer stick gets going. She blows a stream of smoke into the air. "Why not just tell that reporter guy what you know. Let him track down the facts. That's what reporters do."

I roll down my window. "I can't do that."

"Oh, you're too good for—"

"*No.*" I stick my head out the window, yearning for fresh air. "This isn't about pride, Helen. It's about knowing, figuring out what happened."

"Knowing—what, exactly?"

"The truth."

"The truth?" She barks out a smoky laugh. "The truth's whatever we want it to be."

"*Wrong.*" I wave my hands, trying to push the smoke out the window. "You study art, you won't understand. Just take me home. I'll figure it out by myself."

She blows another stream of smoke at the windshield. I lean across her lap and crank down her window, too. But she doesn't seem to notice what I'm doing. She just sits there, staring out at the newspaper's dull gray building.

"Helen, you can take me home."

She doesn't hear me.

"Helen!"

"No." She turns, facing me.

"What?" I ask.

"I understand."

"You understand—what?"

"When a great sculptor's looks at a huge block of marble, he can already see something inside it. Nobody else can, but the sculptor will carve and cut and sand until that image comes out. Or maybe it's released. I don't know. But that's when everyone else understands what he already knew." She nods. "That's what you're like. And Dad. You don't give up until you've got the answers or solved the problem. Especially if someone's been hurt. Like Drew. Or Mom. Or the old people at Sunset Gardens." She takes a long drag on the cigarette, blowing it out like heavy sigh. "It's a pain in the butt. But I admire it, actually."

My throat burns, and not from the smoke. "Thanks."

She looks over. "You're positive this doctor's poisoning people?"

"Yes." I tell her about what I saw in that storage room, how he even printed up the label and put it on the prescription bottle. "And somehow he got everything out of there when he realized I was on to him. I'm thinking he moved it all to his other office."

Helen turns the ignition key. The VW rattles to life.

"Tell me where to go," she says.

THE PAWN SHOPS look grim behind their steel gates. The barbecue joints are flashing neon into the night. And on the street corners, loose-limbed guys stand together, their dark skin melting into the night like they're only shadows. As Helen's rattling car passes, their faces follow.

"Take a left on Second Street," I check the directions on my phone. "And thanks."

She keeps one hand on the wheel, the other grinding her cigarette into the ashtray. "Just don't expect me to go to church, too," she says.

The streetlights dim to amber haloes that barely illuminate the cracked sidewalks. Brick row houses pull back from the curb, lost in the darkness.

"What street number are we looking for?"

I look over. *We.*

Finally. I'm a *we.* And with Helen, no less. I read the address out loud. We are both scanning the city's notorious rough neighborhood. I'm thinking about how the morgue isn't far from here—and how plenty of gunshot victims go from here to there.

"How much gas do you have?" I ask.

"If we turn around right now, I can get us home."

"Funny."

"I'm not kidding."

"What's that, up there?" I point to a brick complex and a lighted plastic sign. It reads, Boatman Plaza. Helen pulls into the parking lot and stops at the front entrance. Another sign is there but it's half-burned out.

"Boatman Plaza," she says. "You think he owns it?"

I don't know. But the sign by the entrance looks like a face with one eye.

"Wait here," I get out of the car.

"Raleigh, don't—"

I shut the door and walk over to the sign. It lists all the businesses inside this "plaza," which doesn't look all that nice. *Boys & Girls Club of Richmond. Urban Assistance League. ElderCare of Central Virginia.*

I lean down, trying to read the sign's burned-out side. *Office of Dr. Robert Boatman.*

"So this is it?"

I turn around. Helen's out of the car, fresh cigarette burning between her fingers.

"He doesn't seem like the type who'd have an office in this part of town." Jackson Ward is like Richmond's version of Harlem, and Dr. Boatman looked like a country club golfer. Nobody's making money in Jackson Ward. "He's tan, dresses nice, your typical rich doctor. Why would he keep an office down here?"

Helen looks around. "It's cheaper."

Greed. I think of that sermon in Titus' church. Greed is poison. I look around again. Windows boarded up. Streets full of litter.

"Hey, how about this?" Helen points at the sign. "Maybe we can finally get a dog."

"*What?*"

"Look." She taps the plastic. "All Fur Love. That's gotta be pet adoption. Maybe down here the dogs are free."

I lean down, reading the name.

"We've begged Dad how many years—ten?"

I read the name again.

And again.

I start wondering if my eyes could lie to me. But, there it is. I even say the name out loud. "All Fur Love."

Helen nods. "That's it."

"No. *All for love.*"

"I got it."

"No. Aunt Charlotte." I describe that day Whitney the white cat flew up the tree. "Aunt Charlotte showed up and called the fire department to save the cat."

"Okay..."

"And she told the fireman, 'Remember, this is all for love.' Then she said it again, later. I thought she meant they were doing this all for love. And then Mr. Halvorsen—"

"Who?"

"He lives at Sunset Gardens, his wife died. But he has a cat. And he said, 'it's all for love.'" I stare at Helen, feeling the idea creep into my mind. "Those cats. At Sunset Gardens. They're all *adopted*. And they've got these behavior problems—they're all coming from All Fur Love."

"So..."

"So what are the chances Dr. Boatman's 'other office' is in the same building as that pet adoption place?" I spread out my arms. "Does this look like a good place for a pet adoption? Or a doctor's office?"

She blows out a stream of smoke.

"Here we go," she says. "You figured something out, didn't you?"

60

"WAIT—WHERE ARE YOU GOING?" Helen asks.

She follows me around the side of the building where faint street-lights glow into a narrow alley. Two green dumpsters are pushed up against the building's brick and a security light gleams overhead. I walk toward them, smelling mildew and wet cardboard. Behind the dumpsters, an old silver car is parked, its hood dented and rusting. Beside it, a door to the building is propped open with a broken brick. I grab the heavy door, glancing inside.

"Raleigh, don't."

I turn around. "Get back in the car, Helen. And lock the doors."

"Where are you going?"

I look down the narrow hallway. Worn blue carpeting. Beige paint. Somewhere further inside, a vacuum is running. "I'm going to check his office."

"What if—"

"There's nobody here but the cleaning person."

"How do you know?"

"Did you see any cars in the parking lot?"

"No, but—"

"But," I nod at the broken-down silver car, "there's no way a rich doctor drives that car."

"I don't want you to go in there."

"I'll just check his office. And that cat adoption place. That's it. I'll be right out."

She hesitates.

"Helen, I promise, if anything's wrong, I'll text. Go wait in the car."

I step into the hallway, quietly setting the door back on the brick stop. With the vacuum's hovering noise, the beige hallway seems to vibrate, the sound rising and falling as someone pushes the machine back and forth. Keeping my back against the wall, I move past the office doors. *Urban Assistance League. Richmond Revitalization Corps.* The hoovering vacuum grows louder and three large trash cans wait outside an open door. Each can is filled with office paper, paper cups, food wrappers. That's probably why door's propped open—one person would need both hands to carry the trash and open the heavy door.

I step closer, but the vacuum shuts off. I press my back to the wall. Someone is talking, almost muttering. Two lean black arms appear, extending through the open doorway. With a grunt, the person deposits a fourth trash can in the hallway. And is gone. Moments later, I hear the sharp *snap* of a plastic bag whipped open. The vacuum starts up again.

I let out my breath, and try to remember the sign outside. The office numbers. Dr. Robert Boatman—it was Suite 200-something. Across from me, the office for *Richmond Action for Aging Network* is Suite 128. So the doctor's office must be upstairs. I lean forward, peering down the hallway. Up ahead, a handrail tilts up a wall. Stairway.

In the open office, the vacuuming person is singing now, but only every third or fourth word. Headphones on? I slide myself toward the doorjamb and see the back of an older black woman. She is not much bigger than the industrial-sized vacuum. I count to three, and leap across the open doorway, sprinting for the stairs. My foot hits the first stair.

"Who's there?!" she yells.

I lunge to the landing, then make it to the second floor. But the hallway splits. I look left—right—left. Which way is his office?

"HOLD IT RIGHT THERE!"

I look down. Her feet pound the stairs, her dark face a wrought-iron fist.

"Where you think you're goin'?"

I try to smile. "I'm looking for Dr. Boatman."

"Dr. Boatman?" The iron fist only tightens. "What for?"

"My grandmother."

"Your *grand-mother*?"

"Yes, she's a patient. He saw her this morning. And I need to talk to him."

"He got a phone." She eyes me. "At night, people *call* their doctor."

"Yes." I'm trying to come up with a decent answer when a door opens on my left.

"Janelle." A male voice. "Is that you?"

Dr. Boatman sticks his head out, sun-streaked hair hanging like wet straw over his tanned face.

"This girl say she got to see you. Somethin' bout her *grand-mother*."

The silence. It feels triangular, crossing between the doctor and this Janelle woman, the doctor and me, me and Janelle. Each of us waiting for the next person to speak.

"Frances Harmon." Sweat bursts through the pores in my skin, prickling across my back. "You saw her this morning. Sunset Gardens?"

The silence continues to hang.

"I knew something ain't right." Janelle starts walking up the rest of the stairs. "You want me to call the po-lice, Dr. Boatman?"

"No, thank you, Janelle." He steps into the hallway. "I can handle this from here."

"If you say so." She heads back down the stairs, completely trusting this terrible man. "I'm 'bout near done but you need anything, just holler."

"Thank you," he says. "I will."

61

DR. BOATMAN HOLDS his door open, as if inviting a featured guest inside.

I glance over my shoulder. Suddenly I want the angry cleaning lady to come back.

"I'm very glad you came," he says.

The vacuum sounds far, far away. A plane passing overhead at 30,000 feet.

"I can explain," he says. "Will you listen?"

His tan looks like melting amber. The hair greasy and flat. But there's something else in his face—something sad. And almost honest. A pleading expression in his eyes, like he knows where all the facts all line up. The place where that bigger truth appears.

I take my phone from my pocket.

"Please don't call the police," he says. "I can explain. Everything. Really."

"I need to call my sister." I tap Helen's number. She immediately picks up.

"Helen, I'll call you in five minutes. If I don't, call the police."

"Raleigh, that's too—"

I disconnect the call.

Dr. Boatman walks back into the office. For several moments, I stand at the doorway, surveying his waiting room. Chairs lined up along the wall. Magazines for old people stacked on a low coffee table. I step inside. The air smells crisp, like chemicals. After a moment I recognize the smell—it's the same one in the library's basement when I use the Xerox machine. Toner—ink toner.

The doctor moves to the receptionist's counter. Medical folders spill across the top, the white paper spreading over the surface like ocean waves. He's been making copies.

I take one more step into the room.

Dr. Boatman lifts a folder, holding it in both hands. It reminds me of my dad's courtroom. The bailiff cradles the Bible this way, right before a witness places their hand on it and swears to tell the truth, the whole truth, and nothing but the truth.

"I need the truth," I tell him. "And if you try anything, I will—"

"I love my patients," he says.

His face looks desperate—haggard and desperate, the tan skin sagging.

"And I love my work," he says. "You need to know that."

"I need to know that? You're poisoning them."

He takes one step forward.

I step back, feeling my spine touch the doorjamb. "Stay right there." I lift my phone. "Or I'm calling the cops."

"All my life I wanted to help people. Do you understand?" He raised the medical file in his hands. "I just wanted to help people. But the world makes it very difficult. Especially for poor people."

I say nothing. But I can sense the larger truth, hovering in the air. Only it's confusing me. The man in front of me is so broken up, so vulnerable. It's not what I expected at all.

He shakes his head. "I've helped hundreds of people in this very office. Hundreds. Right here, where you're standing."

"And what about Sunset Gardens?" I hold my breath. *This is it.* My thumb hovers above the phone's screen, ready to call Helen, the cops. "Answer me."

He looks at me, but says nothing.

"Hey. I asked you a question."

His whole body slouches, like something invisible touched him. And his gaze shifts. He stares over my shoulder.

"Hello, Raleigh."

I whirl.

Karlene is smiling. But it's nothing like her usual smile. This smile is bitter and chemical, like the smell in here. She raises her hand, clutching a gun. A pistol. She stabs the barrel into my side, pushing me into the room and closing the door. Never taking her eyes off us.

"Was I interrupting you two?" she asks, in her honey-Georgia accent. "Please continue. I'd love to hear what y'all were talking about."

I glance at Dr. Boatman. His skin shines with perspiration.

"Karlene, leave the girl out of this," he says. "She doesn't need to be involved."

"Too late, Bob." Karlene shakes her head. "This *girl* is why we're in trouble."

I am sliding my thumb across the phone when Karlene snatches my wrist, twisting my hand until the fingers spasm open.

The phone drops to the floor.

Karlene points the gun at my head. "Pick it up."

I reach down.

She takes the phone, glancing at the screen and reading out loud. "Are you okay? Should I call the cops?" Karlene smiles at me. "Sweet. Must be from that girl chain-smoking in that crappy car." Karlene hands me the phone. "Text back, tell her you're fine."

I stare at the screen.

Karlene shoves the gun barrel into my neck. "Write, I am fine."

My fingers are numb as I tap out the lie.

"There," she says, dropping the phone back on the floor. She turns to Dr. Boatman. "I see you took a cab tonight. You think you're smarter than me, *doctor*? I knew you'd come down here."

Dr. Boatman looks at me. "I'm sorry."

"Oh, please, Bob. You're not sorry. You went along with everything. And I can prove it."

He shakes that file at her. "I made mistakes, but for the greater good."

"The greater good." Karlene flashes her smile at me. "I caught the doctor double billing Sunset Gardens. In other words, insurance fraud."

"I was helping my other patients. They have no money." His voices pitches upward. "I saved lives."

"That's what *you* say. But everyone else is going to see you're a thief. You're going to prison, Bob."

"Blackmail." He looks at me, pleading. "It was all blackmail, that's how this mess got started."

"No, Bob. You brought it on yourself by stealing."

"You threatened me. You never let me—"

"I never made you do anythi—"

I lunge, grab the doorknob. It slips from my sweaty hand. I grab it again but Karlene hurls herself at me, knocking me sideways. I try to stand up. My foot slides on the phone. When she hits me again, I crash into the coffee table. The magazines slide off, smothering the floor. I stand, slowly, my feet slipping on the shiny pages.

Karlene keeps the gun pointed at my head. I stare at the long metal barrel. Old, aged, weathered metal. And I can see the round chambers holding brass bullets. My heart drops, drops all the way into my churning stomach.

"Larry Siegel's revolver," I say. "The one from the Korean War."

She laughs. "Come here, Raleigh."

I don't move.

"Have it your way." She walks over to the doctor and sticks the gun's barrel against his right temple. "Come over, Raleigh, or I'll shoot him."

I stand, step over the magazines. But I can't breathe. My lungs aren't working.

"You're such a predictable person." She grabs my right arm. "Always trying to save people."

The doctor drops the file in his hands, the pages spilling on thin blue carpeting. "Let the girl go. You can shoot me. I'm ruined. But let the girl go."

"Don't worry, Bob. You'll get shot. Just not right this second."

He lifts both hands, holding them in the air. "This was all her idea."

"Shut up, Bob."

"She wanted them to get sick—they had to go to the infirmary. Get their affairs in order. Leave money in their wills to her fake cat charity and then—"

"*Shut up.*"

"*You,*" he cries. "You killed them. You gave them more than I prescribed. You rotten—"

Karlene yanks me to her side. My knees feel watery, like I'm going to collapse. She pushes the steel barrel into my cheek. But I barely feel the pain.

"One more word, I'll kill her."

Dr. Boatman closes his mouth. His eyes pleading with me.

Karlene lifts my numb hand. "Raleigh's going to shoot you."

Blood rushes into my ears, pounding on my skull. The doctor's face blurs.

"And everyone is going to forgive you, Raleigh, when they learn you shot the doctor because he was killing all those nice old people at Sunset Gardens. Because the doctor wanted all their money for his fake cat charity."

I open my mouth, my voice shaking. "All Fur Love."

"*Her* charity," he cries.

"Sorry, Bob, but All Fur Love is now in your name. You own it. Your signature's on every document. All I was doing was finding homes for those pitiful cats, for all those lonely old people."

"Dear God." His chin quivers. "What have you done?"

I force words out of my mouth. "How—how did you know the silica would work?"

"I didn't." She laughs again. "It was that crazy waiter, Niko. Toots kept complaining about him reading all the time. But the residents loved him. So I didn't fire him. He came to me one day with some silly save-the-earth nonsense. He had all this information about those Do Not Eat packages. He explained what they were used for— to dehydrate things. And just like that, the idea hit me. Dehydration is *very* serious. It can kill people. So when I discovered Bob here was double billing the insurance companies—"

"Medicare," he cries. "Not the patients. I didn't steal from any patients."

"Sorry, Bob. The government won't see it that way. It's fraud. The feds are going to enjoy hearing about all that money you stole."

"I stole it to help poor people—for the patients who can't afford to pay. Don't you see?"

"Yes, I see." Her voice is bitter. "You're a regular Robin Hood."

A terrible feeling washes through me. The bigger truth—it's nothing like I imagined. It's so much worse. I cut my eyes to Karlene, pushing words from my mouth. "You were planning to frame Toots. You stole those things, to pin this on her."

"Raleigh." She makes a *tsk-tsk* sound. "Did you just figure that out? I thought you were smarter."

I clench my hands. Fists shaking. "But Toots is innocent."

"*Toots* made it so easy. She kept storing up those packets. It made it look like she was planning this whole thing. But then you—" She stabs the barrel deeper into my cheek. "*You* called that freaking detective. I barely had time to alert Bob here and have him move out all the supplies. Meanwhile, I deleted the film from the camera."

"But the time stamp—"

"The camera's motion-activated, Raleigh. It's very easy to splice."

Dr. Boatman lowers his hands. "Karlene, she's a kid. Let her go. Please."

"Do you know what it feels like?" She seethes. "Spending your entire life taking care of people who can't even remember what day it is?"

"Yes," he says. "I do know."

"No, you don't!" She swings the gun barrel toward him. "You have *money*."

"Money that I use to help the poor."

"Spare me your martyrdom, Bob. Everything's going to come out. All Fur Love?" She laughs, sharp as shattered glass. "People are going to say, 'More like, All For Money'."

She grabs my wrist again, prying open my fingers. She presses the gun in my sweating palm and covers my hands with her own. "Now, Raleigh, you need to pull the trigger. Dr. Boatman deserves to die for killing those sweet old people."

My eyes are burning. I stare at Dr. Boatman, his forehead glistening with sweat. His body trembling.

The larger truth. I found it. Here.

"You killed Cabell Fielding," I said.

"That's right," Karlene whispers in my ear.

"You almost killed Myra."

"*Exactly*," Karlene says. "Myra, dear old Myra."

"And my grandmother—you gave her those pills, too. Why, because of my aunt's money? Was that it—get my aunt to donate more money to your fake *charity*?"

Dr. Boatman closes his eyes.

Karlene purrs in my ear. "Now you understand."

I aim the gun. Her breath is close, quick against my ear, panting.

Dr. Boatman whispers. "Do it. I deserve it."

"You heard him," Karlene shrieks. "Do it!"

I tilt my head, sighting down the gun's barrel, lining up my target. I take a deep breath, holding it just like my dad taught me to steady my aim. Holding, holding. Then I let it out.

"Bang!" I yell, jabbing my elbow into her soft stomach.

I pivot, wrenching it. She doesn't let go. I sweep my left foot out, catching her knee. She buckles. But her grip tightens on the weapon.

"You stupid girl," she hisses.

I twist down, slam our wrists into the floor. Sharp pain shoots through my arm, into my shoulder, but disappears just as quickly. We're both still holding the gun, pointed at the floor. I drive my index finger forward until I catch the trigger. I squeeze. The shot rings out —followed immediately by a high-pitched whine stinging my ears.

Karlene twists sideways, wrenching the gun from my sweaty palm. She's winning. I can feel her superhuman strength, the radiating greed flashing through her system.

I lift my head. The doctor—is he doing something—anything?

He's running for the door.

"No!" I yell.

But before the doctor reaches the door, it swings opens.

The tallest man in Richmond fills the doorway.

"Freeze," says Detective Holmgren.

62

DETECTIVE HOLMGREN SHOVES Karlene facedown on the floor. The doctor is already down, nose to the worn blue carpet. His back shakes. Sobbing.

Karlene turns her head, struggling to look up at Detective Holmgren. "Mike, you have this all wrong."

"Really." With one hand, Holmgren yanks a pair of handcuffs off his belt. He pulls her wrists back. Karlene doesn't resist.

"Yes, I came down here to save Raleigh. Dr. Boatman was going to kill her."

Holmgren squints at me, his deep-set eyes searching. "That true?"

"No. And that gun was stolen, by the way."

Holmgren squeezes the cuffs, so tight the metal cuts into her wrists. He kicks away the magazines on the floor and lifts Karlene like she's a bag of sugar. He drops her into one of the waiting room chairs. With a pen, he picks up the gun by its trigger guard.

"That is Larry Siegel's service revolver," I tell him. "Karlene stole it. And enough other stuff to meet the standard for grand larceny. Drew has a list with all the numbers."

"I'm sure she does." He places the gun on the reception counter.

The doctor is still sobbing on the floor.

"Who called you?" I rub my wrist. It's starting to really hurt. "My sister?"

"No," Holmgren says. "That obit guy from the newspaper called homicide. I'm working the night shift and he asks if we have any charges pending against one Dr. Robert Boatman. That made me wonder. Same doctor you called me about, saying he poisoned patients. I start checking our records, and then a call comes over the scanner. Some white girl's parked in Jackson Ward, demanding a patrol car drive over. Her little sister just went into a medical building and isn't answering all her texts." He raises an eyebrow. "I knew something was up. I drove over. Just as the cleaning lady was leaving. She said a girl was in the doctor's office."

Dr. Boatman raises his head from the floor. "I can explain everything."

"And you will," Holmgren says.

"Then hurry up with the Miranda," I tell him. Otherwise, nothing these two say will be admissible in court.

"Raleigh." Holmgren shakes his head. "You know too much."

He turns to Karlene and the doctor, and begins reciting the Miranda warning. "You have the right to remain silent. You have the right to—"

But there's a commotion beyond the office. Holmgren steps to the door. It sounds like a herd of elephants are storming up the stairs. Suddenly three cops appear in their blue uniforms. Hands on holstered weapons.

"You're just in time," Holmgren says.

63

THE NEXT DAY, I shuffle through my classes.

My mind's foggy. My ears still ring from gunfire. But I get through History. Muddle through Math. Take a nap in Latin.

And in English, I'm so out of it that when Sandbag moves toward me, he seems to be floating across the room, poetry book in his hand. Somewhere on my left, Tinsley is tittering. But everything feels far away. Like it doesn't matter. At all. Last night I went through hours of interrogation by the Richmond Police. And another hour when Helen and I stumbled into the house and my dad was waiting, demanding to know what happened. I told him everything. About Dr. Boatman's insurance fraud at Sunset Gardens and how he used the money to care for his Jackson Ward patients. How Karlene blackmailed him. And how Gockey almost took those pills, thanks to his sister, my Aunt Charlotte.

And now here is Sandbag. He is reciting like an actor on stage.

"LIVES of great men all remind us
    We can make our lives sublime,
    And, departing, leave behind us

Footprints on the sands of time..."

I STARE DOWN at my open book. Inside Karlene, something invisible lurked. Deep inside her heart. Greed, absolutely. But also cruelty. And bitterness.

"Miss Harmon?"

I look up. My eyes feel like they're made of sandpaper. "Yes, sir?"

"Since you were *in absentia* yesterday," Sandbag drones, "would it be possible for you to grace us with a recitation of the poem's final stanza? Or perhaps you would rather continue to daydream away the life that you've been given, thus countering the poem's theme."

The man is beyond annoying.

But I open my mouth, the words right there, as if my heart memorized them instead of my head.

"LET US, then, be up and doing,
     With a heart for any fate;
     Still achieving, still pursuing,
     Learn to labor and to wait."

SANDBAG LOOKS SURPRISED. But he recovers. "In the future, I'll expect more of the same from you."

He turns, finding a fresh victim.

I lay my head on my desk.

64

THE NEXT DAY—WEDNESDAY—I ride my bike down Grove Avenue.

And Drew Levinson rides in front of me.

Not on my handlebars.

Pedaling her purple Schwinn, she flicks her head sideways, checking to see if I'm *right there*.

"I'm here," I call out.

What she told me about energy is true. It can't be created or destroyed. Energy can only be transformed. And Drew Levinson has transformed all that energy of fear into courage.

That whole *up and doing* that Longfellow wrote about? Drew's doing it. Now. *With a heart for any fate.*

"Raleigh?"

"Right here!"

The wind tries to comb her wild hair, the crazy hair that makes it seem like I can see all the invisible thoughts inside her beautiful head. Thoughts that are beyond my brain capacity. Thoughts that sometimes scare me, even bother me. But I know one thing for certain. There isn't one cruel thought inside Drew Levinson's head. Not one. And after discovering somebody we trusted was actually trying to kill our families, that innocence in Drew seems like the biggest gift in the whole universe.

I lean forward, riding my brakes so I don't pass her. "Drew. you're doing awesome."

"Overstatements are a form of lying." She flicks her head back. "But thanks."

And *that.*

Drew Levinson—the least socially aware human being on this big blue planet—is now recognizing feelings, emotions. And maybe that's the whole point of suffering. Everybody suffers. Everybody. But when the suffering ends, it's like we have to choose what to do with that pain—that energy. Karlene suffered taking care of old people, and chose to lie and steal and ultimately kill. The doctor suffered for his patients, and convinced himself he could steal money because it supposedly helped other people.

I glance over my shoulder. Twenty yards back, DeMott's truck follows us, his hazard lights blinking to warn other drivers that he's going this slow. Lifting his hand from the steering wheel, he gives me a thumbs-up. When I called him last night, he didn't hesitate. Not for one second. *Of course,* he said. Of course he would drive to Drew's house and pick up her purple bike. Of course he would bring it to Sunset Gardens. Of course he would follow us back to Drew's house, because she might not be strong enough to bike the whole way home.

I take in a deep breath. DeMott suffered—his favorite uncle died. But DeMott transformed grief into compassion...even for Drew.

After school yesterday, I went by Sunset Gardens to tell Drew about what happened Monday night. Some of the details she already knew—Karlene didn't show up for work on Tuesday. But when I laid out the larger truth, the real surprise was the change in Drew. Her hypothesis had been right, but didn't go far enough. For a long while, she was silent. Finally, looking at me with those soulful brown eyes, she said, "Bubbie told me life is short. She wants me to go outside. She says even if it scares me—*especially* if it scares me—I have to do it. Because one day I'm going to be old, and I will regret not making the most of every day."

Now, I lift my face for another deep breath of this perfect spring air. Six days ago, I thought I'd be okay if I died right then.

But I was wrong. And Longfellow was right.

Learn to labor and to wait.

"Look!" Drew stands on her pedals, skinny legs shaking with the effort. "Raleigh, look at me!"

"You got it!"

She cruises down the last stretch of Grove Avenue, banking to the right, hair blowing like a wheat field full of wind. Her laughter blows back to me. My eyes burn.

She coasts into her driveway, brakes, drops the bike. "Raleigh, I did it!"

I heel down my kickstand, blink away the tears. "Drew, you are amazing."

She laughs, giddy, and races up the back steps—counting by twos to arrive at the perfect magic number six. Flinging open the screen door, she calls out for Sir Isaac Newton.

Her cat.

Personally, if I never see another cat, I'll be just fine.

I walk over to her bike, pick it up, lean it against the back porch. DeMott's truck is coming down the driveway. He's giving me another thumbs-up through the windshield. I wave back, and my phone buzzes with a text. My Dad, I'll bet. Probably wondering how this trip went. I take the phone from my pocket. But I don't recognize the number. And there's no name attached. I scroll through the message.

My heart stops beating.

"Nice job, Raleigh." DeMott gets out of the truck, walks toward me. He's wearing his white baseball uniform. "You realize she's come full circle? Only better."

I nod. My hands are numb again.

The screen door squeals open.

"Raleigh!" Drew stands on the top step, halo of brown hair framing a face that looks like it belongs to the world's most alive person. "We need to go *do* something."

I squeeze the phone in my hand.

She counts down the steps by twos. "...six—where can we go next?"

DeMott laughs. "I've got practice. You two alright on your own?"

I nod again. My voice comes out like a croak. "Thanks. For everything."

"You're welcome." He turns to Drew, placing his hands on her narrow shoulders. "You're my new hero."

She smiles.

He gets back in the truck, waves goodbye, and drives away.

"Think he'll ever dump Tinsley?" Drew asks.

I lift the phone, holding it up to her.

"What is it?" she asks.

"Read the text."

She reads it out loud. "It's me, Tex." She frowns. "Okay. Who's Tex?"

I bite my lip. "That guy from Texas?"

She shakes her head.

"From the science contest—I met him on Ocracoke?"

"Oh, *that* guy. But I thought he was dead. You told me he was dead. Right?"

As I'm staring at the text, the phone buzzes again.

I read the next words out loud. "I'm in Virginia Beach. Come play in the ocean."

My hands are shaking. I can't breathe. I look at my best friend.

But my agoraphobic-OCD-genius best friend suddenly unleashes her biggest grin. Her brown eyes crinkle until they're almost shut.

"Cool!" she says. "Did you know the ocean's orbital waves begin when wind blows on the open sea?"

"No."

"And that the particles in ocean waves move in a circular clockwise direction?"

"No."

"And did you know that I've never been to the ocean?"

"Really."

She tilts her head. "Will you take me with you?"

I lower the phone, telling my heart to calm down. "Whenever you're ready."

"Raleigh." Drew smiles. "I'm ready."

THE END

A PSALM OF LIFE

What The Heart Of The Young Man Said To The Psalmist.
　　Tell me not, in mournful numbers,
　　　Life is but an empty dream!
　　For the soul is dead that slumbers,
　　　And things are not what they seem.

Life is real! Life is earnest!
　　And the grave is not its goal;
　　Dust thou art, to dust returnest,
　　　Was not spoken of the soul.

Not enjoyment, and not sorrow,
　　Is our destined end or way;
　　But to act, that each to-morrow
　　　Find us farther than to-day.

Art is long, and Time is fleeting,
　　And our hearts, though stout and brave,
　　Still, like muffled drums, are beating
　　　Funeral marches to the grave.

In the world's broad field of battle,
　　In the bivouac of Life,
　　Be not like dumb, driven cattle!
　　Be a hero in the strife!

Trust no Future, howe'er pleasant!
　　Let the dead Past bury its dead!
　　Act,— act in the living Present!
　　Heart within, and God o'erhead!

Lives of great men all remind us
　　We can make our lives sublime,
　　And, departing, leave behind us
　　Footprints on the sands of time;

Footprints, that perhaps another,
　　Sailing o'er life's solemn main,
　　A forlorn and shipwrecked brother,
　　Seeing, shall take heart again.

Let us, then, be up and doing,
　　With a heart for any fate;
　　Still achieving, still pursuing,
　　Learn to labor and to wait.
　　Henry Wadsworth Longfellow

THANK YOU

Thank you for spending time with Raleigh Harmon. After writing these many mysteries about her—with more to come—Raleigh seems like a best friend. I hope she feels that way to you, too.

If you enjoyed *Stone and Sunset*, please consider leaving a review. That helps other readers find the book.

To find out about new Raleigh Harmon books, sign up for my newsletter. Along with sneak peaks and giveaways, you'll also receive a free Raleigh Harmon short story, *HERS*. To sign up, go to www.sibellawrites.com or for those of you reading on digital devices, click HERE.

"There are worse crimes than burning books," poet Joseph Brodsky once said. "One of them is not reading them."

Thanks for reading.

With warmest affection,

—Sibella

THE RALEIGH HARMON MYSTERIES

Stone and Spark

Stone and Snow

Stone and Sand

The Stones Cry Out

The Rivers Run Dry

The Clouds Roll Away

The Mountains Bow Down

The Stars Shine Bright

The Waves Break Gray

The Moon Stands Still

And More To Come...

ACKNOWLEDGMENTS

Books get written in solitude. But they require a team before presenting themselves in public.

Team Raleigh Harmon gets support from some very special people: editor Lora Doncea (www.editsbylora.com) who keeps me honest *and* grammatically correct; the prince of forensic geology, Ray Murray, who read an early version of this manuscript while cruising near Antarctica; two keen readers, Nicole Petrino-Salter and Rel Mollett; and the beautiful family of Niko Baruffi, a very cool Seattle kid, who generously allowed me to use his name. And Bill and Joan Goddeau, for being Raleigh's steadfast friends from the beginning.

As always, my team captains are my heroes: Joe, Daniel, and Nico. Thank you for all the steadfast love and support—and laughter, always.

ABOUT THE AUTHOR

After riding a motorcycle across the United States, Sibella Giorello spent ten years writing feature stories for newspapers. Among other national awards, her stories earned two nominations for the Pulitzer Prize.

Sibella now writes the bestselling mystery series featuring forensic geologist Raleigh Harmon. The first book in the series, *The Stones Cry Out*, won a Christy Award. The series also includes prequel mysteries in which teenager Raleigh Harmon learns about life and how mineralogy can solve crimes. In the prequels, her father is still alive—and her mother is still crazy.

Contact Sibella through her website, www.sibellawrites.com. Or through social media.